Arbor T

The Cat Who Talked to Ghosts

Also available in Large Print
by Lilian Jackson Braun:

The Cat Who Had Fourteen Tales
The Cat Who Went Underground
The Cat Who Ate Danish Modern
The Cat Who Sniffed Glue
The Cat Who Knew Shakespeare
The Cat Who Saw Red

The Cat
Who Talked
to Ghosts

Lilian Jackson Braun

G.K. HALL & CO.
Boston, Massachusetts
1991

Dedicated to Earl Bettinger,
the husband who . . .

Library of Congress Cataloging-in-Publication Data

Braun, Lilian Jackson.
    The cat who talked to ghosts / Lilian Jackson Braun.
       p. cm.—(G.K. Hall large print book series)
    ISBN 0-8161-5081-8
    1. Large type books. I. Title.
[PS3552.R354C366 1991]
813'.54—dc20   90-28150

One

Jim Qwilleran is a very rich man—the richest individual in Moose County, to be exact. Moose County, as everyone knows, claims to be 400 miles north of everywhere, a remote rockbound outpost comfortably distant from the crime, traffic, and pollution of densely populated urban areas to the south. The natives have a chauvinistic scorn for what they call Down Below.

Before Qwilleran inherited his enormous wealth he had been a journalist Down Below, covering the crime beat on major newspapers for twenty-five years. His name (spelled with the unconventional Qw) and his photograph (distinguished by a luxuriant moustache) were known to millions. Then, at the uneasy age of fifty, he became heir to the Klingenschoen fortune and retired to Moose County.

Currently he lives quite simply in Pickax City, the county seat (population: 3,000), sharing a modest bachelor apartment with two Siamese cats, writing a column for the local newspaper, driving an energy-efficient car, dating a librarian, and ignoring the fact that he owns half of Moose County and a substantial chunk of New Jersey. The tall husky man with a prominent moustache is frequently seen riding a bicycle in Pickax, dining in restaurants, and going into the secondhand bookstore. He reads much, and although his mournful eyes and drooping moustache give his countenance an aspect of sadness, he has found contentment.

Not surprisingly Qwilleran has retained his interest in crime, possessing a natural curiosity and a journalist's cynicism that can scent misdoing like a cat sniffing a mouse. Recently he was haunted by private suspicions following an incident that others accepted as a whim of fate. The initial circumstances are best related in his own words. He recorded the following on tape shortly after his midnight ride to North Middle Hummock:

I knew the telephone was about to ring. I knew it a full ten seconds before it interrupted the first act of *Otello*. It was a Sunday night in early October, and I was in my pajamas, taking it easy, listening to an opera cassette that Polly Duncan had brought me from England. The Siamese also were taking it easy, although not necessarily listening. Koko was on the coffee table, sitting tall and swaying slightly, with a glazed expression in his slanted blue eyes. Opera puts him in a trance. Yum Yum was curled up on my lap with her paws covering her ears—a feline commentary on Verdi, no doubt. I'm not a great opera-lover myself, but Polly is trying to convert me, and I admit that Verdi's *Otello* is powerful stuff.

Suddenly, during the tense build-up to the drunken brawl scene, Yum Yum's body stiffened and her toes contracted. At the same instant Koko's eyes opened wide and his ears pointed toward the telephone. Ten seconds later . . . it rang.

I consulted my watch. In Pickax not many persons venture to call after midnight.

"Yes?" I answered brusquely, expecting to hear a befuddled voice asking for Nadine or Doreen or Chlorine against an obbligato of late-night bar hubbub. Or the caller might say abruptly, "Whoozis?" In that case I would say grandly, "*Whom* are you calling, sir?" And he would hang up immediately without even an expletive. Of all the four-

3

letter words I know, the speediest turn-off in such circumstances is *whom*.

It was no barfly on the line, however. It sounded like Iris Cobb, although her voice —usually so cheerful—had a distinct tremor that worried me. "Sorry to call so late, Mr. Q, but I'm . . . terribly upset."

"What's the trouble?" I asked quickly.

"I'm hearing . . . strange noises in the house," she said with a whimper.

Mrs. Cobb lived alone in an old farmhouse rather far out in the country, where noise is an uncommon factor and any slight sound is magnified at night. The thumps and clicks from a furnace or electric pump, for example, can be unnerving, and a loose shutter banging against the house can drive one up the wall.

"Does it sound," I asked, "like a mechanical problem or something loose on the outside of the house?"

"No . . . no . . . not like that," she said in a distracted way as if listening. "There! I just heard it again!"

"What kind of noise, Mrs. Cobb?" My curiosity was aroused at that point.

She hesitated before replying timidly, "It's frightening! Sort of . . . unearthly!"

How should I react? Mrs. Cobb had always thought it amusing to have a resident ghost in an old house, but tonight her voice expressed abject terror. "Could you describe the sounds specifically?"

"It's like knocking in the walls . . . rattling . . . moaning . . . and sometimes a scream."

I ran a questioning hand over my moustache, which always perks up at moments like this. It was October, and Moose County likes to celebrate Halloween for the entire month. Already there were pumpkins on every front porch and ghostly white sheets hanging from trees. The pranksters might be getting an early start—perhaps some kids from the nearby town of Chipmunk, which is noted for its rowdies. "You should call the police," I advised her calmly. "Tell them you suspect prowlers."

"I called them the night before last," she said, "and everything was quiet when the sheriff got here. It was embarrassing."

"How long has this been going on? I mean, when did you first hear mysterious sounds?"

"About two weeks ago. At first it was just knocking—now and then—not very loud."

Her voice was more controlled now, and I thought the best course was to keep her on

5

the line. She might talk herself out of her fears. "Have you mentioned the situation to anyone around there?" I asked.

"Well . . . yes. I told the people who live at the end of the lane, but they didn't take it seriously."

"How about reporting it to Larry or Mr. Tibbitt?"

"Somehow I didn't want to do that."

"Why not?"

"Well . . . in the daylight, Mr. Q, when the sun is shining and everything, I feel foolish talking about it. I don't want them to think I'm cracking up."

That was understandable. "I suppose you keep the floodlights turned on in the yard after dark."

"Oh, yes, always! And I keep peeking outside, but there's nothing there. It seems to be coming from inside the house."

"I agree it's a puzzling situation, Mrs. Cobb," I said, trying to appear interested and helpful but not apprehensive. "Why don't you jump in your car and drive over to Indian Village and spend the night with Susan? Then we'll investigate in the morning. There's sure to be some logical explanation."

"Oh, I couldn't!" she said with a faltering

cry. "My car's in the barn, and I'm afraid to go out there. Oh, Mr. Q, I don't know what to do! . . . Oh, my God! There it goes again!" Her words ended with a shriek that made my flesh creep. *There's something outside the window!*"

"Get hold of yourself, Mrs. Cobb," I said firmly. "I'll pick you up and take you to Indian Village. Call Susan and tell her you'll be there. Pack a bag. I'll see you in twenty minutes. And drink some warm milk, Mrs. Cobb."

I pulled on pants and a sweater over my pajamas, grabbed the car keys and a jacket, and bolted out of the apartment, half stumbling over a cat who happened to be in the way. Mrs. Cobb had a health problem, and the noises might very well be imaginary, the result of taking medication, but that made them no less terrifying.

The farmhouse in North Middle Hummock was thirty minutes away, but I made it in twenty. Fortunately there was no traffic. This was late Sunday night, and all of Moose County was at home, asleep in front of the TV.

The old paving stones of Main Street, wet from a recent shower, glistened like a night scene in a suspense movie, and I barreled through the three blocks of downtown Pickax at sixty-five and ran the town's one-and-only red light. At the city limits the streetlights ended. There was no moon, and it was hellishly dark on the country roads. This had been a mining region in the nineteenth century. Now the highway is bordered with abandoned mineshafts, rotting shafthouses, and red Danger signs, but on this moonless night they were obliterated by the darkness.

I drove with my country-brights, following the yellow line and watching for the Dimsdale Diner, a lonely landmark that stays open all night. Its lights glimmered faintly through dirty windows, identifying the intersection where I had to turn onto Ittibittiwassee Road. There the highway was straight and smooth. I pushed up to eighty-five.

Beyond the Old Plank Bridge the route became winding and hilly, and I slowed to a cautious sixty-five, thinking about this woman who was depending on me tonight. Poor Mrs. Cobb had survived more than her share of tragedies. A few years ago, when I lived Down Below and wrote for the *Daily Fluxion*, she was my landlady. I rented a furnished room over her antique shop in a blighted part of the city. After the murder of her husband she sold the shop and moved to Pickax, where she applied her expertise to museum work. Now she was resident manager of the Goodwinter Farmhouse Museum, living in one wing of the historic building.

It was not surprising that she phoned me in her desperation. We were good friends, although in a formal sort of way, always addressing each other as "Mrs. Cobb" and "Mr. Q." I suspected that she would like a closer relationship, but she was not my type. I admired her as a businesswoman and an expert on antiques, but she played the clinging vine where men were concerned, and it could be cloying. She also played the witch in the kitchen. I'll admit to being a pushover for her pot roast and coconut cake, and the Siamese would commit murder for her meatloaf.

So here I was, speeding out to North Middle Hummock in my pajamas to rescue a helpless female in distress. For a brief moment it crossed my mind that her agonized phone call might be a ploy to get me out there in the middle of the night. Ever since inheriting all that damned Klingenschoen money I've been wary of friendly females.

And ever since Mrs. Cobb arrived in Pickax with her vanload of cookbooks and her worshipful attitude, I've been on my guard. I enjoy a good meal and have always considered her a great cook, but she wore too much pink and too many ruffles—not to mention those eyeglasses with rhinestone-studded frames. Besides, I was involved with Polly Duncan, who was intelligent, cultivated, stimulating, loving . . . and jealous.

Hunting for North Middle Hummock in the dark was literally going-it-blind. It had been a thriving community in the old days when the mines were operating, but economic disaster after World War I had reduced it to a ghost town, a pile of rubble overgrown with weeds and totally invisible on a moonless night. With no streetlights and no visible landmarks, all trees and bushes looked alike. Finally my headlights picked out the white rail fence of the Fugtree farm, and I gave three cheers for white paint. After another dark stretch there was a white-painted cottage with a flickering light in the window; someone was watching TV. The cottage marked the entrance to Black Creek Lane, and the lane dead-ended at the Goodwinter place. I felt a flood of relief.

Mrs. Cobb had inherited the historic

Goodwinter farmhouse from Herb Hackpole, her third husband, after a shockingly brief marriage. She immediately sold it to the Historical Society for use as a museum —sold it for one dollar! She was that kind of person, good-hearted and incredibly generous.

As I drove down the gravel lane I noticed that the Goodwinter farmyard, which should have been floodlighted, was in darkness. So was the house. Power failures are common in Moose County . . . and yet, I remembered seeing lights in the Fugtree farmhouse, and someone was watching TV in the cottage up at the corner. I felt a tingling sensation on my upper lip.

Driving around to the west side of the sprawling farmhouse, I parked with the headlights beamed on the entrance to the manager's apartment and took a flashlight from the glove compartment. First I banged the brass knocker, and when there was no answer I tried the door and was not surprised to find it unlocked. That's customary in Moose County. Flashing my light around the entrance hall I found a wall switch and flipped it experimentally, still thinking the power might be cut off. Unexpectedly the

11

hall fixture responded—and on went four electric candles in an iron chandelier.

"Mrs. Cobb!" I called. "It's Qwilleran!"

There was no answer, nor was there any knocking or rattling or moaning. Certainly no screaming. In fact, the rooms were disturbingly silent. An archway at the left led to the parlor, and its antique furnishings were illuminated as soon as I found the wall switch. Why, I asked myself, had this frightened woman turned out all the lights? The roots of my moustache were sending me anxiety signals: Sometimes I wish it were less sensitive.

Across the hall the bedroom door was standing open, and there was an overnight case on the bed, partly packed. The bathroom door was closed. "Mrs. Cobb!" I called again. Somewhat reluctantly I opened the bathroom door and steeled myself to look in the stall shower.

Still calling her name, I continued down the hall to the old-fashioned kitchen with its fireplace and big dining table and pine cabinets. I flipped on the lights, and in that instant my instincts told me what I would find. There was a milk carton on the kitchen counter, and on the floor was a sprawled figure in a pink skirt and pink sweater, the eyes staring, the round face painfully contorted. There were no signs of life.

Two

When Qwilleran discovered Mrs. Cobb's lifeless body he reacted with more sorrow than shock. He had sensed the worst as soon as he turned down Black Creek Lane and found the premises in darkness. Now, looking down at the pink-clad figure —pink to the very end!—he pounded his moustache with his fist, pounded it in sadness mixed with anger. It was unthinkable that this good woman should slip away in the prime of life, at the apex of her career, at the height of her joy. She had won the admiration of the community; her last husband had left her well-off; and at the age of fifty-five she was a grandmother for the first time. But then, he reminded himself, Fate had never been known for its good timing.

Finding the kitchen telephone, he punched the police emergency number and reported the incident without emotion, stating all the necessary details. The phone stood on a relic from an old schoolhouse: a cast-iron base supporting a wooden seat and a boxlike desk with lift-up top. The writing surface was grooved for pens and pencils and inkwell, and it was carved with generations of initials. Also on the desk was an alphabetized notebook containing phone numbers; it was open to *E*. Qwilleran called Susan Exbridge in Indian Village, and she answered on the first ring.

"Susan, this is Qwill," he said somberly. "Did Iris call you a short time ago?"

"Yes, the poor thing was frightened out of her wits for some reason or other. She was almost incoherent, but I gathered that you're bringing her over here to spend the night. I've just put pink sheets on the guestbed."

"That was the plan. I'm at the farmhouse now. She won't be able to make it."

"Why? What happened, Qwill?"

"I found her on the kitchen floor. Not breathing. No pulse. I've called the police."

Susan wailed into the phone. "How terrible! How perfectly awful! What will we do without her? I'm devastated!" She had a tendency to be dramatic and a personal reason to feel bereft. The two women were partners in a new enterprise in downtown Pickax, and the gold lettering had just been painted on the shop window: Exbridge & Cobb, Fine

15

Antiques. The formal opening was scheduled for Saturday.

Qwilleran said, "We'll talk tomorrow, Susan. The sheriff will be here momentarily."

"Is there anything I can do?"

"Get some rest and prepare for a busy day tomorrow. I'm calling Larry, and I'm sure he'll need your help with arrangements."

Larry Lanspeak was president of the Historical Society and chairperson of the Goodwinter Farmhouse Museum as well as owner of the local department store. As merchant, civic leader, and talented actor in the Pickax Theatre Club he brought boundless energy to everything he undertook. Qwilleran put in a call to the Lanspeak country house in fashionable West Middle Hummock, and, although it was almost two o'clock, Larry answered the phone as briskly as he would in midday.

"Larry, this is Qwill. Sorry to disturb you. We have trouble. I'm calling from the museum. Iris called me in hysterics not long ago, and I rushed out here. You know about her heart condition, don't you? I was too late. I found her dead on the kitchen floor. I've called the police."

There was a prolonged silence at the other end of the line.

"Larry . . . ?"

In a hollow voice Larry said, "It can't be! We need her! And she was too young to go!"

"She was our age." Qwilleran's tone was understandably morose.

"I'll throw on some clothes and get there as soon as possible. God! This is terrible news. Carol will be floored!"

Qwilleran turned on the yardlights and turned off his headlights just as the sheriff's car came down the lane.

A young officer in a wide-brimmed hat stepped out. "Somebody report a dead body?"

"It's Mrs. Cobb, manager of the museum. She called me in a panic, and I came out to see if I could help. I'm Jim Qwilleran from Pickax."

The deputy nodded. Everyone knew the outsize moustache that belonged to the richest man in the county.

They went indoors, and Qwilleran pointed the way to the kitchen.

"Emergency's on the way," said the deputy. "They'll take the body to Pickax Hospital. The medical examiner will have to sign the death certificate."

"He might want to check with Doctor

17

Halifax. She was being treated for a heart condition."

The deputy nodded, writing up his report.

Qwilleran explained, "Mrs. Cobb called me because she was hearing strange noises and was afraid to stay here."

"She put in a call a couple of nights ago. I checked it out, but I couldn't find anything irregular. No evidence of prowlers on the grounds. Are you next of kin?"

"No. She has a son in St. Louis. He'll have to decide where we go from here. I'd better call him and break the news."

At that moment the emergency vehicle arrived, and silent attendants removed the pink-clad remains of one who had captivated the community with her generosity, her cheerful personality, and her encyclopedic knowledge of antiques. And her baking, Qwilleran thought. Whenever there was a charity bazaar or civic reception, Mrs. Cobb stayed up all night baking cookies—not just chocolate chip but an array of lemon-coconut squares, butterscotch pecan meringues, apricot-almond crescents, and more. Ironically, there were Moose County citizens who would remember Iris Cobb chiefly for her cookies.

Qwilleran leafed through the notebook on

the school desk in search of her son's phone number. Unfortunately he was unable to remember the young man's name. He had a vague recollection that it was Dennis. The last name was not Cobb but something like Gough, pronounced Goff . . . or Lough, pronounced Luff . . . or Keough, pronounced Kyow. Under *H* he found a listing with a St. Louis area code, and he punched the number. A man's sleepy voice answered.

Many a time Qwilleran had been enlisted to notify a victim's next of kin, and he did it with sensitivity. His voice had a richness of timbre and a sympathetic gentleness that gave the impression of genuine feeling.

"Dennis?" he said in a sober monotone. "Sorry to wake you at this hour. I'm Jim Qwilleran, a friend of your mother, calling from North Middle Hummock."

The young man was immediately alarmed. "What's wrong?" he demanded. His gulp was audible.

"I received a phone call from Iris after midnight. She was afraid to stay at the farm alone, so I offered to drive her to a friend's house . . ."

"What's happened? *Tell me what's happened!*"

"I found her on the kitchen floor. No

19

doubt she'd had a heart attack. It pains me to bring you this news, Dennis."

Her son groaned. "Oh, God! I was flying up there to see her tomorrow—I mean, today. Her doctor suggested it."

"Her going is a great loss. She made many friends here and won over the entire community."

"I know. She told me in her letters how happy she was. For the first time in her life she felt as if she really belonged."

"That brings up the matter of funeral arrangements, Dennis. What should we do! It's your decision, although the Klingenschoen Memorial Fund would consider it a privilege to cover all expenses. Had Iris ever expressed her wishes?"

"Gosh, no," said her son. "She was too busy living! I don't know what to say. This is so totally unexpected. I've got to think about it—talk it over with Cheryl."

"Call me back, here at the farmhouse, soon as possible. The hospital is waiting for instructions."

Returning the receiver to the cradle Qwilleran noticed the shelf of paperback cookbooks on the wall—a sad substitute for the three-dozen hardbound cookbooks she had lost in a disastrous fire. Other shelves displayed antique pewter plates, porringers, and tankards; the overhead beams were hung with copper pots and baskets; around the fireplace were wrought-iron utensils used in the days of open-hearth cooking. It was a warm and friendly place. Mrs. Cobb loved her kitchen.

Absently he browsed through her phone book, where the listings were written with bold-tip pen in large block letters, a sign of her failing eyesight. The book contained the numbers of museum volunteers for the most part . . . also someone named Kristi . . . and Vince and Verona, whoever they were . . . and Dr. Halifax. Both his home and office numbers were listed. In Pickax one could call the doctor at home in the middle of the night. HB&B obviously was the law firm of Hasselrich, Bennett and Barter. No doubt they had handled her inheritance and drawn up her will. Mrs. Cobb had realized a sizable estate from her third husband, although she chose not to use his name.

As he waited Qwilleran wandered about the apartment, looking for clues to the final minutes of her life. In the open luggage on her bed were a pink robe and pink slippers. The milk carton was still on the kitchen counter, and he put it in the refrigerator.

21

There was a mug of milk in the microwave; the oven had been turned off, but the milk was warm. He poured it down the drain and rinsed the mug. The door leading from the kitchen into the main part of the museum was unlocked, and he was browsing through the exhibit rooms when the phone rang. He was pleased that Dennis would call back so soon. The voice he heard, however, was that of a woman.

"This is Kristi at the Fugtree farm," she said. "Is Iris all right? I saw a police car and ambulance going down the lane."

"I regret to say," he announced solemnly, "that Mrs. Cobb has had a fatal attack."

"Oh, no! I'm so sorry. I knew she was seeing Doctor Hal, but I didn't know it was so serious. Is this Mr. Lanspeak?"

"No, just a friend from Pickax."

"How did it happen?" She sounded young and breathless.

"The details will be in tomorrow's paper, I believe."

"Oh . . . Well, I'm very sorry. I really am! I was sitting up with my sick kids and I saw the flashing lights, so I just had to call."

"That's all right."

"Well, thank you. What's your name?"

"Jim Qwilleran," he mumbled.

Most women would have reacted with an excited "Ooooooh!" as they realized they were talking to an eligible and very wealthy bachelor, but this young woman merely said, "My name is Kristi Waffle."

"It was good of you to call. Good night."

He heard a car pulling into the farmyard and went to meet Larry Lanspeak. Despite the man's elevated standing in the community he was unprepossessing. Ordinary height, ordinary coloring, and ordinary features gave him an anonymity that enabled him to slip into many different roles for the Theatre Club.

"What a tragedy!" he said, shaking his head and speaking in the well-modulated tones of an actor. He walked into the apartment with the deliberate and elongated stride of a man who wishes he were taller. "No one will ever appreciate how much that woman has done for our community! And she wouldn't take a penny for it! We'll never find a manager to equal—"

He was interrupted by the telephone bell.

"This will be her son calling from St. Louis," Qwilleran said as he picked up the receiver, but he winced at the first words he heard.

"Say! This is Vince Boswell!" It was a loud piercing voice with a nasal twang. "I called to see about Iris. Something happen to her? The wife and me, we were sort of watching a video, and we saw the ambulance lights."

Qwilleran replied coolly, "I regret to say that Mrs. Cobb has had a fatal attack."

"No kidding! That's a damn shame!" said the ear-shattering voice, adding with muffled volume as he turned away from the mouthpiece, "Some guy says Iris had a fatal attack, honey!" Then he shouted into the phone, "We liked Iris a helluva lot, my wife and me. Anything we can do?"

Qwilleran was holding the receiver six inches from his ear. "I don't believe so, but thanks for calling."

"We're right close by if you need any help at the museum, understand? Glad to pitch in at a time like this."

"That's kind of you. Good night, Mr. Bosworth."

"Boswell," the man corrected him. "We're staying in the cottage up at the corner, the wife and me. Larry Lanspeak is a friend of ours."

"I see. Well, good night, Mr. Boswell. We appreciate your concern."

Qwilleran hung up and said to Larry, "Who's Boswell?"

"Haven't you met Vince and Verona? She's one of our volunteers, and Vince is cataloguing the antique printing presses in the barn. He's writing a book on the history of printing."

Qwilleran thought, Does the world need another book on the history of printing? "Where did you find this guy, Larry?"

"He came up here from Pittsburgh."

Must have been a coach for the Steelers, Qwilleran thought.

Larry went on, "Vince offered to do the job gratis, so we let him live in the hired man's cottage rent-free. Now that Iris is gone we should have someone living on the premises for security reasons. I'm thinking the Boswells might fill in temporarily."

"I'll be willing to move in until you locate a permanent resident," Qwilleran said.

"That's a kind offer, Qwill, but it would be an imposition."

"Not at all. I've been wanting to spend some time at the museum—especially in the document collection—digging up material for my column."

"If you're serious, Qwill, it would solve our problem, and you wouldn't have to be involved with the museum operation. It's a separate telephone line, and the volunteers come and go with their own key. No one would bother you."

"I'd have the cats with me, of course," Qwilleran pointed out. "Koko is a self-appointed security officer, and Yum Yum once distinguished herself by catching a museum mouse. Iris used to invite them over here once in a while, and they never did any damage."

"I'm not worried about that," Larry said. "I know they're well-behaved, and they could have a ball, socializing with the barn-cats and stuffing themselves with fieldmice."

"They're indoor cats," Qwilleran quickly corrected him. "I'm very careful not to let them out."

The telephone rang again, and this time it was Dennis. "We've talked it over, Mr. Qwilleran, and Cheryl and I think the funeral and burial should be up there, where Mother had so many friends. I'll fly up today as I originally planned, and in the meantime you can make whatever decisions have to be made. She always wrote about you in her letters. You were very good to her."

"I'm glad you're coming up, Dennis. I'll meet your plane at the airport and make a reservation for you at the Pickax Hotel, but I don't have your last name."

"It's H-o-u-g-h, pronounced Huff."

"Are you catching the five o'clock shuttle out of Minneapolis?"

"That's right . . . and Mr. Qwilleran, there's something I want to tell you when I arrive, something that was happening to my mother in the last week or so. It had to do with the museum. She was greatly disturbed."

Qwilleran touched his moustache tentatively. "I certainly want to hear about it."

"Thanks for everything, Mr. Q. Isn't that what Mother always called you?"

"Most people call me Qwill. You do the same, Dennis."

As he slowly hung up the phone, questions about Iris Cobb's mental state raced through his mind. It had to be the medication!

"What's the decision?" Larry asked.

"The arrangements are all up to us. Funeral and burial here. Her son will arrive this evening. I'll have the Klingenschoen Fund cover expenses, and I want everything done right."

"I agree. We'll use the Dingleberry funeral home and have the service at the Old Stone Church."

"Would you be good enough to make a couple of phone calls while I rustle up some instant coffee?" Qwilleran asked. "We should line up Dingleberry and inform the hospital. If they need to know the next of kin, it's Dennis H-o-u-g-h, pronounced Huff. Then I'll call WPKX and the night desk at the paper. They can run a bulletin on page one, and I'll write an obituary for Tuesday."

Larry said, "Tell them the museum will be closed for the entire week."

They sat at the dining table in the kitchen, pushing aside the pink candles in milk-glass holders and swigging coffee from majolica mugs as they worked out the details: friends invited to call at Dingleberry's Tuesday evening, final rites to be held at the church on Park Circle Wednesday morning, the Pickax Funeral Band to lead the procession of cars to the cemetery. As past president of the chamber of commerce Larry was sure that all places of business would close on the morning of the funeral. As current president of the board of education he would ask that schools also close for half a day.

"Grades K to twelve have all made field trips to the museum," he said, "and Iris always had cookies and lemonade for the kids."

For a century or more, funerals had been events of moment in Pickax. The townspeople always turned out en masse to pay their respects and count the number of vehicles in the procession. These statistics became a matter of record, to be memorized and quoted: ninety-three cars for Senior Goodwinter's funeral the year before; seventy-five when Captain Fugtree was buried. Most spectacular of all was Ephraim Goodwinter's funeral in 1904; fifty-two buggies, thirty-seven carriages, more than a hundred mourners on foot, and seventeen on bicycles. "Everything but camels and elephants," one irreverent bystander was heard to remark on that occasion. Ephraim, owner of the Goodwinter Mine, was intensely disliked, and his funeral procession resembled a march of triumph, but that was a long story, veiled in hearsay and prejudice—one that Qwilleran hoped eventually to research.

Next came the question of flowers or no flowers. "I'm sure Iris would like flowers," he said. "There's a certain sentimentality in floral tributes, and our friend was a sentimental soul."

29

"And how about eulogies? Iris was modest to a fault."

"Yes, but she craved approval. When she first came to Pickax I introduced her at a city council meeting, and the audience applauded as a matter of courtesy. Iris was so touched by the applause that she went home and cried. So I vote for eulogies."

"Good! We'll line up the mayor and the president of the county commissioners. Or should we have a woman give one of the eulogies? Susan, perhaps. Or Carol."

"Knowing Iris, I'd say the eulogies should be given by men."

"Maybe you're right. We'll ask Susan to pick out the casket and something for Iris to wear." Larry leaned back in his chair. "Well, I believe that's all we can do tonight. I have Columbus Day specials at the store tomorrow—I mean, today—and if I rush home now I can snatch about three hours of sleep."

Qwilleran said, "I'd like to mention one thing: Iris complained of hearing peculiar noises after dark. Did you ever hear anything unusual?"

"Can't say that I did. I've been here many times at a late hour when we were setting up

30

exhibits, and all I ever heard was crickets and frogs and maybe a loon."

"When I arrived tonight, Larry, the whole place was in darkness. I thought it was a power failure, but when I tried the wall switches, everything worked. How do you explain that?"

"I don't know," said Larry, obviously tired and impatient to leave. "When we found out her eyesight was getting bad, we told Iris not to try to conserve electricity, but she had thrifty habits. I'll get you some keys from the office." He went through the doorway to the museum and soon returned, holding up two keys. "This one is for the front door of the apartment, and this one is for the barn. You might want to put your car in the barn in bad weather. There's a good supply of wood for the fireplaces, too."

"Which barn?"

"The new steel barn. The old barn is full of printing presses."

"How about this door to the museum? Does it lock?"

"No, we've never bothered to install a lock, and Iris always left it open except when she was cooking."

"I'll keep it closed," Qwilleran said, "because of the cats. I don't want them prowling around the museum."

"Do whatever you wish, Qwill. I don't know how to thank you for coming to our rescue. I hope you'll be comfortable. Let me know how it works out."

The two men walked to their cars and drove up Black Creek Lane, Larry in the long station wagon that signified a moneyed country estate, and Qwilleran in his economy-model compact. He drove back to Pickax at a normal speed, thinking:

Someone turned off the lights—switch by switch, room by room, indoors and out.

Someone turned off the microwave oven.

Someone closed the door between the kitchen and the museum.

Three

It was almost dawn when Qwilleran arrived at his apartment in Pickax. The city was eerily silent. Soon alarm clocks would jolt the populace awake, and the seven o'clock siren on the roof of the city hall would rout late sleepers out of bed. They would turn on their radios and hear about the death of Iris Cobb, whereupon the Pickax grapevine would go into operation, relaying the shocking news via telephone lines, across back fences, and over coffee cups at Lois's Luncheonette near the courthouse.

Qwilleran labored wearily up the steep narrow stairs to his rooms over the Klingenschoen garage. Waiting for him at the top of the flight were two disgruntled Siamese— Yum Yum giving him her reproachful look and Koko giving him a piece of his mind. With glaring eyes, switching tail and stiff-legged stance he delivered a single high-intensity syllable, "YOW!" that said it all:

Where have you been? The lights were on all night! Nobody fed us! You left the window open!

"Quiet!" Qwilleran protested. "You sound like Vince Boswell. And don't weary me with petty complaints. I have news that will turn your ears inside out. We've lost Mrs. Cobb! No more homemade meatloaf for you two reprobates!"

He shooed them into their own apartment—a room with soft carpet, cushions, baskets, and TV—and then fell into bed. He slept through the seven o'clock wailing of the siren, and he slept through the first blast of the pneumatic drill on Main Street, where the city was digging up the pavement again.

At eight o'clock he was jerked back to consciousness by a phone call from Arch Riker, his lifelong friend, now publisher of the local newspaper.

Without greeting or apology Riker blurted, "Did you hear the newscast, Qwill? Iris Cobb was found dead at her apartment last night!"

"I know," Qwilleran replied, grumpy and hoarse. "I was the one who found the body, called the police, notified next of kin, planned the funeral, phoned the news to the

34

radio station and your news desk, and got home at five o'clock this morning. Got any more hot breaking news?"

"Go back to sleep, you old grouch," said Riker.

At eight-thirty Polly Duncan called. "Qwill, are you up? Did you hear the distressing news about Iris Cobb?"

Qwilleran controlled his umbrage and gave her a gentler version of his tirade to Arch Riker. Then in the next half hour he was called by Fran Brodie, his former interior designer; Mr. O'Dell, his janitor; and Eddington Smith, who sold secondhand books, all of them taking seriously their commitment to the Pickax grapevine.

In exasperation he rolled out of bed, pressed the button on his computerized coffeemaker, and opened a can of red salmon for the Siamese. As he gulped the first welcome swallows of the hot beverage he watched them eat—bodies close to the floor, tails horizontal, heads snapping sideways. After that, they performed a primitive ritual with wide-open jaws and long pink tongues, followed by a laving of mask and ears with moistened paws, all painstakingly choreographed. And this mundane chore was done with elegance and grace by a pair of fawn-furred, brown-pointed, blue-eyed objects of living art. Qwilleran had discovered that watching the Siamese was therapeutic, relieving fatigue, frustration, irritability, and restlessness—a prescriptionless drug with no adverse side effects.

"Okay, you guys," he said, "I have more news for you. We're moving to the Goodwinter Farmhouse Museum." It was his policy to communicate with them in straightforward terms. As if they understood what he said, they both scooted from the room; they abhorred a change of address.

Qwilleran loaded his car with writing materials, an unabridged dictionary, two suitcases of clothing for the nippy weather ahead, his portable stereo, a few cassettes including *Otello*, and the turkey roaster that served as the cats' commode. Then he produced the wicker hamper in which they were accustomed to travel.

"Let's go!" he called out. "Where are you rascals?" Eighteen pounds of solid cat-flesh had suddenly evaporated. "Come on! Let's not play games!" Eventually, crawling on hands and knees, he found Yum Yum under the bed and Koko in the farthest corner of the clothes closet, hiding behind a pair of running shoes.

Limp and silent they allowed him to drop them into the hamper, but they were hatching a countertactic. As soon as he headed the car for North Middle Hummock they began their program of organized squabbling and hissing. Their lunges at each other rocked the hamper, and their snarls suggested bloody mayhem.

"If you heathens will shut up," Qwilleran yelled, "I'll give you a running commentary on this trip. We are now headed north on Pickax Road and approaching the defunct Goodwinter Mine. As you may recall, it was the scene of a disastrous explosion in 1904."

There was a momentary lull in the backseat racket. The cats liked the sound of his voice. It had a resonance that soothed the savage breasts under that pale silky fur.

He continued in the style of a tour director. "Coming up on the right is the Dimsdale Diner, famous for bad food and worse coffee. Windows haven't been cleaned since the Hoover administration. Here is where we turn onto Ittibittiwassee Road."

His passengers were quietly contented now. The sun was shining; the sky was an October blue with billowing white clouds tinged with silver; the woods were aflame with autumn color. The journey was far dif-

37

ferent from the game of blind-man's buff that Qwilleran had played the night before.

"Hold on to your teeth," he said. "We are about to cross the Old Plank Bridge. Next we'll be rounding some sharp curves. On the left is the infamous Hanging Tree."

After that came the ghost town that had once been North Middle Hummock . . . then the white rail fence of the Fugtree farm . . . and finally the sign carved on barnwood:

GOODWINTER FARMHOUSE MUSEUM
1869
Open Friday through Sunday
1 *to* 4 P.M. *or by appointment*

Black Creek Lane was lined with trees in a riot of gold, wine red, salmon pink, and orange—living reminders of the ancient hardwood forests that had covered Moose County before the lumbermen came. At the end of the vista was the venerable farmhouse.

"We're here!" Qwilleran announced. He carried the hamper into the west wing of the rambling building. "You'll have two fireplaces and wide windowsills with a view of assorted wildlife. That's something you don't get in downtown Pickax."

The Siamese emerged from the hamper cautiously, and then made straight for the kitchen, Yum Yum to the place where she had caught a mouse four months before and Koko to the exact spot where Mrs. Cobb had collapsed. He arched his back, bushed his tail, and pranced in a macabre dance.

Qwilleran shooed them out of the kitchen, and they proceeded to explore methodically, sniffing the rugs, leaping to tabletops with the lightness of feathers, testing the seats of chairs for softness and congenial contour, checking the view from the windowsills, and examining the bathroom, where their commode had been placed. In the parlor Koko recognized a large pine wardrobe—a Pennsylvania German *Schrank*—that had come from the Klingenschoen mansion. It was seven feet high, and he could sail to the top of it in a single calculated leap. On the bookshelves he found only a few paperbacks, most of the space devoted to displaying antique bric-a-brac. Chairs were covered in dark velvet, the better to show cat hairs, and the polished wood floors were scattered with antique Orientals, good for pouncing and skidding.

While the Siamese inspected the premises, Qwilleran brought in the luggage. The writing materials he piled on the dining table in the kitchen. The stereo equipment he placed on an Austrian dower chest in the parlor. His clothing was a problem, however, since the bedroom was filled with Mrs. Cobb's personal belongings. Worse still, in his opinion, was the bedroom furniture: chests and tables with cold marble tops, a platform rocker too dainty in scale, and an enormous headboard of dark wood, intricately designed and reaching almost to the ceiling. It looked as if it might weigh a ton, and he had visions of the thing toppling on him as he lay in bed.

"Tonight will be the test," he said to the prowling Siamese. "Either this old house emits weird noises after dark, or they were all in the poor woman's head. But I doubt whether we'll ever solve the mystery of the darkened house and yard. How many lights were on before she collapsed? There would be light in the kitchen where she was warming milk, perhaps in the bedroom where she was packing a bag, certainly in the yard because she was expecting me. And obviously the microwave had been in use."

Koko said "ik ik ik" and scratched his ear.

Qwilleran locked both cats out of the

kitchen while he sat at the dining table and typed Mrs. Cobb's obituary on her own typewriter. He needed no notes. He was well aware of her credentials as an antique dealer and licensed appraiser, of her accomplishments in cataloguing the vast Klingenschoen collection, of her generous gift to the Historical Society and her tireless efforts in restoring it as a living museum, wheedling cash donations and treasured heirlooms from tight-fisted Moose County families. She had staged programs for schoolchildren, infecting them with a germ of interest in their heritage. And Qwilleran could not end his paean without lauding the cornucopia of cookie delights that poured from her kitchen.

He omitted the fact that all three of her husbands had died unnatural deaths: Hough from food poisoning, Cobb from a murderous accident, and Hackpole . . . Qwilleran preferred not to think about Hackpole.

The obituary finished, he telephoned it to the copydesk of the *Moose County Something* for Tuesday's edition. Admittedly this was an unusual name for a newspaper, but Moose County took pride in being different.

The work had given Qwilleran an appetite, and he foraged in the freezer, putting

41

together a lunch of beef-barley soup and homemade cheese bread.

Before he could finish his repast, the banging of the brass knocker summoned him to the front door. The caller proved to be a scrawny man of middle age, sharp-eyed and sharp-nosed.

"I saw your car in the yard," said a loud twangy voice. "Is there anything I can do for you? I'm Vince Boswell. I've been working on the printing presses in the barn."

It was the voice he had heard on the telephone, the kind that punctures the eardrums like a knife. Qwilleran winced. He said coolly, "How do you do. I've just moved in and I'll be living here for a few weeks."

"That's just fine! Then I don't need to worry about the place. I sort of kept an eye on the museum when Iris was away. You must be Jim Qwilleran that writes for the *Something*. I see your picture in the paper all the time. Will you be spending much time here?"

"I'll be coming and going."

"Then I'll watch the place when you're away. I'm a writer, too—technical stuff, you know. I'm writing a book on the history of the printing press and cataloguing the antique equipment in the barn. Big job!" Boswell looked past Qwilleran and down at the floor. "I see you've got a kitty."

"I have two," Qwilleran said.

"My little girl loves kitties. Maybe my wife could bring Baby over to meet them some day."

Qwilleran cleared his throat. "These are not your usual cats, Mr. Boswell. They're Siamese watch-cats, highly temperamental, and not accustomed to children. I wouldn't want . . . your child to be accidentally scratched." He was aware that Moose County courtesy required him to invite the caller in for a beer or a cup of coffee, but Boswell's clarion voice annoyed him. He said, "I'd ask you in for a cup of coffee, but I'm leaving for the airport. Someone is coming into town for the funeral."

Boswell shook his head sadly. "My wife and me, we felt bad about that. Iris was a nice lady. When is the funeral? Will there be a visitation at the mortuary?"

"I believe the information will be in tomorrow's paper." Qwilleran glanced at his watch. "I'm sorry, but you'll have to excuse me, Mr. Boswell. I want to be there when the plane lands."

"Call me Vince. And let me know if there's anything I can do, you hear?" He left with a wave of the hand that included the cat. "Goodbye, kitty. Nice to meet you, Mr. Qwilleran."

Qwilleran closed the door and turned to Koko. "How did you react to that noisy oaf?"

Koko laid his ears back. Qwilleran thought, No one has ever called him "kitty." A more appropriate form of address would be "Your Excellency" or "Your Eminence."

Before leaving for the airport he telephoned Susan Exbridge at her apartment in Indian Village. He said, "Just want you to know I've moved into Iris's quarters, in case you need me for anything. How's it going?"

The vice president of the Historical Society had energy and enthusiasm to match that of the president. She said, "I'm beat! I rushed out to the museum early this morning and selected some clothes for Iris to be buried in. I decided on that pink suede suit she wore for her wedding last year. Then I chose the casket at Dingleberry's. Iris would love it! It has a pink shirred lining, very feminine. Then I discussed the music with the church organist and lined up hosts for tomorrow night at the funeral home and hired the marching band. I also talked the florists into flying in special pink flowers from Minneapolis. Moose County goes in for rust and gold mums, which would be ghastly with the pink casket lining, don't you think?"

"That sounds like a full day's work, Susan."

"It was! And all so emotional! I haven't had time to cry yet, but now I'm going to drink two martinis and have a good wet weep for poor Iris . . . What did you do today, Qwill?"

"I wrote her obit and phoned it in, and now I'm leaving for the airport to pick up her son," Qwilleran said. "I'll take him to dinner and drop him off at the hotel. His name is Dennis H-o-u-g-h, pronounced Huff. Will you and Larry do the honors tomorrow?"

"What did you have in mind?"

"You might see that he's taken to lunch and dinner and escorted to Dingleberry's at the proper time."

"Is he attractive?" asked Susan without missing a beat. Recently divorced, she was constantly alert to possibilities.

"It depends upon your taste," Qwilleran said. "He's five feet tall, weighs three hundred pounds, and he has a glass eye and dandruff."

45

"Just my type," she said airily.

Qwilleran changed his clothes, found cold roast beef in the refrigerator, which he warmed for the Siamese, and then drove to the airport.

Two years before, the Moose County airport had been little more than a cow pasture and a shack with a windsock, but a grant from the Klingenschoen Fund had upgraded the airstrip and terminal, built hangars and paved a parking lot, while the local garden clubs had landscaped the entrance and planted rust and gold mums.

In the terminal, copies of the Monday *Something* displayed this news on the front page, within a black border:

BULLETIN

Iris Cobb Hackpole was found dead at her apartment in North Middle Hummock early this morning, following an apparent heart attack. She was resident manager of the Goodwinter Farmhouse Museum and partner in a new antique shop opening in Pickax. She had been in ill health. Funeral arrangements to be announced.

As the two-engine turboprop landed and taxied toward the terminal, Qwilleran wondered if he would recognize Dennis from their previous meeting Down Below. He remembered him as a clean-cut, lean-jawed young man just out of college, who worked for an architectural firm. Since then Dennis had married, fathered a child, and started his own business as a building contractor— developments that had brought joy to his mother's heart.

The young man who now walked toward the terminal showed the evidence of a few added years and responsibilities, and his gaunt face showed the evidence of grief and weariness.

Qwilleran gave him a sincere handshake. "It's good to see you again, Dennis. Sorry it has to be under these circumstances."

The son said, "That's the hell of it! My mother kept inviting Cheryl and me up here for a visit, but we were always too busy. I could kick myself now. She never even saw her grandson."

As they started the drive to Pickax Qwilleran asked him, "Did Iris tell you anything about Moose County? About the abandoned mines and all that?"

"Yes, she was a good letter writer. I've

saved most of her letters. Our son can read them some day."

Qwilleran glanced at his passenger and compared his lean and melancholy face with Mrs. Cobb's plump and cheery countenance. "You don't resemble your mother."

"I guess I resemble my father, although I never knew him or even saw his picture," Dennis said. "He died when I was three years old—from food poisoning. All I know is that he had a lousy disposition and was cruel to my mother, and when he died there was a snotty rumor that she poisoned him. You know how it is in small towns; they don't have anything else to do but peddle dirt. So we moved to the city, and she brought me up alone."

"I have profound sympathy for single parents," Qwilleran said. "My mother faced the same challenge, and I'll be the first to admit it wasn't easy for her. How did Iris get into the antique business?"

"She worked as a cook in private homes, and one family had a lot of antiques. Right away she was hooked. We used to study together at the kitchen table—me doing my math and her studying about drawer construction in eighteenth-century highboys or whatever. Then she met C. C. Cobb, and they opened the Junkery on Zwinger Street where you lived. I guess you know the rest."

"Cobb was a rough character."

"So was Hackpole, from what I hear."

"The less said about that zero, the better," said Qwilleran with a frown. "Are you hungry? We could stop at a restaurant. Pickax has a couple of good ones."

"I had some chili in Minneapolis while I was waiting for the shuttle, but I could stand a burger and a beer."

They went to the Old Stone Mill, a century-old grist mill converted into a restaurant, with the waterwheel still turning and creaking. Dennis had his beer, and Qwilleran ordered Squunk water with a twist.

"It's better than it sounds," he explained. "It's a local mineral water that comes from a flowing well at Squunk Corners." Then he said, "I'm sorry Iris didn't live to see the opening of Exbridge and Cobb. It's a far cry from the Junkery on Zwinger Street. Her apartment at the museum is also filled with important antiques. You'll probably inherit them."

"I don't think so," said Dennis. "She knew I didn't go in for old furniture and stuff. Cheryl and I like glass and steel and that molded plastic from Italy. But I want to see the museum. I used to work for a firm that restored historic buildings."

"The Goodwinter farmhouse is a remarkable example, and its restoration was all her brainwork. It's about thirty miles out of Pickax, and I questioned the advisability of her living there alone."

"So did I. I wanted her to get a Doberman or a German shepherd, but she vetoed that idea in a hurry. She wouldn't like a dog unless it had Chippendale legs."

"Did you two keep in touch regularly?"

"Yes, we had a good relationship. I phoned every Sunday, and she wrote once or twice a week. Do you know her handwriting? It's impossible!"

"Only a cryptographer could read it."

"So I gave her a typewriter. She loved that machine! She loved the museum. She loved Pickax. She was a very happy woman . . . and then the wings fell off."

"What do you mean?"

"She went to the doctor for indigestion and found out she'd had a silent coronary. Her cholesterol was sky-high; her blood sugar was iffy; and she was about fifty pounds overweight. Psychologically she crashed!"

"But she always looked healthy."

"That's why it was such a bummer. She

got depressed, and then she began to turn off about the museum . . . Do you believe in ghosts?"

"I'm afraid not."

"Neither do I, but Mom was always interested in spirits—friendly ones, that is."

"I know all about that," Qwilleran said. "On Zwinger Street she claimed there was a playful apparition in the house, but I happen to know that C. C. Cobb was playing tricks. Every night he got out of bed without disturbing her and put a saltshaker in her bedroom slippers or hung her underpants from the chandelier. He must have worked hard to think up a new prank every night."

"That's what I call devotion," Dennis said.

"Frankly, I think she knew, but she didn't want C. C. to know that she knew. That's *real* devotion!"

The hamburgers were served, and the two men ate in silence for a few minutes. Then Qwilleran said, "You mentioned that Iris began to be disillusioned about the museum. I was not aware of that."

Dennis nodded soberly. "She began to think the place was haunted. At first she was amused, but then she got frightened. Cheryl and I tried to get her down to St. Louis for a visit. We thought a change of scene would do her some good, but she wouldn't leave until after the formal opening of the shop. Maybe it was her medication—I don't know—but she kept hearing noises she couldn't explain. That can happen in an old house, you know—creaking timbers, mice, drafts in the chimney . . ."

"Did she give you any particulars?"

"I brought some of her letters," Dennis said. "They're in my luggage. I thought you could read them and see if anything clicks. It doesn't make sense to me. I want to ask her doctor about it when I see him."

"Doctor Halifax is a wonderful, humane being, willing to listen and explain. You'll like him."

They drove to the New Pickax Hotel, as it was called, Qwilleran warning Dennis not to expect state-of-the-art accommodations. "The hotel was 'new' in the 1930s, but it's convenient, being right downtown and handy to the funeral home. Larry Lanspeak will be in touch with you tomorrow—or even tonight. He's president of the Historical Society and a great guy."

"Yeah, Mom raved about the Lanspeaks."

They parked in front of the hotel, and

Qwilleran accompanied Dennis to the front desk, where the presence of the famous moustache assured deluxe service from the hotel staff. The night desk clerk was one of the big good-looking blond men who were in plentiful supply in Moose County.

Qwilleran said to him, "Mitch, I made a reservation for Dennis Hough, spelled H-o-u-g-h. He's here for Mrs. Cobb's funeral. See that he gets the best . . . Dennis, this is Mitch Ogilvie, a member of the Historical Society. He knew your mother."

"I was sorry to hear the bad news, Mr. Hough," said the clerk. "She was a terrific person, and she loved the museum."

Dennis mumbled his thanks and signed the register.

"Good night, Dennis," Qwilleran said. "I'll see you at the funeral home tomorrow evening."

"Thanks for everything, Qwill . . . Hold it!" He took an envelope from his carry-on duffel and handed it over. "These are photocopies. You don't need to return them. They're some of her recent letters. The last one arrived Saturday. Maybe you can figure out what was going on at the museum . . . or whether it was . . ." He tapped his forehead.

Four

After dropping Dennis Hough at the hotel Qwilleran drove to North Middle Hummock through a cloud of spectral blue vapor—moonlight mixed with wisps of fog settling in the valleys of the Hummocks. When he arrived home and turned off his headlights, the farmyard and the farmhouse were bathed in a mystic blueness.

He let himself in and turned on the four-candle ceiling fixture. Only three candles lighted. At the same time two shadowy forms came slinking from the dark parlor and blinked at him.

"What happened to the lights?" he asked them. "Last night all four were operating."

The Siamese yawned and stretched.

"Have you anything to report? Did you hear any unusual sounds?"

Koko groomed his breast with a long pink tongue, and Yum Yum rubbed against Qwilleran's ankles, suggesting a little something to eat. This was the first time they had been left alone here, and Qwilleran looked for tilted pictures, books on the floor, dislodged lampshades, and shredded bathroom tissue. One could never guess how they might react to abandonment in a new environment. Happily, only a few cat hairs on a blue velvet wing chair and some dried weeds on the parlor floor testified to their feline presence; they had chosen Mrs. Cobb's favorite chair as their own, and one or both of them had leaped to the top of the seven-foot *Schrank* to examine the dried arrangement that filled a Shaker basket.

Qwilleran made a cup of coffee before sitting down to read Iris Cobb's last letters, thankful that Dennis had given her the typewriter. The first letter was dated September 22 and began with grandmotherly questions about Dennis Junior, comments on the fine weather, raves about the new antique shop scheduled to open October 17, and a lengthy recipe for a new high-calorie dessert she had invented, after which she wrote:

I'm having so much fun at the museum. The other day I thought it would be nice if we displayed a long-handled bedwarmer in one of our exhibit bedrooms, and I remembered that someone had donated a bed-

warmer in poor condition. I looked it up on the computer. (The Klingenschoen Fund paid to have our catalogue computerized. Isn't that nice?) Sure enough, it said the brass pan was dented and the handle was loose but it was worthy of restoration. So I went downstairs to look for it.

The basement is a catchall for damaged stuff, and I was poking around, looking for the bedwarmer, when I heard a mysterious (did I spell that right?) knocking sound in the wall. I said to myself—Oh, goody! We've got a ghost! I listened and decided which wall it was coming from, and then I picked up an old wooden potato masher that was lying around and went rat-tat-tat on the wall myself. After that there was no more knocking. If it was a ghost, I guess I frightened it away.

I wish you could come for the shop's grand opening. It's going to be very gala. Susan's arranging for champagne punch and flowers and everything.

Love from Mother

Qwilleran thought, Gold and rust mums, no doubt. He turned to the next letter, dated September 30, and discovered a drastic change of mood. Mrs. Cobb wrote:

56

Dear Dennis and Cheryl,

I'm terribly upset. I just got my report from Dr. Hal and everything is wrong!! Heart, blood, cholesterol, everything! I've been crying too hard to talk, or I would have phoned. If I don't go on a strict diet and do certain exercises and take medication, I'll need surgery!! It was a horrible shock. Never thought this would happen to me. I felt so good! Now I feel positively suicidal. Did I spell it right? Forgive me for unloading my troubles on you. Can't write any more tonight.

Mother

Poor Iris, Qwilleran thought. His mother had experienced the same panic when her doctor handed her a sentence of death. He picked up the next letter, pleased to find her in a better frame of mind. It was written five days later.

Dear Kids,

Your phone call cheered me up no end. I should have gone down there when you first invited me, but now I have to stay here for the grand opening. In the daytime I feel okay, but at night I get very nervous and depressed, mostly because of the wierd (did

I spell that right?) noises. I told you about the knocking in the basement. Now I hear it all the time—moaning and rattling too. Sometimes I think it's all in my head, and then I get really worried and that awful tightness in my chest.

I've always said an old house reflects the people who've lived in it, like something gets into the wood and plaster. It sounds crazy, I know, but bad things have always happened to the Goodwinters—suicide, fatal accidents, murder. I can feel it in the atmosphere of the house, and it's making me very uncomfortable. Is it my imagination? Or is it evil spirits?

I've been so concerned about my own troubles that I forgot to ask about little Denny. Did you find out what caused his rash?

Love from Mom and Grandmom

The last letter was not dated, but Dennis had received it on Saturday, the day before his mother died.

Dear Dennis,

I don't know how much longer I can stand it—the noises, I mean. The volunteers don't hear anything. I'm the only one

58

that hears it. I told Dr. Hal, and he took me off medication for a few days, but it doesn't make any difference. I still hear the noises, but only when I'm alone. I hate to tell Larry. He'll think I'm crazy. The museum's open Friday, Saturday, and Sunday, and there'll be people around. I'm going to wait until Monday, and if it isn't any better, I'm going to resign.

Mother

P.S. Now I don't hear it any more.

Dennis, receiving the letter on Saturday, called Dr. Halifax and bought a plane ticket for Monday. On Sunday night she died, her face contorted with pain—or what? She was frightened to death, Qwilleran decided. By what? Or by whom?

After reading the last letter he was in no hurry to go to bed with that monstrous headboard towering over him. He considered sleeping on the sofa, but first he had to conduct an experiment. It was his intention to sit up until midnight with lamps and chandeliers alight in every room and with the stereo blasting at full volume. Then, precisely at midnight, he would turn everything off and sit in the dark, listening.

For Phase One of this strategy he marched

through the apartment, flipping on light switches and activating lamps. In the entrance hall only two candles responded. The night before, it had been four. An hour ago it was three. He huffed into his moustache, having little patience with electrical equipment that failed to do its duty, and he was in no mood to go hunting for spare lightbulbs.

Comfortable in his Mackintosh bathrobe and moosehide slippers, he treated the cats to a sardine and prepared another cup of coffee for himself. Then he inserted the *Otello* cassette into the stereo and settled into the blue velvet wing chair in front of the fireplace. He refrained from building a fire; the crackling logs would spoil the pure tones on the cassette.

This time he hoped to hear the recording from start to finish without interruption. To his consternation, just as Othello and Desdemona approached their love duet in Act One, the telephone rang. He turned down the volume and went to the phone in the bedroom.

"Qwill, this is Larry," said the energetic voice. "I've just talked to Dennis Hough on the phone. Thanks for getting him installed at the hotel. He says his accommodations are very good."

"I hope they didn't give him the bridal suite with the round bed and satin sheets," Qwilleran said moodily, resenting the interruption.

"He's in the presidential suite—the only one with a telephone and color TV. Everything's set for tomorrow. Susan will take him to lunch; Carol and I will take both of them to dinner. Is everything okay at the museum? Are you comfortable there?"

"I expect to have nightmares from sleeping in that monster of a bed."

In a tone of mock rebuke Larry said, "That monster, Qwill, is a priceless General Grant bed that was made a century ago for a World's Fair! Look at the quality of the rosewood! Look at the workmanship! Look at the patina!"

"Be that as it may, Larry, the headboard looks like the door to a mausoleum, and I'm not ready to be interred. Otherwise, all is well."

"I'll say good night, then. It's been a hectic day, and neither of us had much sleep last night, did we? I finally lined up the other pallbearers, so now I'm going to have a much deserved nightcap and turn in."

"One question, Larry. Did you see Iris during museum visiting hours this past week?"

"I didn't, but Carol did. She said Iris looked tired and worried—the result of her medical report, no doubt, and maybe the stress of opening the new shop. Carol told her to go and lie down."

Qwilleran went back to his opera, but he had missed the love duet. He turned off the machine peevishly, checked the cats' whereabouts, doused the lights, and sprawled in the blue wing chair with his feet on the footstool. Then he waited in the dark—waiting and listening for the knocking, moaning, rattling, and screaming.

Four hours later he opened his eyes suddenly. He had a kink in his neck and two Siamese on his lap, their combined weight having caused one foot to be totally numb. Asleep they weighed twice what they weighed on the veterinarian's scale. Qwilleran limped about the room, grumbling and stamping his deadened foot. If there had been noises in the walls, he had slept through them in a blissful stupor. Larry's phone call was the last thing he remembered.

In retrospect there was something about the call that bothered him. Larry had mentioned pallbearers. He said he had lined up "the other pallbearers." What, Qwilleran wondered, did he mean by "other"?

He waited fretfully for seven o'clock, at which time he telephoned the Lanspeak country house. Without preamble he said, "Larry, may I ask a question?"

"Sure, what's on your mind?"

"Who are the pallbearers?"

"The three male members of the museum board and Mitch Ogilvie—in addition to you and me. Why do you ask?"

"Just for the record," Qwilleran said, "no one up to this minute has even hinted that I might be a pallbearer—not that I have any objection, you understand—but I'm glad I happened to find out."

"Didn't Susan talk to you?"

"She talked to me at considerable length about a pink suede suit and a casket with pink lining and pink flowers being flown in from Minneapolis, but not a word about pall-bearing."

"I'm sorry, Qwill. Does it create a prob-lem?"

"No. No problem. I merely wanted to be sure."

The truth was that it created a definite problem. It called for a dark suit—something Qwilleran had not owned for twenty-five years. Neither in his lean years nor in his newly acquired affluence had he found an extensive wardrobe important to his life-style. In Moose County he could get by with sweaters, windbreakers, a tweed sports coat with leather patches, and a navy blue blazer. At the moment he owned one suit, a light gray, purchased when he was best man at Iris Cobb's marriage to Hackpole. It had not been off the hanger since that memorable occasion.

At nine o'clock sharp he telephoned Scottie's Men's Shop in downtown Pickax, saying, "I need a dark suit in a hurry, Scottie."

"How darrrk, laddie and in how much of a hurrry," said the proprietor. He liked to burr his *r*'s for Qwilleran, who always made it known that his mother's maiden name was Mackintosh.

"Very dark. I'm going to be a pallbearer, and the funeral's at ten-thirty tomorrow morning. Do you have a tailor on tap?"

"Aye, but canna say for how long. He were goin' to the doctor. Get over here in five minutes and he can fit you."

"I'm not in Pickax, Scottie. I'm living at the Goodwinter farmhouse. Can you keep him there for half an hour? Bribe the guy!"

"Weel, he's a stubborrrrn Scot, but I'll do my best."

Qwilleran made a dash for his razor, slapped on the lather, and cut himself. Just as he was stanching the blood and muttering under his breath, the brass door knocker clanged.

"Damn that Boswell!" he said aloud. He was sure it was the bothersome Boswell; who else would call at such an hour?

In his short shavecoat and with half a faceful of lather, he strode to the entrance hall and yanked open the door. There on the doorstep stood a startled woman holding a plate of biscuits. She covered her face with one hand in embarrassment. "Oh, you're shavin'! Pardon me, Mr. Qwilleran," she said in a soft southern drawl. Each lilting statement ended with emphasis on the last word and an implied question mark. "I'm your neighbor, Verona *Boswell?* I brought you some fresh biscuits . . . for your *breakfast?*" It was a refreshing sound in Moose County, 400 miles north of North, but Qwilleran had no time for refreshment.

"Thank you. Thank you very much," he said briskly, accepting the plate.

"I just wanted to say . . . *welcome?*"

"That's kind of you." He tried not to be

curt. On the other hand, the lather was drying on his face and Scottie's tailor was pacing the floor.

"Let us know if there's anythin' we can . . . *do for you?*"

"I appreciate your thoughtfulness."

"I hope we can better acquainted after the . . . *funeral?*"

"Indeed, Mrs. Boswell." He had stepped back and was beginning to close the door.

"Oh, please call me . . . *Verona?* You'll see us around a lot."

"I'm sure I shall, but I must ask you to excuse me now. I'm leaving for Pickax on urgent business."

"Then I won't hold you up. We'll probably see you tonight at the . . . *visitation?*" Reluctantly she backed away, saying, "My little girl would love to meet your kitties."

Qwilleran finished dressing with clenched jaw. He had always lived in cities, where one could ignore neighbors and be completely ignored in return. The smothering neighborliness of the Boswells, he feared, might be a problem—not to mention "Baby" who wanted to meet the "kitties." Was that really her name? Baby Boswell! Qwilleran disliked the child even before setting eyes on her. He was sure she would be one of those insufferable tots—cute, vain, and precocious. Like W. C. Fields he had never developed a liking for small children.

As for Verona Boswell, she was not unattractive, and her gentle voice was a welcome contrast to her husband's shrillness. Verona was somewhat younger than Vince, but she had lost her freshness—probably, Qwilleran decided, from listening to his whining harangue. Whatever their neighborly virtues, he determined to see as little as possible of the Boswells.

Driving to Pickax in a huff he was stopped for speeding, but the state trooper looked at his driver's license and the distinctive moustache and merely issued a warning. At the men's store Scottie was waiting with a selection of dark blue suits, while a tailor with a tape measure around his neck stood nervously in the background.

"I don't want to pay too much," Qwilleran said, scanning the pricetags.

"Spoken like a true Mackintosh," said the storekeeper, nodding his shaggy gray head. "That clan always had deep pockets and shorrrt arrrms. Perhaps you'd like to rent a suit if it's only for a funeral."

Qwilleran scowled at him.

"On the other hand, mon, a darrrk suit is

67

handy to have in the closet in case you suddenly want to get married."

Qwilleran made a selection reluctantly, considering all the suits overpriced.

As the tailor checked the fit, hoisting here and tugging there, Scottie said, "So you're stayin' at the Goodwinter farmhouse, are you? Have you seen a dead man sittin' on a keg of gold coins?"

"So far I've been denied that pleasure," Qwilleran replied. "Is he supposed to be a regular visitor?"

"Old Ephraim Goodwinter was a miser, you know, and they say he still comes back to count his money. How do you want to pay for this suit? Cash? Credit card? Ten dollars a week?"

From the men's store Qwilleran drove to the Pickax industrial park, where the *Moose County Something* occupied a new building. Designed to house editorial and business offices as well as a modern printing plant, the building was a costly project made possible by an interest-free loan from the Klingenschoen Fund. The daily masthead on page four listed the following:

ARCH RIKER, *editor and publisher*
JUNIOR GOODWINTER, *managing editor*

68

Qwilleran first walked into the managing editor's office, which was dominated by a large, old-fashioned rolltop desk that dwarfed the young man sitting in front of it. The desk had belonged to his great-grandfather, the miserly Ephraim.

Junior Goodwinter had a boyish face and a boyish build and was growing a beard in an attempt to look older than fifteen. "Hey! Pull up a chair! Put your feet up!" he greeted Qwilleran. "That was a swell piece you wrote about Iris Cobb. I hear you're house-sitting at my old homestead."

"For a while, until they find a new manager. I hope to do some research while I'm there. How's the ancestral desk working out?"

"Not so swift. All those pigeonholes and small drawers look like a good idea, but you file something away and never find it again. I like the idea of the rolltop, though. I can stuff my unfinished work in there, roll the top down, and go home with a clear conscience."

"Have you discovered any secret compartments? I imagine Ephraim had a few secrets he wanted to hide."

"Golly, I wouldn't know where to start looking for secret compartments. Why don't you bring Koko down here and let him sniff around. He's good at that."

"He's been doing a lot of sniffing since we moved into the farmhouse. He remembers Iris and wonders why she's not there. By the way, just before she died she talked about hearing unearthly noises. Did you ever have any supernatural adventures when you lived there?"

"No," said Junior. "I was too busy riding horses and scrapping with my six-foot-four brother."

"You never told me you were an equestrian, Junior."

"Oh, sure. Didn't you know that? I wanted to be a jockey, but my parents objected. The alternatives were a bell-hop or a hundred-ten-pound journalist."

"How's the new baby?" Qwilleran asked, never able to remember the name or sex of his young friends' offspring.

"Incredible kid! This morning he grabbed my finger so hard I couldn't pull away. And only four weeks old! Four weeks and three days!"

Tight-fisted like his great-great-grandfather, Qwilleran thought. Then he pointed toward the door. "Who's that? Is that William Allen?" A large white cat had walked into the office with a managerial swagger.

"That's him in person—not a reincarnation," Junior said. "He escaped from the fire in the old building, miraculously. Probably incurred a little smoke damage, but he cleaned it up without making an insurance claim. We found him a month ago, ten months after the fire. Guess where he was! Sitting in front of the State Unemployment Office!"

Next Qwilleran visited the office of the publisher. Arch Riker was sitting in a high-backed executive chair in front of a curved walnut slab supported by two marble monoliths.

"How do you like working in this spiffy environment?" Qwilleran asked. "I detect the fine hand of Amanda's Design Studio."

"It cramps my style. I'm afraid to put my feet on my desk," said Riker, who claimed to do his best thinking with his feet elevated.

"Those underpinnings look like used tombstones."

"I wouldn't be surprised if they were. Amanda has all the instincts of a grave robber . . . Say, that was a decent obit you wrote for Iris Cobb. I hope you write one that's

71

half that good when it's my turn to go. What's the story behind the story?"

"Meaning what?"

"Don't play dumb, Qwill. You know you always suspect that a car accident is a suicide, and a suicide is a murder. What really happened Sunday night? You look preoccupied."

Qwilleran touched his moustache in a guilty gesture but said glibly, "If I look preoccupied, Arch, it's because I've bought a dark suit for the funeral—I'm one of the pallbearers—and it's a question whether Scottie will have it ready on time. Are you going to Dingleberry's tonight?"

"That's my intention. I'm taking the lovely Amanda to dinner, and we'll stop at the funeral home afterward, if she can still stand up and walk straight."

"Tell the bartender to water her bourbon," Qwilleran suggested. "We don't want your inamorata to disgrace herself at Dingleberry's."

As lifelong comrades the two men had sniggered about their boyhood crushes, gloated over their youthful affairs, confided about their marriage problems, and shared the pain of the subsequent divorces. Currently they indulged in private banter about

72

Riker's cranky, outspoken, bibulous friend Amanda. There were many complimentary adjectives that could apply to this successful businesswoman and aggressive member of the city council, but "lovely" was not one of them.

Riker asked, "Will you and Polly be there?"

"She has a dinner meeting with the library board, but she'll drop in later."

"Perhaps we could go somewhere afterward—the four of us," Riker proposed. "I always need some liquid regalement after paying my respects to the deceased."

Qwilleran stood up to leave. "Sounds good. See you at Dingleberry's."

"Not so fast! How long are you going to be downtown? Can you hang around until lunchtime?"

"Not today. I have to go home and unpack my clothes, and find out where they store the spare lightbulbs, and take inventory of the freezer. Iris always cooked as if she expected forty unexpected guests for dinner."

"Home! You've been there half a day, and you call it home. You have a faculty for quick adjustment."

"I'm a gypsy at heart," Qwilleran said. "Home is where I hang my toothbrush and where the cats have their commode. See you tonight."

Driving to North Middle Hummock he noticed that the wind had risen and the leaves were beginning to fall. On Fugtree Road the pavement was carpeted with yellow leaves from the aspens. It would be a pleasant day to take a walk, he thought. His bicycle was in Pickax, and he missed his daily exercise. He was feeling relaxed and in a good humor; a little banter with his colleagues at the *Something* always put him in an amiable mood. A moment later, his equanimity was shattered.

As he turned the corner into Black Creek Lane he jammed on the brakes. A small child was standing in the middle of the lane, holding a toy of some kind.

At the urgent sound of tires crunching on gravel Mrs. Boswell ran out of the house, crying helplessly, "Baby! I told you to stay in the yard!" She picked up the tiny tot under one arm and took the toy away from her. "This is Daddy's. You're not supposed to touch it."

Qwilleran rolled down the car window. "That was a narrow escape," he said. "Better put her on a leash."

"I'm so . . . *sorry*, Mr. Qwilleran?"

He continued slowly down the lane, experiencing a delayed chill at the recollection of the near-accident, then thinking about Verona's ingratiating drawl, then realizing that the "toy" was a walkie-talkie. As he parked in the farmyard the Boswell van was pulling away from the old barn; the driver leaned out of the window.

"What time is the funeral tomorrow?" trumpeted the irritating voice, resounding across the landscape.

"Ten-thirty."

"Do you know who they got for pallbearers? I thought they might call on me, being a neighbor and all that. I would've been glad to do it, although I'm plenty busy in the barn. Any time you want to see the printing presses, let me know. I'll take time out and explain everything. It's very interesting."

"I'm sure it is," said Qwilleran, stony-faced.

"We're thinking of going to the visitation tonight, the wife and me. If you want to hitch a ride with us, you're welcome. Plenty of room in the van!"

"That's kind of you, but I'm meeting friends in Pickax."

"That's okay, but don't forget, we're here to help, any time you need us." Boswell waved a friendly farewell and drove up the lane to the hired man's cottage.

Plucking irritably at his moustache Qwilleran let himself into the apartment and searched for the cats—always his first concern upon returning home. They were in the kitchen. They looked surprised that he had returned so soon. They seemed embarrassed, as if he had interrupted some private catly rite that he was not supposed to witness.

"What have you two rapscallions been doing?" he asked.

Koko said "ik ik ik" and Yum Yum nonchalantly groomed a spot on her snowy underside.

"I'm going for a walk, so you can return to whatever shady pastime has been giving you that guilty look."

Leisurely, after changing into a warm-up suit, he walked up the lane, enjoying the glorious October foliage and the vibrant blue of the sky and the yellow blanket of leaves underfoot. When he reached the hired man's cottage he hurried past, lest the Boswells should rush out and engage him in neighborly conversation. At the corner he turned east to explore a stretch of Fugtree Road he had never traveled. It was paved but there were no farmhouses—only rocky pastureland, patches of woodland, and squirrels busy in the oak trees. He walked for about a mile, seeing nothing of interest except a bridge over a narrow stream, evidently Black Creek. Then he retraced his steps, hurrying past the Boswell cottage and slowing down in front of the Fugtree farm.

The Fugtree name was famous in Moose County. The farmhouse had been built by a lumber baron in the nineteenth century, and it was a perfect example of Affluent Victorian—three stories high, with a tower and a wealth of architectural detail. The complex of barns, sheds, and coops indicated it had also been a working farm for a country gentleman with plenty of money. Now the outbuildings were shabby, the house needed a coat of paint, and the grounds were overgrown with weeds. The present occupants were not taking care of the Fugtree property in the manner to which it had been accustomed.

As Qwilleran speculated on its faded grandeur, someone in the side yard looked in his direction with hands on hips. He turned away and walked briskly back to Black Creek Lane. Passing the hired man's cottage he was careful to keep his gaze straight ahead. Even so he was aware of the tot running across the front lawn.

"Hi!" she called out.

He ignored the salutation and walked faster.

"Hi!" she said again as he came abreast of her. He kept on walking. As a youngster in Chicago he had been cautioned never to speak to strange adults, and as an adult in a changing society he considered it prudent never to speak to strange children.

"Hi!" she called after him as he marched resolutely down the lane, scattering leaves underfoot. She was probably a lonely child, he guessed, but he banished the thought and finished his walk at a jog-trot.

Arriving at the apartment he flipped the hall light switch out of sheer curiosity. Three candles responded. First it had been four, then three, then two. Now it was three again. Growling under his breath he strode to the kitchen, where Koko was sitting on the windowsill gazing intently at the barnyard. Yum Yum was watching Koko.

Qwilleran said in a louder voice than usual, "Since you two loafers spend so much time in the kitchen staring into space, perhaps you can tell me where to find the spare lightbulbs. Come on, Koko. Let's have a little input.''

With seeming difficulty Koko wrenched his attention away from the outdoor scene and executed a broad jump from the windowsill to the large freezer chest that Mrs. Cobb had left well stocked with food.

"I said lightbulbs, not meatballs," said Qwilleran. He opened and closed the pine cabinets until he found what he needed—a flame-shaped lightbulb intended for use in candle-style fixtures. He carried this and a kitchen chair to the front hall, the Siamese romping alongside to watch the show. Any action out of the ordinary attracted their attention, and a man climbing on a kitchen chair rated as a spectacle.

After Qwilleran had climbed on the chair, he forgot which light needed replacing. He stepped down and flicked the switch. All four candles responded.

"Spooks!" he muttered as he returned the chair to the kitchen and put the lightbulb back into the broom closet.

Five

The Dingleberry funeral home occupied an old stone mansion on Goodwinter Boulevard, one that had been built by a mining tycoon during Moose County's boom years. Though the exterior was forbidding, the interior had been styled by Amanda's Design Studio. Plush carpet, grasscloth walls, and raw silk draperies were in pale seafoam green, accented with eighteenth-century mahogany furniture and benign oil paintings in expensive frames. The decor was so widely admired that most of the fashionable residences in Pickax were decorated in Dingleberry green.

When Qwilleran arrived on Tuesday evening the large parking lot in the rear was filled and all the legal parking spaces on the boulevard were taken, as well as some of the illegal ones. Entering the establishment he heard a respectful babble of voices in the adjoining rooms. Susan Exbridge, handsomely dressed as usual, quickly approached him in the foyer.

"Dennis is darling!" she said in a subdued voice, restraining her usual dramatics of speech and gesture. "I feel so sorry for him. He thinks Iris would still be alive if he had arrived a day earlier, but I did my best to ease his mind. I took him to lunch at Tipsy's and then drove him around the county. He was quite impressed! When he saw the Fitch estate—it's for sale, you know—he said the big house could be converted into condos, and he'd like to live in the other house himself. I didn't mention it to him, but if he inherits Iris's money he could afford to buy the Fitch property and we could get him into the Theatre Club. He's interested in acting, and we could use a handsome man for leading roles—of his age, I mean. I told him Moose County is a good place to raise a family. Of course, I can't imagine why anyone would want to live in St. Louis anyway, can you?"

"You should be selling real estate," Qwilleran said.

"I may do that if the antique shop isn't a big success. How will I ever be able to swing it without Iris? I had the connections, but she had the know-how. Exbridge and Cobb! It sounded so right! Like Crosse and Blackwell or Bausch and Lomb. Would you like to see her? She looks lovely."

Susan accompanied Qwilleran into the Slumber Room, where visitors were gathered in small groups, speaking in low but animated voices. One entire wall was banked with pink flowers, plus a few red and white blossoms for accent, and Iris Cobb in her pink suede suit lay at peace in a pink-lined casket with her rhinestone-studded eyeglasses folded in one hand as if she had just removed them before taking a nap.

Qwilleran said, "Was the pink nail polish your idea, Susan? I never saw her wear nail polish."

"She said she couldn't because she had her hands in water so much, but she won't have to cook any more, so I thought the polish was a nice touch."

"Don't kid yourself. At this moment she's happily concocting some ethereal delicacy for the angels."

"Have the attorneys called you?" she asked.

"No. Why should they?"

"Thursday morning is the reading of the will. They've asked Larry and me to attend. I wonder why. I'm getting nervous."

Qwilleran said, "Perhaps Iris left you her General Grant bed."

A new group of visitors arrived, and Susan excused herself to return to her greeting post in the foyer. Qwilleran sought out the chief mourner, who was eager to see him.

"Did you read her letters?" Dennis asked.

Qwilleran nodded dolefully. "Her decline was very rapid. It was a damn shame."

"I asked Doctor Halifax if the noises she heard could be the result of taking medication. He wouldn't say yes and wouldn't say no, but I saw the results of her tests, and she had really let herself get in bad shape. He said she had a 'crippling fear' of surgery. I knew that. She had been resisting eye surgery, although her vision was beginning to impair her driving."

"When would you like to see the farmhouse?"

"How about tomorrow after the funeral? I'm curious about—"

Dennis was interrupted by a loud voice at the entrance, and he looked toward the foyer. Everyone turned toward the foyer. The Boswells had arrived and were headed toward the bier, the man carrying their small child. For the first time Qwilleran noticed that he walked with a pronounced limp.

"Look, Baby," he was saying in the voice of a sideshow barker. "This is the nice lady who used to give you cookies. She's gone to live in heaven, and we came to say goodbye."

"Say goodbye to Mrs. Cobb, Baby," said the mother's soft voice.

"Bye-bye," said Baby, curling her fingers in a childish gesture.

"Iris looks so . . . *pretty?* Doesn't she, Baby?"

"Why is she in a box?" For a child of her age she was remarkably articulate, Qwilleran thought.

The father set her down and turned to see Qwilleran watching them. "They've got a good turnout here tonight. Parking lot was all parked up," he said in a voice that could be heard throughout the Slumber Room and adjoining areas. "Biggest visitation I ever went to! Will you take a look at those flowers! She was one popular lady! She didn't act like she had much on the ball, but people liked her. You can tell by the big crowd."

Mrs. Boswell, who was clasping her daughter's hand, said, "Baby, this is the nice man who's living at . . . the *museum?* Say hi to Mr. Qwilleran."

"Hi!" said Baby.

Qwilleran looked down at the creature

four feet below his eye level, pathetically puny in her short blue velvet coat and hat and wrinkled white tights. The outfit had obviously been homemade in a hurry. Before he could reply with a stiff "How do you do," the parents had spotted the Lanspeaks and descended on them, leaving him with Baby.

She looked up in wonder at his moustache and said in her clear, precise speech, "What's that thing on your face?"

"That's my nose," said Qwilleran. "Doesn't your father have a nose?"

"Yes, he has a nose."

"How about your mother? Does she have a nose?"

"Everybody has a nose," said Baby with disdain, as if dealing with a dolt.

"Then you should recognize a nose when you see one."

Baby was not fazed by his evasive logic. "Where do you work?" she asked.

"I don't work. Where do you work?"

"I'm too little. My daddy works."

"Where does he work?"

"In the barn."

"What does he do in the barn?"

Baby scuffed the toe of her doll-size shoe. "I don't know. I don't go to the barn."

"Why not?"

"I'll get dirty."

"A likely story," said Qwilleran, glancing around and hoping to be rescued soon.

"They have kitties in the barn," Baby volunteered.

"If you don't go to the barn, how do you know they have kitties?"

This animated dialogue had attracted the rapt attention of surrounding groups, and Mrs. Boswell swooped in and snatched her daughter away. "Don't pester Mr. Qwilleran," she scolded softly.

It was a relief for him to circulate among the adults. The guest register was a who's who of Pickax: civic leaders, wealthy antique collectors, politicians running for office, and members of the Historical and Genealogical societies—the two most important organizations in a county that took pride in its heritage. The Old-Timers Club, which admitted only lifelong residents of advanced age, was represented by numerous white-haired members, many of them dependent upon canes, walkers, and wheelchairs. Qwilleran thought it commendable that Mitch Ogilvie, the young desk clerk from the hotel, paid lavish attention to these oldsters, listening to their stories and encouraging them to talk.

Arch Riker was there, clutching the arm of the unsteady Amanda. Polly Duncan, in the company of library boardmembers, exchanged glances with Qwilleran across the crowded room; they were always discreet in public. The lively Homer Tibbitt, age ninety-four, was accompanied by an elderly woman with well-coifed hair of a surprisingly youthful brown.

Riker said to Qwilleran, "Who's that old fellow who walks like a robot?"

"When you're his age, you won't be able to get out of bed without a derrick," said Qwilleran. "That's Homer Tibbitt, retired school principal, ninety-four and still doing volunteer work for the museum."

Amanda said, "That eighty-five-year-old woman with the thirty-year-old hair is Rhoda Finney. She's been chasing him for years, even before his wife died. She's one of the Lockmaster Finneys, and we all know about *them!*" Amanda's pronouncements always blended rumor, imagination, and truth in no known proportion. "The old fellow that Homer's talking to is Adam Dingleberry, oldest mortician in three counties." She referred to a frail, stooped figure dependent upon a walker. "He's buried more secrets than a dog buries bones. I'll bet some of them come back to haunt him. Look at the two old fogeys with their heads together, snickering like fools! You can bet Adam's telling dirty stories and Homer made his girl friend turn off her hearing aid."

Riker tugged at her arm. "Come on, Amanda; it's time to go."

Qwilleran maneuvered about the room until he caught Polly's eye, then tilted his head three degrees toward the front door. She said good night to her boardmembers and then followed him.

In the lobby Riker said, "Shall we go to the Old Stone Mill? They stay open later than Stephanie's."

"We'll meet you there," said Qwilleran. Then he and Polly walked to their separate cars.

At the picturesque mill the party of four asked for a quiet table and were conducted to a secluded corner overlooking the water-wheel. They were a motley foursome: the Klingenschoen heir with the overgrown moustache; Arch Riker with the equanimity, thinning hair, and paunchy figure of a life-long newspaper deskman; Polly Duncan, the pleasant-faced, soft-voiced, well-informed administrator of the Pickax public library; Amanda Goodwinter of the Drinking Goodwinters, as her branch of the prominent clan was known. Polly had a matronly figure, a penchant for plain gray suits, and graying hair that was noticeably unstyled, but she was a paragon of fashion compared to Amanda, on whom every new garment looked secondhand and every hair looked purposely out of place. Nevertheless, Riker enjoyed her crotchety company for perverse reasons that Qwilleran could not fathom.

Amanda had her usual bourbon; Polly asked for dry sherry; Riker wanted Scotch; and Qwilleran ordered pumpkin pie and coffee.

Polly said, "Qwill, that was a beautiful obituary you wrote for Iris. In everyday life she was so self-effacing that one tended to forget all her skills and knowledge and admirable qualities."

Amanda raised her glass in a toast. "Here's a wet one to Saint Iris of the Hummocks!" Then she winced and scowled at Riker, who had kicked her under the table.

Polly raised her glass and quoted from *Hamlet:* "And flights of angels sing thee to thy rest."

The two men nodded and sipped in silence. Riker asked, "How was your summer in England, Polly? Did you floor them with your knowledge of Shakespeare?"

She smiled pleasantly. "I had no chance to show off, Arch. I was too busy answering their questions about American movies."

"At least," Qwilleran said, "the English know that the Bard of Avon is an Elizabethan playwright and not a cosmetics distributor."

"Here come the big guns," Amanda muttered as another foursome arrived.

On the way to their table the Lanspeaks, Dennis Hough, and Susan Exbridge stopped to speak to Qwilleran's group, and Polly said to them, "That was a remarkable display at Dingleberry's. All color-coordinated! Even to the pink nail polish!"

"Give Susan the credit for that," Carol Lanspeak said.

"I might have guessed!" said Polly sweetly in what passed as a compliment to Susan's exquisite taste, except that she raised her eyebrows slightly. Qwilleran and Riker exchanged knowing glances. Polly's dim regard for Susan was no secret.

As the new arrivals went on to their table Riker asked, "Is it true that Dingleberry will bury you free if you're a hundred or older?"

"They can afford to," Amanda grumbled. "They're making money hand over fist, but

I've had a helluva tough time collecting my decorating fee."

"They expect to take it out in trade," Qwilleran said.

"The Dingleberry enterprise," said Polly, "involves five generations. Adam Dingleberry's grandfather was a coffin maker. The next generation combined a furniture store with an undertaking parlor, as it used to be known. The present operation is run by Adam and his sons and grandsons."

Amanda said, "Who was that cretin with a jack-hammer voice that came in and disturbed the peace?"

"You made a hit with his kid, Qwill," said Riker. "Who are they?"

"My neighbors at the museum. He's cataloguing the printing presses for the Historical Society . . . Incidentally, Arch, the obituary I submitted referred to visiting hours at the funeral home. Someone changed it to 'visitation' hours. I know it's considered genteel in certain circles, but it's a ridiculous euphemism that doesn't belong in a newspaper with any class. A 'visitation' is a divine manifestation."

"Or a spirit communication," added Polly. "Shakespeare refers to the visitation of Hamlet's father's ghost."

"Speaking of ghosts," Qwilleran said, "has there ever been a rumor that the Good-winter farmhouse is haunted?"

Belligerently Amanda said, "If it isn't, it should be! Three generations died violent deaths, starting with that old tightwad Ephraim, and they all deserved it!"

Her escort rebuked her with quiet amusement. "You're speaking of your blood relatives, Amanda."

"That's not my branch of the family tree. We're crazy but Ephraim's branch has always been rich and mean."

"Quiet, Amanda. People are staring at you."

"Let them stare!" She glowered at surrounding tables.

Still protesting, Riker said, "Our managing editor is a direct descendent of Ephraim, and he's neither rich nor mean. Junior is poor and likable."

"He's only a kid," Amanda growled. "Give him time! He'll turn out rotten like all the rest."

Winking at Qwilleran and gently changing the subject, Riker asked, "Does anyone at this table believe in ghosts?"

"They're hallucinations caused by drugs,

delirium, and other physical and mental disorders," Qwilleran said.

"But they've been around for thousands of years," said Polly. "Read the Bible, Cicero, Plutarch, Dickens, Poe!"

Riker said, "When our kids were young we took a vacation in a rented cabin in the mountains. Our dog went with us, of course. He was a big fearless boxer, but every night that animal would grovel on the cabin floor, whining and cringing like a coward. I never saw anything like it! Later we found out that a former tenant had been murdered by a tramp."

"I have a tale to relate, too," said Polly. "I was traveling in Europe when my mother died. I didn't even know she was ill, but one night I woke up and saw her standing by my bed as clear as could be—in her gray coat with two silver buttons."

"Did she speak?" Riker asked.

"No, but I sat up in bed and said, 'Mother! What are you doing here?' Immediately she vanished. The next morning I learned she had died several hours before I saw her image."

Qwilleran said, "That's known as a delayed crisis apparition, a kind of telepathy caused by intense emotional concentration."

"Hogwash!" said the lovely Amanda.

Qwilleran and Polly murmured a discreet good night in the parking lot of the Old Stone Mill and drove home in separate cars after an affectionate "I'll call you" and "à bientôt."

It was another one of those dark nights when cloud cover hid the moon. Unlike the reckless drive to answer Iris Cobb's cry for help, this journey was taken in a leisurely manner as Qwilleran thought about Polly Duncan and her melodious voice, her literate background, her little jealousies, and her haughty disdain for Susan Exbridge. (Susan had her hair done at Delphine's, spent money on clothes, drove an impressive car, wore real jewelry, lived in Indian Village, served on the library board of directors even though she never read a book—all things of which Polly disapproved.) It surprised him, however, that Polly accepted supernatural manifestations; he thought she had more sense.

He could see a light in the Fugtree farmhouse, and the TV was flickering in the Boswell cottage, but the museum yard was dark. What it needed was a timer to turn on lights automatically at dusk. He parked and

94

reached for the flashlight in the glove compartment, but he had left it in the house. Turning on his headlights he found his way to the entrance, at the same time catching a glimpse of shadowy movement in one of the windows. The cats, he surmised, had been on the windowsill watching for him and had jumped down to meet him. When he opened the door, however, only Yum Yum made an appearance. Koko was elsewhere; he could be heard talking to himself in a musical monologue interspersed with yiks and yowls.

Stealthily Qwilleran stole to the rear of the apartment and observed the cat meandering about the kitchen with his nose to the floor like a bloodhound, sniffing here and there as if detecting spilled food. Mrs. Cobb's cooking habits had been casual. A handful of flung flour often missed the bowl; a vigorously stirred pot splashed; a wooden spoon dripped; a tomato squirted. Yet the floor looked clean and freshly waxed. Koko was following the memory of a scent; he was investigating something known only to himself; and he was giving a running commentary on his discoveries.

Qwilleran changed into night attire before making another attempt to hear the recording of *Otello*. The Siamese joined him in the parlor, but at the first crashing chords they flew out of the room and remained in hiding throughout the storm scene. At one point they thought it safe to come creeping back, but then the trumpets sounded, and they disappeared again.

Just as the triumphant Othello was making his dramatic entrance, the telephone rang. Qwilleran groaned his displeasure, turned down the volume, and took the call in the bedroom.

"Our office has been trying to reach you, Qwill," said the genial attorney who handled legal matters for the Klingenschoen Fund. "As attorneys for Mrs. Cobb we would like to suggest that you attend the reading of her will on Thursday morning."

Qwilleran huffed into his moustache with momentary annoyance. "Do you have a good reason for asking me to be there?"

"I'm sure you will find it interesting. Besides the major bequests to her family, she wished to leave certain remembrances to friends. Eleven o'clock Thursday morning in my office."

Qwilleran thanked him with little enthusiasm and went back to *Otello*. He had been following the libretto in English, and now he had lost his place and lost the drift of the opera. He rewound the tape and punched Play. Again the Siamese staged their absurd pantomime of wild flight and stealthy return; it was becoming a game. This time the tape unreeled as far as the opening scene of Act Two. The villainous Iago was launching into his hate-filled *Credo* when . . . the telephone rang again. Qwilleran shuffled into the bedroom once more.

A woman's voice said, "Mr. Qwilleran, your lights are on."

Lost in the mood of the opera, he hesitated. Lights? What lights? Yardlights? *"My car lights!"* he yelped. "Thanks. Who's calling?"

"Kristi at the Fugtree farm. I can see your place from an upstairs window."

After thanking her again Qwilleran dashed outdoors and turned off his headlights. The beam had faded to a sick yellow, and he knew the battery was down. He was right; the motor refused to turn over. Leaning back in the driver's seat he faced the facts: Country garages close at nine o'clock; It is now past midnight; The funeral is at ten-thirty in the morning; I have to pick up my suit at nine; My battery is dead.

There was only one thing to do. Disagreeable though it might be, it was the only solution to the problem.

Six

Early Wednesday morning Qwilleran clenched his teeth, bit his lip, swallowed his pride, and telephoned the cottage at the top of Black Creek Lane. It was important, he realized, to strike the right tone—not too suddenly friendly, not too apologetic, yet a few degrees warmer than before, with a note of urgency to mask embarrassment.

"Mr. Boswell," he said, "this is Qwilleran. I have a serious problem."

"How can I be of service? It's a privilege and a pleasure," said the voice that knifed the eardrums.

"I neglected to turn off my headlights last night, and my car won't start. Are you, by any chance, equipped to give my battery a jump?"

"Sure thing. I'll run down there pronto."

"I hate to bother you so early, but I have to be in Pickax at nine o'clock . . . for funeral preliminaries."

"No problem at all."

"I'll reimburse you, of course."

"Wouldn't think of it! That's what neighbors are for—to help each other. Be there in a jiffy."

Qwilleran loathed the man's syrupy sentiments and hoped he would not be expected to repay the favor by baby-sitting some evening while they went to a movie in Pickax.

Painful though he found it, Qwilleran survived the Boswell brand of friendliness and thanked him sincerely, though not effusively. As he started his drive to Pickax it occurred to him that some small token of appreciation would be in order, since Boswell refused remuneration. A bottle of something? A box of chocolates? A potted plant? A stuffed toy for Baby? He vetoed the toy immediately; such an avuncular gesture would be misconstrued, and Baby would start hanging around, asking questions, and expecting to pet the "kitties." She might even start calling him Uncle Qwill.

As he passed the Fugtree farm he remembered he owed Kristi Waffle a debt of gratitude as well. Chocolates? A potted plant? A bottle of something? He had not even met the woman. She sounded young and spirited. Apparently she had children, but of what age? Did she have a husband? If so, why was he not cutting the grass? They were hardly well-off. The inevitable pickup truck in the driveway was ready for the graveyard. By the time he arrived at Scotties's he was still in a quandary. A fruit basket? A frozen turkey? A bottle of something?

Qwilleran picked up his dark blue suit and rushed to his apartment over the garage. Across the Park Circle the mourners were already gathering at the Old Stone Church. Traffic was detoured, the cars of the funeral procession were lining up four abreast, and the park itself was filled with curious bystanders. Dressing hurriedly he found black shoes and a white shirt and dark socks, but all his ties were red stripes or red plaid or simply red, so it was back to Scottie's for a suitable tie.

When he finally arrived at the church, properly cravatted, he observed three generations of Dingleberry morticians in charge: old Adam propped up in the narthex, his sons handling details with inconspicuous efficiency, and his grandsons marshalling the procession. Within the church the organ was groaning sonorous chords, the pews were filled, the pink flowers were banked in front of the altar, and Iris Cobb lay in a pink casket in her pink suede suit. This was what she would have wanted for her farewell to Pickax. Although she had always appeared modest, she gloried in the attention and approval of others. Qwilleran felt a surge of joy for his former landlady, his former housekeeper, his eager-to-please friend—who had achieved such status.

After the interment he attended a small luncheon in a private room at Stephanie's. Conversation was in a minor key as guests endeavored to say the right thing, dropping crumbs of comfort, sweetly sad regrets, and nostalgic reminiscences.

Dennis Hough was the first to break the pattern. He said, "I've met some good people up here. No wonder my mother was so happy! I wouldn't mind relocating in Moose County."

"It would please Iris immensely," said Susan Exbridge.

"But I don't know how Cheryl will react to the idea. It's so far away from everything. How's the school system?"

Carol Lanspeak spoke up. "Thanks to the K Fund, we've been able to expand our facilities, improve the curriculum, and hire more teachers."

"The K Fund?"

"That's our affectionate nickname for the Klingenschoen Memorial Fund."

Larry Lanspeak said, "The county has several industrial and commercial builders, but we need a good residential builder. I think you should consider it."

After the luncheon, when Qwilleran and Dennis were driving to North Middle Hummock, the younger man asked, "How does the K Fund operate?"

"It manages and invests the Klingenschoen fortune and disburses the income in ways that will benefit the community—grants, scholarships, low-interest business loans, and so forth."

"If I started a business up here, would I stand a chance of getting a loan?"

"I have no doubt, if you applied to the Fund and presented a good case."

"My mother told me the Klingenschoen fortune is all yours."

"I inherited it, but too much money is a burden," Qwilleran explained. "I solved the problem by turning everything over to the Fund. I let them worry about it."

"That's very generous."

"Not generous; just smart. I have all I need. I used to be quite happy living out of two suitcases and renting a furnished room. I still don't require a lot of possessions."

As they passed a hedged field Qwilleran said, "This is where a flock of blackbirds rose out of the bushes and spooked a man's horse. He was thrown and killed. The blackbirds stage guerrilla warfare against the human population at certain times of year."

"Who was the man?"

"Samson Goodwinter. It happened more than seventy-five years ago, but the natives still talk about it as if it were last week."

"My mother's letters said that all the Goodwinters met with violent deaths."

"Let me explain the Goodwinter family," said Qwilleran. "There are forty-nine of them in the latest Pickax phone book, all descended from four brothers. There are the much admired Goodwinters, like Doctor Halifax, and the eccentric Goodwinters, like Arch Riker's friend Amanda. Another branch of the family specializes in black sheep, or so it would seem. But the unfortunate Goodwinters that your mother mentioned are all the progeny of the eldest brother, Ephraim. He jinxed his whole line of descendents."

"How did he do that?"

"He was greedy. He owned the Goodwinter Mine and the local newspaper and a couple of banks in the county, but he was too stingy to provide safety measures for the mine. The result was an explosion that killed thirty-two miners."

"How long ago did that happen?"

"In 1904. From then on, he was violently hated. To thirty-odd families and their relatives he was the devil incarnate. He tried to make amends by donating a public library, but his victims' families wouldn't forgive. They threw rocks at his house and tried to burn down his barn. His sons and the hired man took turns standing guard with shotguns after dark."

"What did he look like? Do you know?"

"The museum has his portrait—a sour-looking villain with side whiskers and hollow cheeks and a turned-down mouth." They were now driving through the hilly terrain known as the Hummocks. "Around the next bend," Qwilleran pointed out, "you'll see a grotesque tree on a hill. It's called the Hanging Tree. It's where they found Ephraim Goodwinter dangling from a rope on October 30, 1904."

"What happened?"

"His family maintained it was suicide, but

the rumor was circulated via the Pickax grapevine that he was lynched."

"Was there ever any proof, one way or the other?"

"Well, the family produced a suicide note," Qwilleran said, "so there was no investigation, and no charges were brought. And if the lynching story is true, it's curious that no one ever squealed on the vigilantes and there were no deathbed confessions. Today there's a fraternal order called the Noble Sons of the Noose. They're supposed to be direct descendents of the lynch mob."

"What do they do? Have you ever met one of them?"

"No one knows who belongs to the order; not even their wives know. The mayor of Pickax might be a Noble Son. Or the Dingleberry boys. Or Larry Lanspeak. It's a secret that has been handed down for three or four generations, and—believe me!—it's not easy to keep a secret in Moose County. They have a gossip network that makes satellite communication look like the pony express. Of course, they don't call it gossip. It's *shared information*."

"Fantastic!" said Dennis with wonder in his face. "This is interesting country!"

When they reached Black Creek Lane

Qwilleran drove slowly to let his passenger enjoy the beauty of the foliage and the approach to the quaint farmhouse. A rusty van was leaving the barnyard as they arrived.

"Brace yourself," said Qwilleran. "Here comes the loud-mouth who livened things up at the funeral home last night."

The van stopped, and Vince Boswell leaned out. "Sorry I couldn't get to the funeral," he said. "I'm trying to finish work on the presses before snow flies. How many cars went to the cemetery?"

"I didn't count them," Qwilleran snapped, and then—remembering Boswell's assistance in getting his car started—he amended his curt reply in a more cordial tone. "There was a marching band, very impressive. The church was filled."

"Must've been quite a sight. I wish I could've been there to say goodbye to the lady." He peered at Dennis. "I don't believe I've been formally introduced to your friend."

Qwilleran made the introductions briefly.

Boswell said, "Coming to pick up some of your mother's things, I suppose. She had a cookbook that my wife would like to have if you don't want it—just as a remembrance, you know. She's always looking for new

107

things to cook. If you two gentlemen would like to come and have supper with us to-night, you'd be very welcome. It won't be fancy, but it'll be home-cooked."

"That's kind of you," said Qwilleran, "but Mr. Hough's time is limited. He simply wants to see the farmhouse."

"Be glad to show you the printing presses in the barn, sir."

"Not this time, thanks."

"Well, let me know if I can be of any assistance," said Boswell.

As the van drove away, Dennis said, "Do you think he's a Noble Son of the Noose?"

"He's a son of *something*," said Qwilleran, "but he bailed me out of a tight situation this morning, and I should be grateful. Maybe that's why he was hinting for your mother's cookbook."

"At the funeral home last night he asked Larry for my mother's job as resident manager. Sort of premature, don't you think?"

"Vince Boswell isn't noted for his finesse."

First they walked around the grounds, Qwilleran pointing out the features of the house. The original section was built of square logs measuring fourteen by fourteen inches, chinked with mortar made of clay, straw, and hog's blood. The east and west wings were added later, and the whole structure was covered with cedar shingles, now weathered to a silvery gray.

Dennis showed no sentiment when they entered his mother's apartment. He strolled about with his hands in his pockets, commenting on the wide floorboards, the extravagant use of milled woodwork, and the six-over-six windows, many of the panes having the original wavy glass. He said nothing about the General Grant bed or the Pennsylvania *Schrank* or the pewter collection in the kitchen—all considered rare treasures by Iris Cobb.

When they entered the kitchen, Koko rose from his huddle on the windowsill, stretched his long body in a hairpin curve, and made a flying leap to the top of the freezer-chest, six feet away.

"Too early for dinner," Qwilleran told him.

"Is that Koko?" Dennis asked. "My mother told me about him. She said he's very smart."

Koko was now on the floor, tracing abstract patterns with his nose, moving his head from right to left, covering the entire room systematically.

"This is his bloodhound act," Qwilleran explained.

As the cat neared the telephone he became excited, hopped to the seat of the old school desk and sniffed the desktop with moist snorts.

"What's in that desk?" Dennis asked.

Qwilleran lifted the lid. "Papers," he said. There were scribbled notes in Iris Cobb's illegible hand, newspaper clippings, index cards, a magnifying glass, and a battered looseleaf notebook, its black covers now gray with waterspots and flour and hard use.

Dennis said, "That looks like her personal cookbook. She told me it was the only thing she saved from the fire last year. That's because it was in her luggage at the time. She was taking it on her honeymoon, if you can believe that."

"Knowing your mother, I can believe it," said Qwilleran as he returned the book to the desk. "There are women in Moose County who would sell their souls to the devil if they could get their hands on this collection of recipes. Would you like to see the museum now?"

Dennis glanced at his watch. "Sure."

The main section of the house was furnished with trestle tables, rope beds, a pie safe, banister-back chairs, ironstrapped chests and other trappings of a pioneer home. The east wing was devoted to collections of textiles, documents, lighting fixtures and the like. Dennis ignored the stenciled walls that had thrilled his mother, and the window curtains that had required so much research, and the heirlooms she had begged from old families in the area.

"It was the basement where she first heard the knocking," he said.

"Okay, let's go downstairs," said Qwilleran.

A sign at the top of the basement stairs explained that the "cellar" originally had a dirt floor and was used for storing root vegetables and apples in winter, and possibly milk and cream from the family cow. Later a coal bin had been added, and a fruit closet for home canning. The basement now had a concrete floor and the latest in heating and laundry equipment, but the exposed joists overhead were fourteen-inch logs with the bark still in evidence.

Qwilleran found a door leading to a storeroom under the west wing, where damaged furniture and household cast-offs were piled without plan or purpose, among them a wooden potato masher. The stone walls were a foot thick, one of them roughly covered with cracked plaster. Had Iris cracked it, Qwilleran wondered, when she tapped out an answer to the ghostly visitor?

"Nothing here to explain the knocking," said Dennis. "The house is built like Fort Knox. Let's go back upstairs. Susan is picking me up and taking me to see the Fitch property. The real estate broker is meeting us there."

"Are you serious about moving to Moose County?"

"I won't know until I talk it over with Cheryl, but when I tell her about the Fitch estate she might get excited."

Don't tell her about Susan, Qwilleran thought. There was an obvious rapport developing between Dennis and the vivacious divorcée. He had observed it at Dingleberry's and at the luncheon following the funeral, and he noticed it again when Susan arrived and whisked the young man away to the Fitch estate. He was at least fifteen years her junior but tall like her former husband and with the same rugged good looks.

When he had waved the couple on their way he went indoors, flicking the hall lights out of sheer curiosity. The previous flick had activated four candles. Now it was three again. Qwilleran huffed into his moustache.

He had expected to spend the afternoon with Dennis, examining the museum exhibits and looking at the printing presses in the barn, after which they might have had drinks at the Shipwreck Tavern in Mooseville, dinner at the Northern Lights Hotel overlooking the lake, and dessert at the colorful Black Bear Café.

Somewhat disappointed he telephoned Polly at the library. "Would you like to go out tonight? We could have dinner at the Northern Lights and finish up at the Black Bear."

"How would you like to come to my place instead?" she asked.

"You shouldn't have to cook after working all day," he protested.

"Don't worry. I can whip up something very easily."

He knew what it would be. They had recently read a play aloud—*The Cocktail Party* by T. S. Eliot—and since then Polly had been whipping up curried dishes instead of broiling fish or pan-frying chops. He liked Indian fare, but Polly was whipping a good idea to death. Her cottage was beginning to have a permanent aroma of Bombay, as if it had seeped into the carpet and upholstery. "Are you sure you want to take the trouble?" he asked.

"Of course I do! Besides, I have a surprise for you."

"What is it?" Qwilleran hated to be surprised.

"If I tell you, it won't be a surprise, will it? Come at six-thirty. That will give me time to go home and change clothes."

And find the curry powder, he thought. Reluctantly he agreed. He would have preferred broiled whitefish or stuffed porkchops at the Northern Lights.

Now he had time to kill, and it occurred to him that he had never raked leaves. He had interviewed kings; he had been strafed on a Mediterranean beach; and briefly he had been held hostage by a crazed bank robber, but he had never raked leaves. He changed into jeans and a red plaid shirt and went to the steel barn to find a rake.

A year ago the barn had been the scene of an auction when the Goodwinters' household goods were liquidated. Now it functioned as a garage and utility shed, housing garden tools, a work bench, odds and ends of lumber, and stacks of firewood. Mrs. Cobb's station wagon was parked there, and he assumed it would be sold. It was larger than his downscale compact and would more easily accommodate the cats' carrier and their commode. It might be enjoyable to take them on a few trips around the country. The Lanspeaks had been raving about the Blue Ridge Mountains. He wondered if the altitude would hurt their ears.

Finding a rake, Qwilleran embarked on a new experience—pleasant exercise that activated the muscles without engaging the mind. It gave him time to think about the irritating Vince Boswell, Koko's discovery of Iris Cobb's cookbook, the all-too-obvious attraction between Susan Exbridge and Dennis Hough, Polly's promised surprise, and the prospect of another dinner of curried something-or-other.

From the corner of his eye he was aware of someone small approaching him.

"Hi!" said Baby.

Qwilleran grunted a reply and raked faster.

"What are you doing?"

"Raking leaves."

"Why?"

"For the same reason you brush your teeth. It has to be done."

She considered this analogical reasoning

briefly and followed up with, "How old are you?"

"That's classified information. How old are you?"

"Three in April."

"What kind of car do you drive?" Qwilleran asked.

"I don't have a car," she said with a pretty pout. He had to admit she was a pretty child as well as articulate.

"Why not?"

"I'm too little."

"Why don't you grow up?"

As Baby pondered an answer to this baffling question her mother came running down the lane. "Baby? Baby?" she called out in her gentle and ineffectual way. "Daddy doesn't want you to come down here. I'm sorry, Mr. Qwilleran. Was she bothering you? She's always asking annoying . . . *questions?*"

"She's training to be a journalist," Qwilleran said, raking industriously.

He finished his chore with satisfaction, heaping the leaves in piles for the yard crew to remove. Then he went indoors to feed the Siamese. The freezer-chest contained, he estimated, a two-month supply of spaghetti sauce, chili, macaroni and cheese (his favorite), vichyssoise, pot roast, turkey tetrazzini, shrimp gumbo, deviled crab, Swedish meatballs and other Cobb specialties—nothing in curry sauce, he was glad to note.

He thawed some pot roast for the cats, and while they were devouring it he took Mrs. Cobb's personal cookbook from the small desk and looked for his favorite coconut cream cake with apricot filling, but the handwriting defeated him. Over the years the pages had been spotted with cook's fingerprints and smeared with tomato, chocolate, egg yolk, and what appeared to be blood. He thought, One could boil this and make a tasty soup. Koko had probably smelled the presence of the book and tracked it to its hiding place in the desk. Remarkable cat! Sniffing the book himself, he could detect no noticeable scent. He returned it to the desk and dressed for dinner.

Polly lived in a small house on the old MacGregor farm. The last of the Mac-Gregors had died, the main farmhouse was for sale, and the intelligent goose that used to patrol the property was no longer around. For one dark moment as he parked the car Qwilleran envisioned curried goose as Polly's surprise, but when he approached the front door the aroma of curried shrimp assailed his nostrils and he half expected to hear raga music.

"Don't tell me! I can guess what's for dinner," he said.

Her greeting was unusually ardent. She bubbled with an excitement unlike her normal air of subdued happiness.

"Shall we have an Attitude Adjustment Hour before dinner?" she asked, blithely jingling ice cubes in glasses. She served him Squunk water with a twist and passed a plate of olive-and-cheese hors d'oeuvres. Then, raising her sherry glass she said, "Eat thy bread with joy and drink thy Squunk water with a merry heart."

"You're in a good mood tonight," he said. "Did the library board vote you a raise?"

"Guess again."

"They approved a new heating system for the library?"

Polly jumped up. Ordinarily she rose gracefully, but she jumped up saying, "Close your eyes," as she hurried to the bedroom. When she returned he heard a faint squeak, and he opened his eyes to see her holding a small basket in which lay a small white kitten with large brown ears, large brown feet, a dark smudge on his nose, and the indescribably blue eyes of a Siamese.

"Meet my little boy," she said proudly. "He came all the way from Lockmaster on the bus today, traveling by himself."

"Is this what Siamese look like when they're young?" Qwilleran asked in astonishment. He had adopted both Koko and Yum Yum after they were grown.

"Isn't he adorable?" She lifted him from the basket and nuzzled her face against his fur. "We love him to pieces! He's such a sweetheart! . . . Are you my little sweetheart? . . . Yes, he's my little sweetheart. Listen to him purr."

She placed the kitten carefully on the floor, and he lurched across the carpet like a windup toy, his skinny legs splayed at odd angles and his large brown feet flopping like a clown in oversize shoes. Polly explained, "He's still unsteady on his legs, and he doesn't quite know what to do with his feet. Of course, he's a little dismayed, being away from his mother and siblings . . . Aren't you, sweetums?"

Qwilleran had to admit he was an appealing little creature, but he found Polly's commentary cloying. He occasionally called Yum Yum his little sweetheart, but that was different. It was a term of endearment, not maudlin gush. "What's his name?" he asked.

"Bootsie, and he's going to grow up to be just like Koko."

Fat chance, Qwilleran thought, with a name like that! Koko bore the dignified cognomen of Kao K'o Kung, a thirteenth-century Chinese artist. He said, "You told me you didn't want a pet. You always said you were too busy and too often out of town."

"I know," she said, sweetly sheepish, "but the librarian in Lockmaster had a litter, and Bootsie was just too irresistible. Do you want to hold him? First I have to give him a kiss-kiss so that he knows he's loved."

Qwilleran accepted the small bundle gingerly. "He must weigh about three ounces. What's he stuffed with? Goose down?"

"He weighs exactly one pound and eight and a half ounces on my kitchen scale."

"Do you feed him with an eyedropper?"

"He gets a spoonful of nutritional catfood four times a day. It doesn't take much to fill up his little tum-tum."

Bootsie was quite content on Qwilleran's lap, his loud purr shaking his entire twenty-four and a half ounces. Occasionally he emitted a small squeak, closing his eyes in the effort.

"He needs oiling," Qwilleran said.

"That means he likes you. He wants you to be his godfather. Give him a kiss-kiss."

"No thanks. I have jealous cats at home." He was glad when Bootsie was returned to the bedroom and dinner was served.

It was curry again—and hot enough to send him catapulting out of his chair after the first forkful. "Wow!" he said.

"Hot?" Polly inquired.

"Like Hades! What happened?"

"I learned how to mix my own curry powder—fourteen spices, including four kinds of pepper. Would you like some ice water?"

Every few minutes Polly peeked into the bedroom to check the kitten. Asleep or awake? In or out of the basket? Happy or unhappy? Qwilleran could hardly believe that an intelligent, sophisticated, middle-aged woman with an executive position in a public library could be reduced overnight to a blithering fool.

For dessert she served a welcome dish of sherbet and suggested having coffee in the living room. "Would you like Bootsie to join us?" she asked coyly.

"No," he said firmly. "I have a serious matter to discuss with you."

"Really?" She said it with a distracted glance at the bedroom door, having heard a squeak, and he knew he would have to drop a bomb to galvanize her attention.

"It's my theory," he said, "that Iris Cobb's death was a case of murder."

Seven

When Polly heard the word "murder," she was aghast. In Moose County homicide was traditionally considered the exclusive property of the cities Down Below. "What leads you to that conclusion, Qwill?"

"Observation, speculation, cerebration," he replied, smoothing his moustache slyly. "At the Old Stone Mill last night, you may remember, I asked if the Goodwinter farmhouse has the reputation of being haunted. I wasn't simply making conversation. Prior to her death Iris complained about noises in the walls—knocking, moaning, and even screaming. In her last letter to her son she was almost deranged by her fears, hinting that there were evil spirits in the house. Then, just before she died, she saw something outside the kitchen window that terrified her."

"How do you know?"

"She was talking to me on the phone at the time. Shortly after, I arrived and found

123

her dead on the kitchen floor. Strangely, all the lights were turned off, inside and outside the house. A heart attack, the coroner said, but I saw the look of terror on her face, and I say it was not a heart attack pure and simple. She was frightened to death, purposely or accidentally, by something outside the window. It could be the same something that turned off the lights, either before or after she collapsed."

Polly gasped and forgot to look at the bedroom door. "Are you implying—a phantom? You've always scoffed at such things."

"I'm simply saying *I don't know*. Something is going on that I don't understand. Koko spends hours gazing out the very window where Iris saw the frightening vision."

"What is the view from that window?"

"After dark, nothing, unless cats can see things that we don't. In the daytime there's only the barnyard and the old barn beyond. The birds have gone south, it appears, and the squirrels are all up on Fugtree Road, raiding the oak trees. Yet something rivets Koko's attention. He also prowls the kitchen floor, sniffing and mumbling to himself."

"Have you heard any of the noises that disturbed Iris?"

"Not as yet. There's a light fixture that

flashes on and off mysteriously, but that's the only spooky occurrence."

Polly said, "I've heard stories about Ephraim's ghost but considered them nonsense. This is a terrible development, Qwill! Why should it happen to that dear woman?"

"There's a possibility that her medication made her susceptible to certain influences in the house that would not disturb anyone else—or even Iris if her health had been normal."

"Should anything be done about it?"

"I don't see how we can act without more evidence," Qwilleran said. "Give me time. After all, it happened only three days ago."

Polly's brow was creased in puzzlement and concern. Not once had she mentioned Bootsie nor glanced in the direction of the bedroom door. With an agreeable feeling of satisfaction Qwilleran made excuses for leaving early.

Driving home to North Middle Hummock he did some serious thinking about Polly and the way she fussed over that kitten. He himself admired and respected his cats—and God knows he indulged them—but he was not sentimental, he told himself. Polly's fatuous prattle was entirely out of character for a sensible woman. Reviewing the course of their friendship he recalled that it was her intelligence that first attracted him. On certain subjects she was quite erudite. After getting off to a slow start, because of her inherent reserve, their relationship had blossomed. Then, with familiarity she became possessive and slightly officious and sometimes jealous. All of this he could understand, and he could handle it, but her gushing over the kitten was more than he could stomach. There would be no more relaxing country weekends at Polly's cottage with just the two of them—reading Shakespeare aloud and playing music—not while Bootsie diffused her attention. Bootsie! It was a vile name for a Siamese, Qwilleran insisted. Considering her passion for Shakespeare, why didn't she name him Puck?

The reading of Iris Cobb's will took place in the office of Hasselrich, Bennett and Barter on Thursday morning in the presence of Dennis Hough, Larry Lanspeak, Susan Exbridge, and Qwilleran, who attended reluctantly. The senior partner was noted for his affability and buoyant optimism. He was the kind of attorney, Qwilleran had once said, who made it a pleasure to be sued, or divorced, or found guilty—an elderly, balding man with quivering jowls and a slight stoop.

When all were assembled Hasselrich remarked, "I well remember the day Iris Cobb Hackpole came to me to draft her last will and testament. This was three months before her health started to decline. There was nothing morbid about the occasion. She was happy in the knowledge that her possessions would go to those she loved and respected, and to causes she embraced."

He opened cabinet doors behind his desk, rolled out a video screen and touched a remote control. There on the screen was Iris Cobb in her pink suede suit and rhinestone-studded eyeglasses. She was smiling. Her round face was glowing. A hush fell on the viewers.

From the speaker came the cheerful voice: "I, Iris Cobb Hackpole, a single woman of Pickax City in Moose County, being of sound mind and memory but mindful of the uncertainties of life, do hereby declare this instrument to be my last will and testament, hereby revoking any and all wills made by me at any time heretofore."

Swift looks passed between the listeners as she went on to bequeath her extensive financial holdings to her son and his family.

To Susan Exbridge she left her share of the assets of Exbridge & Cobb. She wished the Historical Society to liquidate her antique collection, her car, and her personal belongings, the proceeds to benefit the museum. Excluded were only two items: She wished James Qwilleran to have the Pennsylvania German *Schrank*—for reasons he would understand—and her personal recipe book.

The image on the screen faded, and there was a moment of silence followed by appropriate exclamations and some murmured platitudes from Hasselrich.

Susan said to Qwilleran, "I'll make a deal. You give me the cookbook, and you can have Exbridge and Cobb." To Dennis she said, "Now you can move up here and take over the Fitch property."

"I like the idea," he said, and Qwilleran observed a meaningful stare lingering between them.

When a clerk appeared with a silver tray, Hasselrich himself poured coffee and passed the cups, pointing out proudly that they were his maternal grandmother's Wedgwood.

Larry said to Qwilleran, "I didn't know you were a cook."

"I know as much about cooking as I do

about black holes in the universe," he replied, "but Iris had a sly sense of humor. The joke is that no one can read her handwriting. As for the *Schrank*, I'm glad she left me that and not the General Grant bed."

"How's everything at the farmhouse?"

"I'm learning to live with pink sheets and pink towels, but there is one problem. The closets and dressers are filled with Iris's clothing. With my shirts and pants and sweaters draped over chairs and doorknobs, I wake up at night and think I'm surrounded by spectres."

"Just move her things out of your way, Qwill," said Larry. "You'll find some empty cartons in the basement. Our donation committee will take it from there."

"Another thing, Larry. Either we have gremlins or we have faulty wiring in the hall light fixture. It should be investigated by an electrician."

"I'll alert Homer. He'll get a repairman out there right away." Larry went to the attorney's desk and used the phone. Quick decisions and immediate action were his trademark.

Qwilleran had a second cup of coffee, congratulated the heir, and offered him a ride to the airport.

"Thanks, Qwill, but I've decided to stay over until Sunday," said Dennis. "The formal opening of Exbridge and Cobb was scheduled for Saturday, and Susan is going ahead as planned."

Susan said, "The invitations went into the mail last week, Qwill, and I know Iris wouldn't want us to cancel. She'll be with us in spirit, but I feel it's appropriate to have Dennis represent her in the flesh."

Uh-huh, Qwilleran thought.

"People may think the shop is going to limp along on one leg without Iris," she went on, speaking with animation, "but Dennis's presence will give the venture some stability, don't you think? It's terribly kind of him to offer to stay a few more days."

Uh-huh, Qwilleran thought. She was looking unusually happy; her dramatic gestures were more expansive than ever, and Dennis glanced at her too often.

Before leaving, Qwilleran asked Hasselrich if he proposed to notify the newspaper about the terms of the will.

"It has never been our policy to do so," said the attorney.

"In this case you should reconsider. The Hackpole money is news, and Iris was a V.I.P.," Qwilleran argued. "If you don't make an official statement, the Pickax grapevine will start distorting the facts."

"I'll have to cogitate about that," said Hasselrich.

Qwilleran left him cogitating and drove to the office of the *Moose County Something*, where he found the publisher in his richly decorated office.

"Arch, I never noticed this before," said Qwilleran, "but your walls are Dingleberry green."

"That's where I'll end up—at Dingleberry's—so I'm getting used to it a little at a time. What's on your mind? You look purposeful."

"The Cobb-Hackpole bequests have been announced. You ought to send Roger to the attorney's office to get the story."

"Who are the beneficiaries?"

"Her family, her business partner, the Historical Society, and—to a lesser extent—myself."

"You? What do you need? You own half the county already."

"She left me the seven-foot wardrobe that I gave her for a wedding present. Koko always enjoyed sitting on top of it."

"Let Koko sit on a stepladder. That's a Pennsylvania German *Schrank* and worth a

131

small fortune," said Riker, who knew something about antiques. He touched the intercom button and barked, "Iris Cobb's will
has been read. Qwill tipped us off. Get someone over to HB and B."

Qwilleran said, "She also left me a looseleaf notebook containing all her personal recipes, but you don't need to mention that in
the story."

"I thought you were opposed to censor-
ship," said Riker.

"I see it as a provocative headline: MIL-
LIONAIRE WIDOW BEQUEATHS TO BILLION-
AIRE BACHELOR. That has all kinds of
interesting implications."

The intercom buzzer sounded, and a voice
squawked, "Is Qwill there? Ask if he has
any copy for us. We've used up his backlog."

"Did you hear that?" Riker asked. "Has
the *Qwill Pen* run dry?"

"Straight from the Qwill Pen" was the
name of the column that Qwilleran had
agreed to write for the *Something*. "It's like
this," he explained to Riker. "I planned
some interviews, but Iris's death has kept
me off the beat for a few days."

"That's okay. Just give us a quick think-
piece for tomorrow," Riker said. "Remember Mrs. Fisheye."

Driving back to North Middle Hummock Qwilleran did his quick thinking. Both he and Riker remembered their high school English teacher who regularly assigned the class to write a thousand words on such subjects as the weather, or breakfast, or the color green. Fisheye was not her name, but it was her misfortune to have large, round, pale, watery eyes. As a student Qwilleran had done his share of groaning and protesting, but now he could write a thousand words on any subject at a moment's notice.

Surveying the landscape as he drove out on Ittibittiwassee Road and through the Hummocks he decided on his topic: fences! Moose County was crisscrossed with picket fences, hand-split snake fences, barbed wire, four-bar corral, even root fences, each delivering its own message ranging from Welcome to Keep Out. In the fashionable Hummocks there were low stone walls by the mile as well as six-foot grapestake stockades around swimming pools. In the blighted town of Chipmunk there was a fence constructed of old bedsprings. Qwilleran was prepared—if those observations added up to fewer than a thousand words—to quote Robert Frost, allude to Cole Porter, and trace "fence" to its Latin root. He might even dedicate the column to Mrs. Fisheye.

As he drove past the Fugtree farm he noticed that their white fence needed a coat of paint, and he regretted that he had not adequately thanked the woman who had notified him about his headlights. He would like to buy her a paint job for the fence, but such largess might give the wrong impression. Perhaps, he decided, he should simply write a note of thanks.

Turning into Black Creek Lane he spotted two vehicles parked in the museum yard. One was a conservative dark blue four-door, about ten years old. The other was a van from Pickax Power Problems, Inc. The electrician was preparing to leave, and Homer Tibbitt was accepting his bill.

"Get the lights fixed?" Qwilleran called out to them.

"Nothin' wrong but loose lightbulbs," said the electrician. "If you get a lotta vibration it can shake the bulbs loose—make 'em flicker on and off—'specially them flame types. Screw 'em in tight—no problem."

"What could cause vibration?" Qwilleran asked.

"Who knows? Furnace, pump, appliances —any blame thing that's off-balance. Well, so long! Call me again when you gotta soft job like this."

Qwilleran frowned. He could imagine what Pickax Power Problems would charge for a run all the way out to North Middle Hummock. When he unlocked his door and the cats came to greet him, he said, "You heavyweights have got to stop stamping your feet!"

The Siamese were unusually alert and active for midafternoon, which was their scheduled naptime, but that was understandable. Koko as chief security officer had been keeping a wary eye on the electrician, and Yum Yum had been inspecting his shoelaces. In addition, Homer Tibbitt had accompanied the repairman, and the cats had never seen a human who walked like a robot. The chairman of maintenance, remarkably agile for his age, walked briskly with angular flailing movements of arms and legs.

Mr. Tibbitt had returned to the museum, and Qwilleran followed him to apologize. He found the chairman and an elderly brown-haired woman in the exhibit area.

"No need to apologize," said Tibbitt in his high-pitched voice. "It gives me an excuse to come out here and look things over. *She* drives me," he explained with a nod

135

toward his companion. "They won't renew my license any more. That's the advantage of hooking up with a younger woman. Only trouble with Rhoda is her danged hearing aid. She won't get the blasted thing fixed. *Rhoda, this is Mr. Qwilleran.* This is Rhoda Finney. She taught English in my school when I was principal."

Qwilleran bowed over Ms. Finney's hand, and she beamed at him with the serenity of one who has not heard a word that has been said.

Tibbitt said, "Let's go into the office and have some coffee. *Rhoda, do you want some coffee?*"

"Sorry, I don't have any, dear," she said, rummaging in her handbag. "Would you like a throat lozenge?"

"Never mind." He waved her away and led Qwilleran into the bleak office. It was furnished with oak filing cabinets, scarred wooden tables, mismatched chairs, and shelves of reference books. One table was piled with dreary odds and ends under a sign specifying To Be Catalogued. Another table held an array of instant-beverage jars, paper cups, and plastic spoons.

"I'll do a little cleaning," said Ms. Finney,

taking a feather duster from a hook and toddling from the room.

The old gentleman heated water in an electric kettle and measured out instant-coffee crystals for Qwilleran and coffee substitute for himself. "This insipid stuff is all Doctor Hal will let me drink since my last birthday," he explained, "but it's greatly improved with a few drops of brandy." He showed Qwilleran a silver hip flask engraved with his initials. "Leftover from Prohibition days," he said. "Comes in handy now and then . . . What did you think of the funeral? It was a decent send-off, I thought. Even old Dingleberry was impressed. Larry tells me you're living here till they find a manager. Have you noticed anything unusual?"

"Of what nature?" Qwilleran asked, grooming his moustache with a show of nonchalance.

"They say old Ephraim walks around once in a while. Never saw him myself because I've never been here overnight, but he has some kind of secret up his ghostly sleeve. Old Adam Dingleberry knows what it is, but he's not telling. I've twisted Adam's arm five different ways, but he won't budge, for love nor money."

"My cats have been acting strangely since

we moved in," Qwilleran said. "I thought they might be searching for Iris Cobb. She invited them here to dinner a couple of times."

"No doubt they're seeing an invisible presence," said Tibbitt in all seriousness.

"Do you know anyone who has actually seen Ephraim's so-called ghost?"

"Senior Goodwinter told me something shortly before his accident. He said the old man came straight through the wall one night, carrying a rope. He was as silent as the grave. That was almost ninety years after Ephraim died, mind you! It gave Senior a suffocating feeling. Then the vision disappeared into the same wall he'd come from, and a few days later, Senior was dead."

"Which wall?" Qwilleran asked as his thoughts went to Iris Cobb and the potato masher. "Do you know which wall?"

"He didn't tell me that."

"Did any of the family ever see Ephraim looking in a window at night?"

"No one ever mentioned it, but the Goodwinters were inclined to be hush-hush about the whole matter. I was surprised when Senior confided in me. I'd been his teacher in the early grades, and so I guess he trusted me."

"I get the impression that people up here are strong believers in the spirits of the dead."

"Yes indeed! This is a good ghost country—like Scotland, you know. We have a lot of Scots here. Didn't you tell me you're a Scot?"

"My mother was a Mackintosh," Qwilleran informed him with an air of pride, "and she never saw a ghost to my knowledge. Certainly she never talked about ghosts in my presence."

"You need sensitivity and an open mind, of course. Skeptics don't know what they're missing."

"Did you ever see an apparition?"

"I certainly did! Thirty-two of them! You've heard of the explosion at the Goodwinter Mine in 1904? Thirty-two miners blown to bits! Well . . . twenty years after that disaster I had a curious experience— twenty years to the day, May thirteenth. I'd been visiting a young lady who lived in the country. I lived in Pickax, a distance of six miles, and I was walking home. Not many folks in Moose County had automobiles in those days, and I didn't even have a bicycle. So I was walking home around midnight along North Pickax Road. It wasn't paved in those days. Do you know where that hill rises just north of the mine? It was only a slag heap then, and when I reached it I saw some shadows moving across the top of the heap. I stopped and stared into the darkness and realized they were men—plodding along with pickaxes and lunch buckets and with never a sound. Then they disappeared over the hill. I counted; there were thirty-two of them, and every one had a light on the front of his head. In my mind I can still see those bobbing lights as the column of men trudged along. There was no wind that night, but after they passed by, the leaves of the trees rustled and I felt a chill."

Qwilleran was respectfully quiet for a few moments before he said, "Did you say that was in 1924? Prohibition was in effect. Are you sure you hadn't been taking a nip of white lightning from that silver flask?"

"I'm not the only one who saw them," Homer protested. "And it was always on the anniversary of the explosion—May thirteenth."

"Are they still being seen?"

"Not very likely. Now that the road's paved and cars are whizzing by at seventy miles an hour, who could see anything as ephemeral as a ghost? But I'll tell you what!

Next year, on the night of May thirteenth, you and I will go out to the Goodwinter Mine site, park the car, and wait for something to happen."

"I'll mark it on my calendar," Qwilleran said, "but don't forget to take your flask along."

At that moment Rhoda Finney entered the office with her feather duster. Seeing the coffee cups she said, "You naughty men! You didn't tell me you were having coffee!"

Homer glanced at Qwilleran and shrugged hopelessly. Hoisting himself out of his chair, he prepared to measure an instant beverage from the row of jars on the table. *"What kind?"* he shouted.

Ms. Finney looked at her watch. "Seventeen minutes after two, dear." She whisked a few items of office furniture with the duster before sitting down.

Qwilleran said, "This museum operation seems to be very well organized."

"Yes indeed," said Homer. "Larry runs a tight ship. We have twelve active committees and seventy-five volunteers. I ride herd on the maintenance staff. We have high school students doing the yard work, earning points for community service. We have twenty able-bodied volunteers doing the cleaning, if you count Rhoda with her blasted feather duster. We hire professionals—like Pickax Power Problems—to do repairs. For window washing the county sends us jail inmates."

"Do you ever find any loose shutters banging in the wind? Any loose shingles on the side of the house?"

"Nothing's been reported, and if it's not broken, we don't fix it."

"Did you know the plaster is cracked in the basement under the west wing?"

Homer dismissed the matter with an angular wave of the hand. "You mean the magpie nest? That's a repository for junk donated to the museum: broken furniture, rusty tools, moldy books, cracked crockery, stained slop jars and potties."

"The poppies were beautiful this year," Rhoda interrupted. "Too bad they don't have a longer blooming season."

"*I said potties—not poppies!*" Homer shouted in his reedy treble. "*Chamber pots! Thunder mugs! The things they put under beds!*"

Rhoda turned to Qwilleran and explained sweetly, "The garden club maintains our flower beds. Don't you think the rust and gold mums are lovely? We haven't had any frost yet."

"I give up!" said Homer, throwing up his bony hands. "She's a sweet woman, but she'll be the death of me!" With disjointed movements of arms and legs he stomped from the room.

Rhoda asked with a radiant smile, "Was he giving his lecture on old barns again?"

"No, he was giving his *lecture on ghosts!*" Qwilleran replied loudly.

"Oh . . . yes," she said as she hung the feather duster on a hook behind the door. "They have quite a few at the Fugtree farm, you know."

Qwilleran bowed out quickly, shouting that the phone was ringing in the west wing.

It was Roger MacGillivray, reporter for the *Moose County Something*, who was calling. "Qwill, I got the info on Iris Cobb's will," he said, "but there's one thing that isn't clear. What is this cookbook she left you?"

Qwilleran, who was adept at extemporaneous prevarication, said, "That is her personal collection of recipes that she wished to have published posthumously." He spoke with the deliberation of one who is authorized to make a statement for publication. "The Klingenschoen Fund will underwrite the printing costs, and proceeds will go to the Iris Cobb Memorial Scholarship. For home economics studies," he added as an afterthought.

"Great!" said Roger. "That wraps it up. Thanks a lot."

Qwilleran dashed off his column for Friday's paper and phoned it in to the copydesk. It was late, therefore, when he started thinking about dinner, but he found one of his favorite dishes in the freezer—lamb shank cooked with lentils—and he thawed a hearty portion in the microwave. It was a large piece of meat, and before sitting down to eat, he sliced off a generous chunk for the Siamese, dicing it and putting it on their plate under the telephone table. Yum Yum attacked it with enthusiasm, but Koko was virtually glued to the kitchen windowsill, staring at the darkness outside.

"We've had enough of this ridiculous performance, young man!" Qwilleran said. "We'll find out what's bugging you!" With flashlight in hand he stormed out of the building, beaming the light around the exterior, in shadowy places not illuminated by the yardlights. He saw nothing unusual, nothing moving. A slight tremor on his upper lip made him wonder, What are cats seeing when they're gazing into space? Koko had left the windowsill, and Qwilleran was ready to give up the search when the flashlight beam picked out some depressions in the ground under the kitchen window. They looked like footprints. That rules out disembodied spirits, he told himself. It could have been some kid from Chipmunk . . . a juvenile Peeping Tom . . . a window washer from the county jail.

He hurried indoors and looked up Homer Tibbitt's phone number. He wanted to know when the windows had last been washed.

The maintenance chairman lived at October House, a residence for seniors, and the operator said, "I'm sorry, but I can't ring Mr. Tibbitt at this hour. He retires at seven-thirty. Do you wish to leave a message?"

"Just tell him Jim Qwilleran called. I'll try again tomorrow morning."

Both cats seemed to have enjoyed their portion of lamb; they were washing their masks, whiskers, and ears with satisfaction. Qwilleran popped his own dinner plate into the microwave for another shot of heat and immediately pulled it out again, staring at it in disbelief. All that remained on his plate was a mess of lentils and a shank bone, gnawed clean.

Eight

As Qwilleran prepared breakfast for the Siamese on Friday morning his mind was still on the footprints outside the kitchen window. If the window washers had been there since last weekend, the footprints could be theirs. If not, the telltale depressions had doubtlessly been left in the soft soil Sunday night, when Iris Cobb was making her last phone call. It had rained earlier that evening; since then the weather had been dry.

He placed the plate of tenderloin tips on the floor under the telephone table and once again called October House.

"Mr. Tibbitt," said the operator, "is not available. Would you care to leave a message?"

"This is Jim Qwilleran."

"Oh, yes, Mr. Qwilleran. You called last night."

"Will Mr. Tibbitt return soon?"

"I'm afraid not. He's gone to Lockmaster."

"Is he all right?" Qwilleran asked hastily. Lockmaster, in the county to the south, had a medical center noted for its geriatric department.

"Oh, yes, he's fine. Ms. Finney drove him down there to see the autumn color in horse country. They say it's gorgeous."

"I see," Qwilleran mused. "When do you expect them to return?"

"Not until Sunday afternoon. They're visiting friends down there. Shall I have him call you?"

"No. Don't bother. I'll catch up with him at the museum."

Qwilleran now faced an uncomfortable task—packing Iris Cobb's personal belongings in cartons from the basement. He had done it once before, after his mother died, and it was a heart-wrenching chore. He had done it often when he worked in a nursing home during college days, and in that situation it was a routine job. But it was an embarrassingly intimate rite to perform for a woman who had been his former landlady and housekeeper. He felt like a voyeur as he gathered her pink pantsuits, pink robes, pink underwear, and pink nightgowns from closets and dresser drawers. Most painful of all was the invasion of the top drawers with its jumble of smeared lipsticks, broken earrings, used emery boards, pill bottles, a hair brush with stray hairs clinging to the bristles, and the magnifying glass with silver handle that he had given her on her last birthday.

When the cartons were packed, he labeled them and carried them to the museum office. Koko wanted to accompany him.

"Sorry," Qwilleran said. "The sign stipulates no smoking, no food or beverages, and no bare feet."

When the chore was completed, however, Koko was still bouncing up and down at the door to the museum, trying to turn the doorknob. He had been allowed in the exhibit area once before when Mrs. Cobb was alive, and on that occasion he had been attracted to some model ships.

Qwilleran finally acquiesced. "All right, but you'll be disappointed," he told the cat. "The ship exhibit has been dismantled."

As soon as the connecting door was opened, Koko bounded into the museum, ignoring the pioneer rooms and heading for the east wing, which housed the theme exhibits, study collections, and the museum office. He scampered directly into the office, looked behind the door, and started jumping to reach Ms. Finney's feather duster.

"You devil!" Qwilleran said. "How did you know it was there?" He removed the cat and closed the office door, then watched him closely as he explored.

Koko bypassed the room that had formerly featured model ships; the door was closed, and a sign announced a new exhibit opening soon. He showed no interest in historic documents or the distinguished collection of early lighting devices. What fascinated this remarkable cat was an exhibit that everyone considered the most boring in the museum: textiles. It consisted of bed linens and table linens yellow with age; quilts faded from laundering with lye soap; hand-woven blankets perforated with moth holes; hand-hooked rugs dingy with wear; dreary dishtowels made from flour sacks; a stained mattress stuffed with straw; curtains dyed with berries and onion skins. Yet, the identification cards stated proudly the names of the early settlers who had woven, quilted, hooked, dyed, and stuffed these artifacts. Koko especially liked a bed pillow made from a flour sack and filled, according to the ID card, with chicken feathers from the

Inchpot Centennial Farm. He sniffed it intently.

"Chicken feathers! I might have known!" said Qwilleran. "Let's go home." He picked up the cat, who squirmed from his grasp and rushed back to the Inchpot pillow. Curiously, a similar pillow from the Trevelyan Farm, dating somewhat earlier in Moose County history, was totally overlooked. Qwilleran got a stranglehold on Koko and wrestled him back to the apartment.

They were met by Yum Yum, who touched noses with Koko and proceeded to groom the historical odors out of his fur. This business finished, Koko undertook a new mission: staring at the freezer compartment at the top of the refrigerator.

"There's nothing in that freezer for cats," Qwilleran advised him. "You're barking up the wrong tree. You can have some meatloaf from the big freezer, but not until dinnertime."

Koko persisted, prancing on his hind legs. To prove his point, Qwilleran opened the freezer door, exposing stacks of cinnamon doughnuts, blueberry muffins, chocolate brownies, banana nutbread, and other confections. It was then that an idea flashed into his mind: A package of Mrs. Cobb's pecan rolls would make an ideal thank-you for the family at the Fugtree farm, a gift beyond price and with a touch of sentiment. Later he might present a cherry pie to the Boswells, if he could do so without getting involved in neighborly chitchat. Mrs. Boswell was all right, but her husband's voice made Qwilleran's blood curdle, and Baby was a little pest.

It was early afternoon, a suitable time to pay an impromptu visit. He thawed the pecan rolls and drove to the Fugtree farm. Although it was within walking distance, he reasoned that dropping in on foot would suggest back-fence familiarity, and even the obligatory sharing of refreshments. Arriving by car appeared more businesslike, and he could make a quick getaway. He decided to drive.

At close hand the neglected farmhouse was even more dilapidated than it appeared from the highway. Obviously the front door had not been used for years; even the steps were sprouting weeds. He drove around to the side door, and as he did so a young woman came walking from the nearest barn, wearing grubby coveralls and a feed cap. She had a designer figure, but they were not designer coveralls; rather, they had the air of the

Farmers' Discount Store in North Kennebeck.

"You're Mr. Qwilleran," she greeted him. "I recognized you from your picture in the paper. Excuse the way I look; I've been mucking the barn."

Her manner and her speech seemed incompatible with mucking barns, and Qwilleran's curiosity was kindled. Stepping out of the car he handed her the package of pecan rolls. "I came to thank you for telling me about my car lights Tuesday night. This is something from Mrs. Cobb's freezer. I thought your family might enjoy it."

"Thank you, I don't have a family," she said, "but I love Iris's baking. I'm sorry we've lost her. She was such a neat lady."

Qwilleran was puzzled. "When you first called about Iris . . . you mentioned . . . that your youngsters were ill," he said hesitantly.

Her face went blank for a moment and then brightened. "I guess I said I was taking care of my sick kids. I meant . . . baby goats."

"Pardon my ignorance. I'm a recent refugee from Down Below and I haven't mastered the vocabulary up here."

"Please sit down," she said, waving to-

152

ward some rusty garden chairs. "Would you like a glass of wine?"

"Thanks, Ms. Waffle, but alcohol isn't on my list of vices."

"Kristi" she said. "Call me Kristi, spelled K-r-i-s-t-i. Then how about some fresh lemonade made with honey from local bees?"

"Now you're speaking my language."

He sat down carefully in one of the infirm garden chairs and surveyed the farmyard. It was a scene of unfinished chores, uncut grass, unpainted barns, unmended fences. What was she doing here alone? he wondered. She was young. About thirty, he guessed. But serious in her mien. She was cordial, but only her lips smiled. Her eyes were heavy with sorrow, or regret, or worry. An interesting face!

Along with the lemonade came crackers and a chunk of soft white cheese. "Goat cheese," she explained. "I make it myself. Are you going to be staying at the museum?"

"Only until they find a replacement for Mrs. Cobb." Trying not to stare at the neglected grass and shabby house, he said, "How long have you had this place?"

"Ever since my mother died, a couple of years ago. I grew up here, but I've been away for ten years. When I inherited the house, I came back to see if I could make a living with goats. I'm the last of the Fugtrees."

"But your name is Waffle."

"That was my married name. After my divorce I decided to keep it."

Qwilleran thought, Anything is better than Fugtree.

"Anything is better than Fugtree," she said as if reading his mind.

"I'm not familiar with your family history, although I understand Captain Fugtree was a war hero."

Kristi sighed ruefully. "My earlier ancestors made a lot of money in lumbering, and they built this house, but the captain was more interested in being a war hero, which doesn't pay the bills. When my parents inherited the house, they struggled to keep it up, and now that they're gone, I'm trying to make it go. People tell me I should sell the land to a developer for condominiums, like the ones in Indian Village, but it would be a crime to tear down this fabulous house. At least, I want to give farming a try," she said, smiling sadly.

"Why goats?"

"For several reasons." She brightened perceptibly. "They're really sweet animals and not expensive to feed, and there's a growing market for goat products. Did you know that? I raise dairy goats now, but someday I'd like to have some Angoras and spin their hair and weave it. I studied weaving in art school."

"This sounds like material for the 'Qwill Pen' column," said Qwilleran. "May I make an appointment with you and the goats?"

"That would be neat, Mr. Qwilleran!"

"Please call me Qwill," he said. He was feeling comfortable and somewhat captivated. The lemonade was the best he had ever tasted, and the goat cheese was delectable. Kristi's soft, sad eyes were mesmerizing. He had no desire to leave. Looking up at the house, he said, "This is a unique example of nineteenth-century architecture. What was the reason for the tower? Was it simply a conceit?"

"I don't know exactly. My ancestors were gentlemen farmers, and my mother thought they used the tower as a lookout—to spy on the field hands and see if they were loafing."

"And what do you use it for?"

"I go up there to meditate. That's how I knew you'd left your car lights on."

"What's up in the tower?"

"Mostly flies. Flies love towers. Spraying doesn't do much good. They're always buzzing and sunning and multiplying. Would you like to see the house?"

"Very much so."

"I should warn you. It's a mess. My mother was an absolutely mad collector. She went to auctions and bought all kinds of junk. It's a disease, you know, bidding at auctions."

"I had an acute attack of auctionitis— once," said Qwilleran, "and I can see how the germ could get into anyone's blood and cause a chronic condition for which there is no cure."

They entered the house through the side door, picking their way among shopping bags stuffed with clothing, shoes, hats, dolls and umbrellas; rusty tricycles and a manual lawnmower; open cartons loaded with dented pots and pans, chipped platters, bar trays and old milk bottles; wooden buckets and galvanized pails; an oak icebox and a wicker fern stand; stacks of magazines and bushels of books. Having been too long in attics and basements, these relics were giving their musty scent to the entire house.

Kristi said with a rueful smile, "I've been trying to thin out her accumulation—selling some and giving some away, but there's tons of it!"

The dining room alone harbored two large tables, twenty chairs, three china cabinets, and enough china to start a restaurant.

"See what I mean?" she said. "And this is only the beginning. The bedrooms are worse. Try not to look at the clutter. Look at the carved woodwork and the sculptured ceilings and the stained glass windows, and the staircase."

From the foyer a wide staircase angled up to the second floor. The newel post and handrail were massive, and the balusters were set extravagantly close together, harking back to the days when lumber was king. It was all black walnut, Kristi said.

"But this is not the original staircase," she pointed out. "The first one spiraled up into the tower and was very graceful. My great-grandfather replaced it and sealed off the tower."

"Too many flies?" Qwilleran asked. "Or too hard to heat?"

"That's a long story," she said, turning away. "Do you feel like climbing four flights?"

After they reached the third floor she un-bolted a door leading to the tower. Here the stairs were plain and utilitarian, but they ended in a small enchanting room no bigger than a walk-in closet, with windows on four sides and windowseats cushioned in threadbare velvet. On a shabby wicker table there were binoculars, a guttered candle, and a book on yoga in a brown paper cover. Iridescent bluebottle flies were sunning on the south window.

Qwilleran picked up the glasses and looked to the north, where the big lake shimmered just below the horizon. To the west a church spire rose out of a forest of evergreens. To the east was the Goodwinter property with Boswell's van in the barnyard, a blue pickup in the museum drive, and half a dozen energetic young persons raking leaves, bagging them, and loading them in the truck.

Qwilleran asked, "What is the purpose of the diagonal line of trees cutting across the fields?"

"That's Black Creek," Kristi said. "You can't see the stream, but trees thrive on its banks, and there are some very old willows hanging over the water."

"This house," Qwilleran said as they went back down the four flights of stairs, "should be registered as a historic place."

"I know." Kristi's eyes filled with melancholy. "But there's too much red tape, and

I wouldn't have time to do research and fill out the forms. And then the house and grounds would have to be fixed up, and that's more than I could afford to do."

Qwilleran patted his moustache smugly, thinking, This might be a project for the Klingenschoen Fund to underwrite. The Fugtrees were pioneers who helped develop the county, and their house is an architectural showplace worthy of preservation. Eventually it might be purchased by the Historical Society and opened to the public as a museum. He could visualize Fugtree Road becoming a "museum park" with the Goodwinter farmhouse demonstrating the life of the early settlers and the Fugtree mansion showing Moose County during its boom years. Even the antique presses in the barn had possibilities as a "Museum of the Printed Word." Qwilleran liked the name. One or two good restaurants might open in the vicinity, and the ghost town of North Middle Hummock would rise again, with the inevitable condominiums on the other side of Black Creek. The fact that Kristi was an attractive young woman had nothing to do with his enthusiastic speculations, he told himself.

"Would you like another glass of lemonade?" she asked to break the silence that fell after her last statement.

"No thank you," he said, snapping out of his reverie, "but how about two o'clock tomorrow afternoon for the interview?"

As she walked with him toward his car, he mentioned casually, "The Klingenschoen Fund might help you with the historic registration. Why don't you write a letter to the Fund in care of Hasselrich, Bennett and Barter? And see what happens."

Her eyes lost their melancholy for the first time. "Do you really think I'd stand a chance?"

"No harm in trying. All you have to lose is a postage stamp."

"Oh, Mr. Qwilleran—Qwill—I'd hug you if I hadn't been mucking the barn!"

"I'll take a raincheck," he said.

Arriving back at the farmhouse Qwilleran ignored the Siamese and looked up "goat" in the unabridged dictionary. Then he called Roger MacGillivray at the newspaper office. "Glad I caught you, Roger. I have a favor to ask. Are you free for dinner tonight?"

"Uh . . . yeah . . . but it would have to be early. I promised to be home by seven o'clock to baby-sit."

"I'll buy your dinner at Tipsy's if you'll

stop at the Pickax library and bring me some books on goats."

There was a pause. "Spell that, Qwill."

"G-o-a-t-s. I'll meet you at Tipsy's at five-thirty."

"Let's get this straight, Qwill. You want books on *goats?*"

"That's right! Horned ruminant quad-rupeds. And Roger . . ."

"Yes?"

"You don't need to let anyone know the books are for me."

Nine

Tipsy's was a popular restaurant in North Kennebeck that had started in a small log cabin in the 1930s and now occupied a large log cabin, where serious eaters converged for serious steaks without such frivolities as parsley sprigs and herbed butter. Potatoes were peeled and Frenched in the kitchen without benefit of sodium acid pyrophosphate. The only vegetable choice was boiled carrots. The only salad was cole slaw. And there was a waiting line for tables every night.

Qwilleran and his guest, being pressed for time, used their press credentials to get a table, and they were seated directly below the large portrait of a black-and-white cat for whom the restaurant was named.

Roger slapped a stack of books on the table: *Raising Goats for Fun and Profit, Debunking Goat Myths*, and *How to Start a Goat Club*. "Is this what you want?" he asked incredulously.

"I'm interviewing a goat farmer," Qwilleran said, "and I don't want to be totally ignorant about which sex gives milk and which sex has B.O."

"Find out if it's true they eat tin cans," Roger said. "Who's the farmer? Do I know him?"

"Who said anything about *him?* It's a young woman at the Fugtree farm next to the Goodwinter museum. Her name is Kristi, spelled with a *K* and an *I.*"

"Sure, I know her." Having grown up in Moose County and having taught school for nine years before switching to journalism, Roger's acquaintance was vast. "We were in high school together. She married a guy from Purple Point with more looks than brains, and they moved away—somewhere Down Below."

"She's moved back again, and she's divorced," Qwilleran said.

"I'm not surprised. He was a jerk, and Kristi was a talented girl. Flighty, though. She hopped from one great idea to another. I remember when she wanted to make macramé baskets for the basketball hoops."

"She seems to have her feet on the ground now."

"What is she like? She had big serious eyes

and wore weird clothes, but then all the art students wore weird clothes."

"Now she wears dirty coveralls and muddy boots, and her hair is tied back under a feed cap. She still has big serious eyes. I think she has worries beyond her ability to cope."

The steaks were served promptly, and the two men applied themselves with concentration. The beef at Tipsy's required diligent chewing, but the flavor was world-class. It was homegrown, like the potatoes and carrots and cabbage. There was something in Moose County soil that produced flavorful root vegetables and superior browse for cattle.

Qwilleran said, "I suppose you know I'm living at the Goodwinter farmhouse until they find a new manager."

"Be prepared to dig in for the winter," Roger advised him. "They'll have a tough time replacing Iris Cobb."

"Did you know any of the Goodwinters when they were living there?"

"Only the three kids. We were all in school at the same time. Junior is the only one left around here. His sister is on a ranch in Montana, and his brother is somewhere out West."

"Did they ever say anything about the place being haunted?"

"No, their parents wouldn't let them mention the ghost rumor . . . or their grandfather's murder . . . or their great-grandfather's 'sudden death,' as it was called. The whole family acted as if nothing unusual had ever happened. Why do you ask? Are you seeing spooks?"

Qwilleran touched his moustache gingerly, undecided how much he should confide in Roger. He said, "You know I don't buy the idea of ghosts and demons and poltergeists, but . . . Iris was hearing unearthly noises in the Goodwinter house before she died."

"Like what?"

"Like knocking and moaning and screaming."

"No kidding!"

"And Koko's behavior has been abnormal since we moved in. He's always talking to himself and staring into space."

"He's talking to ghosts," Roger said with a straight face.

Qwilleran could never be sure whether the young reporter was serious or not. He said, "Iris had a theory that a house exudes good or evil, depending on its previous occupants."

"My mother-in-law preaches the same thing," said Roger.

"How is Mildred, by the way? I haven't seen her lately."

"She's up to her eyebrows in good causes, as usual. Still trying to lose weight. Still carrying the torch for that husband of hers. I think she should get a lawyer and untie the knot."

"And how's Sharon and . . . the baby?"

"Sharon's gone back to teaching. And that kid! I never knew a baby could be so much fun! . . . Well, I can't stay for dessert. I've got to get home so Sharon can go to her club meeting. Thanks, Qwill. Best meal I've had in a month!"

Qwilleran remained and ordered Tipsy's old-fashioned bread pudding with a pitcher of thick cream for pouring, followed by two cups of coffee powerful enough to exorcise demons and domesticate poltergeists. Then he drove back to North Middle Hummock to cram for his interview with the goatherd.

After skimming through chapters on breeding, feeding, milking, de-horning, castrating, hoof trimming, barn cleaning and manure management, he made a decision: It

166

would be better to walk the plank than to raise goats. Furthermore, there was the danger of such diseases as coccidiosis, demodectic mange, bloat, and foot rot, not to mention birth defects such as sprung pasterns, pendulous udder, blind teat, leaking orifice, and hermaphroditism. It was no wonder the goat-girl looked worried.

After this briefing he knew, however, what questions to ask, and he felt a growing admiration for Kristi and her choice of career. Perhaps, as Roger said, she was flighty in high school, but who isn't at that age? He was looking forward to the interview. When Polly Duncan called to ask if he planned to attend the reception at Exbridge & Cobb, Qwilleran was glad he had an honest excuse. He said, "I'm interviewing a farmer at two o'clock."

Kristi greeted him on Saturday afternoon in white coveralls. She had been assisting at a kidding, she said. "Buttercup had trouble, and I had to help. Geranium is ready, too, and I have to check her every half hour. You can hear her bleating, poor thing."

"Do you name all your goats?"

"Of course. They all have their own personalities."

167

As they walked toward the goat barns Qwilleran asked how many kids Buttercup had produced.

"Two. I'm building up my own herd instead of buying animals. It takes time, but it costs less."

"How much does a kid weigh at birth?"

"About six pounds. For a while I'll feed them from a bottle three to five times a day."

Qwilleran said, "There's one gnawing question on my mind. How or why did you get involved with goats?"

Kristi said gravely, "Well, I met a goat named Petunia, and it was love at first sight, so I took a correspondence course and then got a job at a goat farm. We were living in New England then."

"What was your husband doing all this time?"

"Not much of anything. That was the problem," she said with a bitter grimace.

They were approaching an area of small barns, sheds, and wire-fenced yards in which were small shade trees with protected trunks. A barncat was squirming to get under the fence. In the nearest yard a dozen goats of different colors were nuzzling each other's heads, lounging on the ground, or standing motionless with passive expressions. They turned sad, gentle eyes to the two visitors, and Qwilleran glanced quickly at Kristi's eyes, which were also sad and gentle.

"I like that big black one with a striped face," he said. "What kind is he?"

"She," Kristi reminded him. "These are all does. That one is a Nubian, and I call her Black Tulip. Notice her Roman nose and elegantly long ears. She's from very good stock. The white one is Gardenia. She's a Saanen. I really love her; she's so feminine. The fawn-colored one with two stripes on the face is Honeysuckle."

"What's that structure in the middle of the yard?"

"A feeder. They get nutritional feed, but they also graze in the pasture. The farmer who leases the Fugtree acreage manages my pastureland. Students come in after school to clean the milking parlor and the feeders and things like that. And then I have a friend who comes out from Pickax on weekends to help."

There was a commotion in the farthest field. Two goats were butting heads, and a third was butting a barrel. "They're bucks," Kristi explained. "We keep them away from the milking area because of the odor."

"Then 'smelling like a billy goat' is not just a figure of speech?"

Kristi was forced to agree. "Would you like to pet the does?" she asked. "They like attention. Don't make any sudden moves. Let them smell your hand first."

The does came to the fence and rubbed against the wire, then turned drowsy eyes toward Qwilleran, purring in a gentle moan, but their coats felt rough to a hand accustomed to stroking cats.

Next Kristi showed him the milking parlor. "I have the milk commercially pasteurized," she explained. "Then it's sold to people who are allergic to cow's milk or find it hard to digest. Would you like a cup of tea and some cheese?"

They went into the house and sat at the table in the kitchen, the only room in the house that appeared habitable. Even so, the table was cluttered with collectibles, including a large leather-bound family bible. Kristi said her mother had bought it at an auction, and the museum might like to have it.

Qwilleran said, "You didn't tell me why your great-grandfather rebuilt the staircase."

"There was scandal involved."

"All the better!"

"You won't put this in your column, will you?"

"Not if you object."

"Well," she began, "it happened early in this century. My great-grandfather had a beautiful daughter named Emmaline, and she fell in love with one of the Goodwinter boys, Ephraim's second son. His name was Samson. But her father disapproved, and Emmaline was forbidden to see her lover. Being a spunky girl she used to climb the spiral staircase to the tower and flash a light, which could be seen from the Goodwinter house, and Samson would meet her on the bank of the Black Creek under the willows. Then tragedy struck! Samson was thrown from his horse and killed. A few months later, Emmaline gave birth to a child, a horrible disgrace in those days. Her family despised her, and her friends deserted her. Then, one night during a thunderstorm, she climbed the spiral staircase and threw herself from the tower."

"A tragic story," Qwilleran said. "Is that why her father remodeled the stairs?"

"Yes, he ripped out the lovely spiral staircase and substituted the angular one we have now. When I was growing up, the door to the tower was always locked."

"How do you know the spiral staircase was lovely. Do you have a photograph?"

"No . . . I just know," she answered mysteriously.

"What happened to Emmaline's child?"

"Captain Fugtree brought him up as his own son. He was my father."

"Then Emmaline was your grandmother!"

"Oh, she was so beautiful, Qwill! I wish I had her looks."

"I'd like to see a picture of her."

"Her photos were all destroyed after she killed herself. Her family pretended she had never existed."

"Then how do you know she was beautiful?"

Kristi cast her sad eyes down and was slow in answering. When she looked up, her face was radiant. "I don't know whether I should tell you this . . . I see her whenever there's a thunderstorm." She waited to see Qwilleran's reaction, and when he looked sympathetic she went on. "She walks upstairs in a flowing white robe, very slowly, up into the tower—and then disappears . . . She walks up the spiral staircase that's not there!"

Qwilleran stared at the granddaughter of

the phantom Emmaline and searched for the right thing to say. She had paid him a compliment by confiding this personal secret, and he had no desire to spoil her story by asking hard-nosed questions. He was saved by the telephone bell.

Kristi reached for the kitchen phone. "Hello?" Then she turned pale, staring straight ahead as if paralyzed. After listening for a few moments, she hung up without another word.

"Trouble?" Qwilleran asked.

She gulped and said, "My ex-husband. He's back in town."

He sensed from her distracted air that there would be no more interview, no more tea. "Well," he said, standing up, "perhaps I should leave now. It's been an instructive afternoon. Thank you for your cooperation and the refreshments. I may call you again to check on details. And let me know if there's anything I can do for you."

She nodded and moved toward the refrigerator like a sleepwalker. "Here's some cheese to take home," she said in a trembling voice. "And don't forget to take the bible for the museum."

As Qwilleran drove the short distance to the Goodwinter place he had more than goats

173

on his mind. He wondered about the Emmaline story. Kristi was quite emotional about her grandmother; perhaps she only imagined that she saw her walking upstairs in flowing white robes. He would like to be there during the next thunderstorm . . . But more serious at the moment was the phone call and Kristi's terrified reaction. He hesitated to intrude in her personal affairs, but he was definitely concerned. She lived there alone. She could be in danger.

As he was about to turn into Black Creek Lane he heard a truck approaching from the west, and he looked back in time to see a pickup turning into the Fugtree drive. As soon as he arrived at the museum he dropped the cheese and the bible on the dining table and immediately called Kristi's number. To his relief she answered in a normal voice.

"This is Qwill," he said. "I forgot to ask how much milk a goat can produce in a day."

"Black Tulip is my best doe, and she gives three thousand pounds a year. We always figure annual weight, not volume per day." She was brief and businesslike in her answer. "And you can say that she was a Grand Champion at the county fair."

"I see. Well, thank you. Is everything all right over there?"

"Everything's okay."

"That phone call just before I left seemed to upset you, and I was concerned."

"That's kind of you, Qwill, but my friend is here from Pickax, and everything's under control."

"Good! Have a nice evening," said Qwilleran.

Was the phone message really from her ex-husband? he wondered. And who was this "friend" who suddenly appeared and made everything right? He turned back to the table where he had dropped Kristi's two donations. Yum Yum, was eating one of them, and Koko was sitting on the other.

Ten

 Qwilleran had a reason for inviting Roger's mother-in-law to dinner. He wanted to know more about Kristi Fugtree Waffle—not to flesh out his goat interview but to satisfy his curiosity—and Mildred Hanstable was the one to ask. A lifelong resident of Moose County, she had taught school for almost thirty years, and she knew two generations of students as well as their parents and grandparents, the past and present members of the school board, the county commissioners—in short, everyone.

When Qwilleran phoned her in Mooseville she squealed with her usual exuberance, "Qwill! So good to hear from you! Roger tells me you're house-sitting at the museum. That was such a shock—losing Iris! She always looked so healthy, didn't she? Perhaps she was a little overweight, but . . . oh, Lord! so am I! I'm going on a diet right away."

"Start your diet tomorrow," he said. "Are you free to have dinner tonight?"

"I'm always free to have dinner. That's my problem."

"I'll pick you up at six-thirty, and we'll go to the Northern Lights Hotel."

Qwilleran thawed some lobster meat for the Siamese, wondering if the waterfront hotel in Mooseville would offer anything half as good. Then he showered and dressed in something he considered commendable for the occasion. When dating Polly Duncan, who was not attuned to fashion, he wore what was readily available, and clean. Mildred, on the other hand, taught art as well as home ec, and she had an eye for color, design, and coordination. For Mildred he tried harder. For Mildred he wore a camel's-hair cardigan over a white open-neck shirt and tan pants, an ensemble that enhanced the suntan he had acquired during recent months of biking. Admiring himself in Mrs. Cobb's full-length mirror, a nicety that was lacking in his Pickax apartment, he noted that the shades of tan flattered his graying hair and luxuriant pepper-and-salt moustache.

In a mood of self-congratulation he drove from the rolling hills and cultivated fields of the Hummocks to the wild, wooded lake-shore, experiencing once again the miraculous change in atmosphere near the lake. It was not merely the aroma of a hundred miles of water and a fleet of fishing boats; it was an indescribable element that elevated one's spirit and made Mooseville a vacation paradise.

Mildred greeted him with a platonic hug. "You're looking wonderful! And I love your tan and white combination!" She was licensed to hug platonically, being not only Roger's mother-in-law but Qwilleran's former neighbor and the food writer for the *Moose County Something* and the loyal wife of an absentee husband.

Qwilleran returned the compliment, admiring whatever it was she was wearing. "Did you design it, Mildred?"

"Yes, it's intended to be a flattering cover-up for a fat lady."

"Nonsense! You are a handsome mature woman with a mature figure," he said with a declamatory flourish.

"I always love your choice of words, Qwill."

As they drove toward downtown Mooseville there were signs that the vacation season was coming to a close. They encountered less tourist traffic, fewer recreation vehicles, and almost no boats on trailers. Summer cottages were boarded up for the winter. There were not many fishing boats bobbing alongside the municipal piers that bordered Main Street, and the seagulls were screeching their last hurrah of the season.

"It's kind of sad," Mildred observed, "but it's pleasant, too. October belongs to us and not to those loud, swaggering tourists from Down Below. Fortunately they throw their money around and keep our economy going. I just wish they had better manners."

The Northern Lights Hotel was a barracks-like building with three floors of plain windows in dreary rows, but it was a historic landmark that had served the community in the nineteenth century when sailors and loggers—likewise lacking in manners—patronized the free-lunch saloon and rented a room for two bits.

As Qwilleran and his guest seated themselves in the dining room at a window table overlooking the docks, Mildred said, "A hundred years ago people looked out this very same window and saw three-masted schooners taking on passengers in bustles and top hats, and new-fangled coal steamers taking on cargoes of lumber and ore." She glanced at the menu. "And a hundred years ago this hotel served slumgullion to deckhands and prospectors, instead of broiled whitefish and petite salads to dieters. What are you having, Qwill? You never have to worry about calories."

"Since the cats are having lobster tonight, I think I'm entitled to French onion soup, froglegs, Caesar salad, and pumpkin pecan pie."

"How do the cats like their new environment?" she asked.

"They've okayed the blue velvet wing chair, the Pennsylvania German *Schrank*, and the kitchen windowsill. About the General Grant bed, when polled they voted 'undecided.' Gastronomically they're in seventh cat heaven, chomping their way through Iris's twenty-four-cubic-foot freezer."

"I read about Iris's will in yesterday's paper. Did she really want to have her recipes published? Or did you invent that? To me it sounded suspiciously like a Qwilleranism."

"If you read it in the *Something*, it's true," he said.

"Well, when her cookbook is published, I want to buy the first copy."

"I was hoping you'd consent to be the editor, Mildred. The recipes will need editing and testing, I imagine. Iris was one of those casual cooks—a fistful of this, a slug of that. I'll volunteer to be your official taster."

"I'd be honored!" said Mildred.

"Let me warn you: her handwriting looks like Egyptian hieroglyphics."

"After correcting school papers for thirty years, Qwill, I can read anything."

He wanted to quiz her about Kristi but thought it prudent to defer the subject until the dessert course. Whenever he invited Mildred to dinner, it seemed, his motive was to pry information from her incredible memory bank, although he tried to be subtle about it. So he asked her about the new exhibit at the museum, soon to be unveiled. She was chairman of the exhibit committee.

"It was finished three weeks ago," she said, "but we postponed the opening to coincide with the autumn color season—sort of a double feature, you know. The show is all about disasters in Moose County history. The public likes disasters. I'm sure you know that. Didn't the circulation of the *Daily Fluxion* always go up after a major plane crash or earthquake?"

"How do you celebrate a disaster in a small room in a museum?" he asked.

"It takes a certain amount of ingenuity, if

I say so myself. We're covering the walls with photo blowups, and I must tell you about the violent controversy that arose. A member of our committee, Fran Brodie, for your information, found a questionable photo in the museum files with no information as to origin or donor, only a date scribbled on the back: October 30, 1904. Does that ring a bell?"

"Isn't that when Ephraim Goodwinter's body was found?"

"A date that will live forever in coffee-shop gossip! It was just a snapshot—a ghoulish picture of the Hanging Tree with (presumably) a body dangling from a rope. Fran wanted to enlarge it to three by four feet. I said that would be pure sensationalism. *She said* it was local history. *I said* it was pandering to bad taste. *She said* it was objective reportage. *I said* it was probably a roll of carpet trussed up to look like a body."

"Why would anyone take the trouble to do that?"

"Ephraim-haters have gone to great lengths, Qwill, to 'prove' that he was lynched by a posse of men draped in white sheets. In fact, the museum even has a sheet with two eyeholes burned in it, allegedly found near the Hanging Tree on October 30,

1904, by the pastor of the Old Stone Church. I suspect it was planted there for the good reverend to find."

"I detect a note of skepticism in your remarks, Mildred."

"If you want to know, it's my opinion that the lynching story is a hoax. Ephraim's suicide note is in the possession of Junior Goodwinter, and the handwriting checks out. Junior has allowed us to photocopy it for the exhibit. Of course, Fran Brodie—who can be a pain in the you-know-what—said the suicide note could be a forgery. So the hassle began all over again, and Larry had to come in to arbitrate. The result was a compromise. We're calling the Goodwinter Mine disaster "Truth or Myth?" with a big banner to that effect. We're showing the alleged suicide note and the alleged hanging snapshot, but in actual size. No lurid blow-ups!"

"I'm glad you stood by your guns, Mildred. You always do! Was Fran ever a student of yours?"

"Ten years ago, yes. And now that she's an interior designer, she likes to challenge her old teacher. She's talented—I'll admit that—but she was always a brat in school and she's still a brat."

The entrees were served, and Qwilleran asked, "Did you attend the Exbridge and Cobb reception this afternoon?"

"It was fabulous!" she said. "You should have been there. They served excellent champagne and hors d'oeuvres. All the important people were there. Everyone dressed up for the occasion. Susan was looking smashing in a designer original, but then she always does; I wish I had that woman's figure. I met Iris's son; he's very personable. And the antiques—you wouldn't believe! They had a $10,000 Chippendale chair! A side chair! It didn't even have arms! And a $90,000 highboy!"

"Who's going to pay those prices in Moose County?"

"Don't kid yourself, Qwill. There's plenty of old money up here. They don't flaunt it, but they've got it—people like Doctor Zoller, Euphonia Gage, Doctor Halifax, the Lanspeaks, and how about you?"

"I've explained that before, Mildred. I'm not the acquisitive type. If I can't eat it or wear it, I don't buy it. Iris and Susan must have invested a fortune in that shop."

"They did," Mildred said, "and now Susan has it all. She really lucked out." Lowering her voice she added, "Don't repeat it, but—from what I noticed this afternoon—she's got her sights on Iris's son, too. I happen to know that he checked out of the hotel Thursday night but isn't leaving town until tomorrow. The hotel auditor is married to our school counselor, and I saw them both in Lanspeak's store today."

"I would have gone to the reception," Qwilleran said, "but I was interviewing an interesting young woman—Kristi Fugtree."

"I remember her," said Mildred. "I had her in art class—a very good weaver. She had intriguing eyes, like some movie star I've seen, but I can't remember who. She married and moved away. Is she back again?"

"She's back again and living on the family farm, raising goats and selling goat's milk."

"Well, that's different, isn't it? Kristi was always different. When my other students were weaving acrylic and chenille, Kristi was weaving cornhusks and milkweed."

"Do you know the fellow she married? His last name was Waffle."

"I knew him only by sight and reputation, and I thought Kristi made a bad choice. He was a good-looking kid and popular with the girls. Kristi was the only one who didn't run after him, so naturally he pursued her. Probably thought she had Fugtree money. If he had had any brains he would have known that the family fortune was thrown away by Captain Fugtree, who was very well-liked, but he was a snob and a loafer with a large ego. If Kristi's raising goats, at least she has more ambition than her illustrious fore-bear."

Qwilleran said, "The house has been neglected for years, but it's an architectural gem."

"Especially the tower! In my nubile days, when we used to hang out in the Willoway, we could see the tower above the trees, and we thought it looked haunted."

"What's the Willoway?"

"Haven't you discovered the Willoway? You're slipping, Qwill," she said with a mischievous smile. "It's a lover's lane under the willow trees that grow on the banks of the Black Creek. The trail starts at the bridge near the museum and then angles across the back of the Goodwinter and Fugtree property. It's notoriously romantic! You should explore it, Qwill—with a suitable companion!"

On Sunday morning Qwilleran explored the Willoway, alone—although not so alone as he expected.

The expedition was not premeditated. He

had been strolling about the grounds of the museum with his hands in his pockets, inhaling deeply, enjoying the riotous autumn color, when he received the distinct impression that he was being watched. He looked in all directions in a casual way, as if admiring the view.

Had he looked toward the farmhouse he would have discovered two pairs of intensely blue eyes fastened on him, but that did not occur to him. He glanced toward the east and saw farmland; to the north was the barn, minus Boswell's van; to the west one could see the tower of the Fugtree mansion rising above the treetops. Perhaps, he thought with pleasure, Kristi was watching him through the binoculars. It was amazing, he thought, how one could sense the fact from such a distance. He groomed his moustache and straightened his shoulders and decided to explore the Willoway.

The crisp, bright October day was so clear that one could hear the faint sound of church bells in West Middle Hummock three miles away. First he walked up Black Creek Lane, then east on Fugtree Road to the bridge, where he slid down an embankment to the stream. Although narrow and shallow, the creek rippled and gurgled briskly over the stones under the drooping branches of willows, while the trail—soft with decades of humus and now gaudily patterned with fallen leaves— was shaded by maples and oaks.

He found it an engagingly private place and he wondered if Iris had discovered this tranquil spot. Probably not; she was a confirmed indoorswoman. Ambling along the trail that meandered to follow the stream, he occasionally caught a glimpse of the Fugtree tower, which loomed larger as he drew closer. Here in the Willoway Emmaline and Samson had kept their ill-fated trysts.

Except for the bubbling water it was hauntingly quiet, as an October day can be, the dew-drenched trail muffling his footsteps. Once he paused to marvel at the picturesque scene, wishing he had brought his camera, and as he stood there he heard the crackling of underbrush. It was followed by indistinct voices. The inflections suggested the ritual of greeting, but not a joyous meeting. There were fragments of dialogue that he could not catch.

Qwilleran moved cautiously toward the source. Rounding a bend in the trail he ducked quickly behind a tree and listened. A woman was speaking angrily.

"I don't *have* any money!"

"Then get some!" a man said threateningly. "I need a car, too. They're after me."

"Why don't you steal one? You seem to know how." This was followed by a small cry of pain. "Don't you touch me, Brent!"

Qwilleran threw a rock into the stream, and the splash halted the hostile interchange for a few seconds.

"What's that?" the man asked in alarm.

"A fish . . . And you can't stay at the house, Brent, so get that out of your head."

There was incoherent whimpering about "no place to go."

"Go back where you came from, or I'll tell the police you're here!"

The man made a retort that sounded vicious, and Qwilleran threw another rock into the stream.

"Somebody's around," the man said.

"Nobody's here, stupid! And now I'm leaving, and I never want to see you again or hear from you! And I'm warning you, Brent: Don't try anything funny. I have a gun at the house!"

"Kristi, I'm hungry." The voice was pleading. "And it's cold at night."

There was a moment of silence. "I'll leave some bread and cheese on the big stump, but that's the end! Go back to Lockmaster and give yourself up."

Her final words faded away as she turned her back. Qwilleran ventured a stealthy peek around the trunk of an oak tree and saw her running along the trail with noiseless steps. He also saw a man in a dark green jacket with stenciling on the back. Then, hearing the sounds of a zipper and urinating in the stream, Qwilleran turned and made his own retreat, climbing the bank to a dirt access road that led to the rear of the Goodwinter property.

His first action was to move his car to the steel barn and lock the door. Then he phoned Kristi's number. Her voice was shaking when she answered.

"It's Qwill calling again," he said. "You must think I haven't got it all together, but I forgot to ask the names of the bucks."

"Oh . . . yes . . . They're Napoleon . . . and Rasputin . . . and Attila," she said.

"Very appropriate! Thank you, Kristi. It's a beautiful day. How's everything at the farm?"

"Okay." Her reply was not convincing.

"You can expect a lot of traffic on Fugtree Road this afternoon. The museum is opening a new exhibit. I hope the activity won't throw the animals off their feed."

"It won't bother them."

"Let me know if there's any problem, any problem at all. Do you hear?"

"Yes," she said weakly. "Thank you."

Hardly reassured by this conversation, Qwilleran wandered aimlessly about the apartment. Kristi's plight troubled him, but she gave the impression that his intervention was neither needed nor wanted. After all, she had a friend in Pickax with a pickup truck who seemed to be available in emergencies. Qwilleran combed his moustache with his fingers.

What he needed was a strong cup of coffee and something distracting to read—something to pass the time until one o'clock when the museum opened to the public. In Pickax he had been reading Kinglake's *Eothen* aloud to the cats, and there were three secondhand Arnold Bennetts he was eager to start, but he had neglected to bring his books to North Middle Hummock. Mrs. Cobb's magazines were not to his taste; he knew all he wanted to know about brown Rockingham ware and early Massachusetts glass-blowers and Newport blockfronts. As for her bookshelves, they were filled with figurines and cast-iron toys and colored glass. The few books on the shelves were paperback titles that he had read at least twice. He was in no mood for *Gone With the Wind* again.

His rambling thoughts were interrupted by a familiar sound: *thlunk!* Then again, *thlunk!* It was the unmistakable evidence of a paperback book hitting an Oriental rug. Qwilleran could recognize it anywhere. He strode into the parlor in time to see Koko making an exit with the low-slung body and drooping tail that spelled mischief. Two books had been knocked off the shelf. Qwilleran read the titles and went directly to the telephone. The time had come, he concluded, to discuss Koko's behavior with an expert.

There was a young woman in Mooseville who seemed to know all about cats. Lori Bamba was also the free-lance secretary who handled Qwilleran's correspondence when the fan mail became too heavy. He called her number, using the kitchen telephone and taking care to close the door. Otherwise, Koko would make himself a pest. He liked Lori Bamba, and he knew when she was on the line.

Lori answered in the blithe way that made it a pleasure to hear her voice, and Qwilleran opened with the amenities. "Haven't seen you for a while, Lori. How's the baby?"

"He's crawling now, Qwill. Our calico thinks he's a kitten and tries to mother him."

"And how's Nick?"

"Well, he hasn't found a new job yet. Let us know if you have any ideas. He has an engineering degree, you know."

"I'll do that, but tell him not to quit until he's lined up something else. And how about you? Do you have time to write some letters for me?"

"Sure do! Nick goes to Pickax on Wednesdays. He can pick up your stuff."

"I'm not in Pickax, Lori. The cats and I are staying in Iris Cobb's apartment at the museum for a few weeks."

"Oh, Qwill! That was terrible news! We'll miss her."

"Everyone misses her, including the Siamese."

"How do they react to living in a museum?"

"That's why I'm calling you, Lori. Something is bothering Koko. The bird population has gone south, and yet he sits on the windowsill for hours, watching and waiting. One day when I took him into the exhibit area he went directly to a bed pillow stuffed with chicken feathers before World War I, and a few minutes ago he knocked two books off the shelf: *To Kill a Mockingbird* and *One Flew Over the Cuckoo's Nest*."

Without hesitation Lori asked, "Is there enough poultry in his diet?"

"Hmmm . . . We've been using up the food in Iris's freezer," Qwilleran said, "and now that you mention it, I believe it's mostly meat and seafood."

"Try serving more poultry," she advised.

"Okay, Lori, I'll give it a shot."

Qwilleran went in search of the Siamese. Standing in the central hall he called out, "Hey, you gastronomes, wherever you are! Doctor Purrgood wants you to eat more duckling, pheasant, and Cornish hen!"

Yum Yum could be heard scratching the gravel in the commode; it made a characteristic sound when flicked against the metal sides of the turkey roaster. Koko had done his famous vanishing act, however.

"Koko! Where are you?"

The cat had an exasperating way of making himself invisible when the occasion demanded, and Qwilleran always worried when he was out of sight.

Yum Yum soon emerged from the bathroom, walking delicately pigeon-toed. She went directly to one of the Oriental rugs in the parlor. There was a suspicious-looking hump in the middle of it, which she sniffed ardently. The hump wriggled.

Throwing back the rug Qwilleran demanded, "What's wrong with you, Koko? Is the thermostat set too low? Are you hiding from something? What are you trying to tell me?"

Koko drew himself up to his full height, as only a Siamese can do, and stalked loftily from the room.

Eleven

The first cars to arrive at the museum for the opening of the disaster exhibit were those of Historical Society members, looking well-dressed in their church clothes: the men with coats and ties, the women with skirts and heels. Mitch Ogilvie as traffic director instructed them to unload the elderly and infirm at the museum entrance and then park in the barnyard, leaving the regular parking slots for the public. A good turnout was expected following the story on the front page of the *Moose County Something*:

GOODWINTER MUSEUM REOPENS
FEATURING MAJOR DISASTERS

The Goodwinter Farmhouse Museum in North Middle Hummock will resume regular hours Sunday with a new exhibit featuring memorable events in Moose County history. The museum has been closed for a week following the death of Iris Cobb Hackpole, resident manager.

The new show displays photographs and artifacts from lumbering, shipping, and mining days, according to spokesperson Carol Lanspeak. Photo murals portray dramatic views of shipwrecks, forest fires, mine disasters, logjams and other mishaps, including a 1919 "disaster" when the sheriff poured gallons of bootleg liquor on the dump at Squunk Corners. Of special interest, Lanspeak said, is a vignette titled "Truth or Myth?" exploring the controversial death of Ephraim Goodwinter in 1904.

"Goodwinter farm and surrounding countryside are at the height of autumn brilliance," Lanspeak said. "The color show makes a trip to the Hummocks doubly enjoyable." Regular hours are 1 to 4 P.M., Friday through Sunday. Groups may be accommodated by appointment.

At one o'clock Qwilleran dressed for the occasion, wearing a new paisley tie that Scottie had cajoled him into buying by burring his *r*'s. With Kristi's bible tucked under his arm he went directly to the museum office,

197

where Larry was punching keys on the computerized catalogue.

"How's it going, Larry?"

"Good publicity always pays off," said the president. "What's that under your arm? Are you planning to deliver a sermon?"

"It's a bible donated by the young woman at the Fugtree farm. What shall I do with it?"

"Is it the Fugtree bible, I hope?"

"No, just something her mother bought at an auction."

"Too bad. Well, write the donor's name on this card and leave the bible on the catalogue table. The registrar will take care of it."

"Any luck, Larry, in finding a successor for Iris?"

"We've had a couple of nibbles. Iris, as you know, wouldn't take a penny, but we're prepared to pay a decent salary plus the apartment, including utilities. Mitch Ogilvie has applied for the job. He likes antiques, and God knows he's enthusiastic, but he's rather young, and the young ones stay a year and then take off for greener pastures. Susan thinks Vince Boswell would be good. He used to conduct antique auctions Down Below, and he's handy with tools. He could make minor repairs that we're having to pay for now."

198

"In my opinion," Qwilleran said, "Mitch has the better personality for the position. Being on the desk at the hotel he's accustomed to meeting people, and I've observed how he gets along with the elderly. Boswell comes on too strong and too loud. He turns people off. Besides, the manager's apartment is hardly large enough for a family of three."

Larry glanced around the office before answering. "Actually, Verona isn't his wife. If we give him the job he'll ship her and the kid back to Pittsburgh."

"How'd he get his bad leg?"

"Polio. That happened way back before they had the vaccine. Considering he has pain, he does pretty well."

"Hmmm . . . Too bad," Qwilleran murmured. "But Mitch, at least, has clean fingernails."

Larry shrugged. "Well . . . you know . . . Vince is doing all that dirty work in the barn. Some of those presses are filthy with an accumulation of ink and grease."

Qwilleran filled out the donation card and then asked, "What happens out here when snow flies?"

"We keep Black Creek snowplowed, and the county takes care of Fugtree Road. No problem."

"Does anyone visit the museum in winter?"

"Definitely! We schedule busloads of students and seniors and women's clubs, and we stage special events for Thanksgiving, Christmas, Valentine's Day, and so forth. For Halloween we have a marshmallow roast for the kids, and Mitch Ogilvie tells ghost stories. As for the snow, it makes this place really beautiful."

"Incidentally," Qwilleran said, "you should consider putting the yardlights on a timer, to turn on automatically at dusk. Also one or two interior lights for security reasons."

"Good idea," said Larry, taking a small notebook from his pocket and making an entry.

"Another matter I want to draw to your attention is the land grant signed 'Abraham Lincoln' in the document exhibit."

"That's the most valuable document we have," Larry said proudly.

"Except that it was not actually signed by Lincoln."

"You mean it's a forgery? How do you know?"

"I wouldn't suspect any felonious intent. I daresay there were thousands of certificates issued, and Secretary Seward was authorized to sign for the president. He did it with a flourish. Lincoln's signature was small and controlled, and he didn't spell out his first name."

"Glad you told me, Qwill. We'll put that information on the ID card." Out came Larry's notebook again. "The value of the document has just dropped a few thousand dollars, but thanks anyway, old pal."

At that moment Carol Lanspeak burst into the office. "Something's missing in the new exhibit, Larry," she said. "Come and see!"

She left immediately, with her husband close behind. Qwilleran followed but was intercepted every step of the way. Mildred Hanstable and Fran Brodie, chatting together like the best of friends, stopped him to comment on his paisley tie.

Mildred said to Fran, "How does he stay so svelte?"

Fran said to Mildred, "How does he stay so young?"

"I stay sober and single," Qwilleran advised them before moving on.

Susan Exbridge whispered in his ear, "Good news! Dennis Hough has made an offer on the Fitch property. He's going to open a construction business up here."

The bad news, Qwilleran thought, is that he's bringing his wife.

Next, Homer Tibbitt and Rhoda Finney approached him, and Homer said in his high-pitched voice, "Were you trying to reach me? We went down to Lockmaster to see the horse races and fix her hearing aid, and while we were there we got married so it wouldn't be a total loss."

"We've had the license for weeks, but he's a terrible stick-in-the-mud," the new Mrs. Tibbitt said, smiling fondly at the groom.

Qwilleran extended his felicitations and pressed on through the crowd, most of whom were trying to get into the crowded room featuring disasters.

Polly Duncan tugged at his sleeve and said in a half whisper, "I have a great favor to ask, Qwill."

"I'll do anything," he said, "except cat-sit with a three-ounce kitten."

Reprovingly she said, "That's exactly what I was going to ask you to do. There's a seminar in Lockmaster, and I hoped I could leave Bootsie with you for one overnight."

"Hmmm," he mused, searching for good reasons to decline. "Wouldn't two big cats with loud voices frighten him?"

"I doubt it. He's a well-adjusted little fellow. Nothing bothers him."

"Yum Yum might think he's a mouse."

"She's smart enough to know better. He won't be any trouble, Qwill, and you'll love him as much as I do."

"Well . . . I'll give it a try . . . but if he expects me to kiss-kiss, he's grievously mistaken."

Qwilleran pushed his way through the growing crowd, noting the presence of attorney Hasselrich and his wife, Dr. Zoller and his latest blond, Arch Riker and the lovely Amanda, the Boswells with Baby, and several politicians whose names would be on the November ballot. Vince Boswell's voice could be heard above all the rest. "Are they going to have refreshments? Iris used to make the best damned cookies!"

Eventually Qwilleran reached the disaster exhibit. As Mildred had said, the dramatic impact was created with photo murals. They depicted the 1892 logjam that took seven lives, the 1898 fire that destroyed Sawdust City, the wreck of a three-masted schooner in the 1901 storm, and other calamities in Moose County history, but the dominating display was the "Truth or Myth?" vignette, which revived old questions about the mysterious end of Ephraim Goodwinter.

The story of the mine explosion and its aftermath was presented graphically without commentary. Photo blowups and newspaper clippings were grouped under four dates:

May 13, 1904—Photo of rescue crew at Goodwinter Mine. Headlines from Down Below say: 32 KILLED IN MINE EXPLOSION.

May 18, 1904—Photo of weeping widows and children. Excerpt from *Pickax Picayune* of that date: "Mr. and Mrs. Ephraim Goodwinter and family left today for several months abroad."

August 25, 1904—Architect's rendering of proposed library building. Feature story in the *Picayune*: "The city soon will have a public library, thanks to the munificence of Mr. Ephraim Goodwinter, owner and publisher of this newspaper."

November 2, 1904—Photo of Ephraim's funeral procession. Report in the *Picayune*: "Mourners accompanied the earthly remains of the late Ephraim Goodwinter to the grave in the longest funeral procession on record. Mr. Goodwinter died suddenly on Tuesday."

Interspersed with the enlarged photos and clippings were miners' hats, pickaxes, and sledgehammers—even a miner's lunch-bucket with reference to the meat-and-potato "pasties" that they traditionally carried down the mine shaft. A portrait of the sour-faced philanthropist showed the knife slash it received while on display in the lobby of the public library. A fuzzy snapshot of the Hanging Tree with its grisly burden was identified as "unidentified." There was also a photocopy of the alleged suicide note in handwriting remarkably similar to that of A. Lincoln. A ballot box invited visitors to vote: Suicide or Murder?

Qwilleran's elbow was jostled by Hixie Rice, advertising manager for the *Moose County Something*. "I get one message from all this," she said. "What Ephraim needed was a good public relations counselor."

"What he needed," said Qwilleran, "was some common sense."

He retraced his course through the crowd and found the Lanspeaks in the office. "You said something was missing. What is it?"

"The sheet," said Carol.

"What sheet?"

"We displayed a white sheet that the Reverend Mr. Crawbanks found near the Hanging Tree after Ephraim's death."

"Do you mean to say that someone stole it?" Qwilleran asked.

Larry said somberly, "It's the only thing that has ever been removed from our exhibit space, and we've had some valuable stuff on display. Obviously we have a crackpot in our midst. And we know it's an inside job because it was missing when the doors first opened to the public at one o'clock. It's no great loss. The sheet had dubious value even as a historic artifact. But I don't like the idea that we have a petty thief on the staff."

Qwilleran asked, "How many people have keys to the museum. Homer tells me you have seventy-five volunteers."

"No one has a key. The volunteers let themselves in with the official key hidden on the front porch."

"Hidden where? Under the door mat?"

"Under the basket of Indian corn hanging above the doorbell," said Carol.

"We've always considered our people completely trustworthy," said Larry.

Qwilleran excused himself and went in search of the exhibit chairperson. He found Mildred in conversation with Verona Boswell, who was saying, "Baby talked in complete sentences by the time she was eight months old." She was clutching the hand of the tiny girl in blue velvet coat and hat.

"Excuse me, Mrs. Boswell," said Qwilleran. "May I borrow Mrs. Hanstable to explain one of the exhibits?"

"Why, of course . . . Baby, do you know who this is? Say hi to Mr. Qwilleran."

"Hi!" she said.

"Hi," he replied more graciously than usual.

He steered Mildred into the deserted textile room. "It's a quiet place to talk," he explained. "I have yet to see a single visitor looking at this godawful exhibit."

"It's grim, isn't it?" she agreed. "We tried to spark it up with colored backgrounds and clever signs, and we roped it off to make it look important, but everyone loves the red velvet roping and hates the textiles. What's on your mind, Qwill?"

"I'd like to compliment you on the disaster exhibit. It's attracting a lot of attention."

"I thank you, and Fran Brodie thanks you. It will be interesting to see the result of the voting."

"Have you looked at the exhibit today?"

"I haven't been able to get near it. Too many people. Did someone take another poke at Ephraim's portrait?"

"No, Mildred, someone walked off with the Reverend Mr. Crawbanks' sheet."

"Really? You wouldn't kid me, would you?"

"Carol discovered that it was missing. She and Larry are surprised to say the least. They have no idea who might have pilfered it. Have you?"

"Qwill," she said, "I don't pretend to understand anything that's going on in today's society. Why don't you ask Koko whodunit? He's smarter than either of us."

"Speaking of Koko," he said, "I wish you would look at that Inchpot bed pillow. Do you see anything unusual about it?"

She studied the limp pillow critically. "Only that it's been moved." She stepped over the velvet roping, plumped the pillow and arranged it more artfully. "There! Does that look better?"

"Is it a normal occurrence for displayed objects to be moved?"

"Well . . . no. The volunteers are told never to disarrange the exhibits. Why do you ask?"

He lowered his voice. "I brought Koko in here the other day, and he zeroed in on that pillow and sniffed it. He wouldn't leave it alone until I ejected him bodily from the

208

museum. Now, don't tell me it's stuffed with chicken feathers, because the pillow from the Trevelyan farm is also stuffed with chicken feathers, but he ignored it completely."

"Let's see what it says on the ID card," Mildred said, stepping over the roping again and picking up the hand-printed label. "It was used on the Inchpot farm prior to World War I . . . The cover is a washed flour sack. . .It's stuffed with chicken feathers from the Inchpot coops. . .It was donated by Adeline Inchpot Crowe."

"Did you say *Crow?*"

"With an *e* on the end."

"Let's get out of here, Mildred. These seventy-five-year-old chicken feathers give me an acute case of depression. How would you like to have a look at Iris's cookbook while you're here?"

Qwilleran ran interference through the throng and suggested a cup of coffee when they entered the kitchen of the west wing.

"Or a little something else?" Mildred said coyly. "Large crowds make me nervous unless I have a glass in my hand."

"I'll see what I can find. Iris didn't maintain a well-stocked bar."

"Anything will do if it has a little buzz."

Qwilleran started rattling ice cubes. "The

cookbook is in the school desk under the telephone. Lift up the lid . . . I find dry sherry, Dubonnet and Campari. What'll it be?"

There was no response.

"Did you find it?" he asked. "It's just a looseleaf notebook, mixed in with a lot of clippings and scraps of paper."

Mildred was bending over the small desk. "It's not here."

"It's got to be there! I saw it a couple of days ago."

"It's not here," she insisted. "Come and look."

Qwilleran hurried to peer over her shoulder. "Where could it have gone?"

"The cats stole it," she said archly. "Koko lifted the lid, and Yum Yum heisted it with her famous paw."

"Not likely. They're larcenous, but a looseleaf notebook two inches thick is out of their class."

"You may have mislaid it."

"I looked at the handwriting for about ten seconds and then put it back in the desk. Someone came in here and pinched it— someone who knew where Iris kept it. Did she ever invite the museum staff in for coffee or anything?"

"Yes, often, but—"

"There's no lock on the door between here and the museum. Someone had three days to do the job. I've been out every day. We've got to get a lock on that door! What's to stop anyone from coming in and snatching the cats?" He stopped and looked around. "Where are they? They're usually in the kitchen. I haven't seen them. *Where are they?*"

Twelve

After the Siamese had been found asleep on a pink towel in the bathroom (insulated from the museum hubbub), and after Mildred had finished her Campari, and after the crowd had thinned out, Qwilleran went in search of Larry Lanspeak. The president was in the office conferring with a few directors of the museum.

"Come in, Qwill," said Larry. "We were just discussing the incident of the missing sheet."

"Now you can discuss the incident of the missing cookbook," Qwilleran said. "Iris's collection of recipes has disappeared from her desk."

"The cookbook I can understand," said Susan, "but who would take a sheet with holes in it?"

Carol suggested posting a large sign on the volunteers' bulletin board. "We could say, 'Will the volunteers who borrowed the sheet from the disaster exhibit and the cookbook from Iris Cobb's desk please return them to the museum office immediately. No questions asked.' How does that sound?"

Qwilleran said, "The time has come to install a lock on the connecting door between the museum and the manager's apartment. Iris had a large collection of valuable collectibles—small items, easy to pick up. People who wouldn't steal from the living think it's okay to steal from the dead. It's a primitive custom, practiced for centuries."

"Yes, but not around here," said Susan.

"How do you know? The dead never report it to the police. Moose County may have computers and camcorders and private planes, but there are plenty of primitive beliefs. Ghosts, for example. I keep hearing that Ephraim walks through the walls occasionally."

Larry smiled. "That's a popular joke, Qwill, just something to talk about over the coffee cups." He reached for the phone, at the same time glancing at his watch. "I'll call Homer about the lock. I hope he's still up. It's only five-thirty, but his bedtime keeps getting earlier and earlier."

"His new bride will change his habits," Qwilleran said. "She's a live one!"

"Yes," Larry said with a chuckle, "they'll

be sitting up watching television until eight o'clock at night . . . Why are we laughing? When we're Homer's age, we won't even be here!" He completed the call and reported that Homer would round up a locksmith first thing in the morning.

Qwilleran said, "I have another suggestion to make, apropos of locks and valuables. Iris had a lot of private papers in her desk in the parlor. They should be bundled up, sealed, and turned over to her son."

"I'll be happy to do that," said Susan. "I'll be seeing Dennis this week."

Qwilleran gave her an expressionless stare and then turned to Larry.

The president said, "I propose we do it right now. Susan, you and Qwill and I can take care of it. How big a box will we need?"

The three of them trooped to the west wing, carrying a carton, sealing tape, and a felt marker. Koko and Yum Yum met them at the door.

"Hello, cats," said Larry jovially.

The Siamese followed them into the parlor, where the desk occupied a place of prominence.

"This is the ugliest desk I've ever seen," Qwilleran commented. It was basically a flat box with one drawer and a pull-out writing surface, perched on tall legs and topped with a cupboard.

"This is an original handmade Dingle-berry, about 1890," Larry informed him. "Iris bought it at the Goodwinter auction. I was bidding against her, but I dropped out when the bidding reached four figures."

Behind the doors of the cupboard were shoeboxes labeled in large block letters with a felt marker: Bills, Letters, Financial, Medical, Insurance, and Personal. In the drawer were the usual pens, scissors, paper clips, rubber bands, memo pads, and a magnifying glass.

Qwilleran said, "She had magnifying glasses all over the house. She even wore one on a chain around her neck."

"Okay," said Larry. "Let's lock this stuff up in the museum office and have Dennis sign for it when he comes."

"Good idea," said Qwilleran.

Susan had nothing to say. She seemed to be sulking. As they were leaving the parlor she almost tripped over a rug.

Qwilleran caught her. "Sorry," he said. "There's a cat under the rug. This is the second time he's crawled under an Oriental."

"He has good taste," Larry said. "These are all antiques and museum-quality."

"Do you have any more booby traps around?" Susan said testily as she followed Larry back to the museum.

Qwilleran thawed some chicken à la king for the Siamese, who devoured it hungrily, carefully avoiding the pimento and the slivered almonds. He watched the fascinating ritual absently, thinking about the missing sheet, the misplaced pillow, the purloined cookbook, and Susan's eagerness to handle Iris Cobb's private papers.

Something had happened to Susan Exbridge after her husband divorced her for another woman. While she was the wife of a successful developer she had been an active clubwoman, serving on the board of every organization and working diligently for the common good. Since that blow to her ego she had concentrated on working for Susan Exbridge. In a way she was justified. According to the Pickax grapevine, her ex-husband had so maneuvered the divorce settlement that Susan was rich on paper but short of cash, and if she liquidated the securities, she would be liable for a large tax bite.

Rumor also had it that ninety percent of

the Exbridge & Cobb venture was financed by Iris. If that were true, Qwilleran pondered, Susan's inheritance would be substantial. Granted, the two women were good friends as well as business partners, but that was a situation that aroused Qwilleran's suspicion. A more unlikely pair of chums could hardly be found. Iris was neither chic nor sophisticated nor glib, yet Susan had engulfed her with friendship, and Iris was flattered to be taken up by a woman so distinguished in manner, dress, and social connections.

It irritated Qwilleran to think that Iris Cobb had been used; it was her know-how as well as her money that had established the new antique shop. It irritated him also to see Susan making a play for Dennis Hough, who had a wife and infant son as well as the bulk of the Cobb-Hackpole fortune.

He worked off his resentment by concocting a sandwich for himself, using caraway rye bread from one freezer, corned beef from the other, and mustard and horseradish from the refrigerator. The Siamese watched him eat, and he shared the meat. "The spirit of Mrs. Cobb is still with us," he told them.

It was true. Her presence was palpable, invoked by the food she had cooked, the friendly kitchen, her taste in antiques, the pink sheets and towels, and even her magazines and paperback novels. At any moment she might walk into the room and say, "Oh, Mr. Q, would you like some of my chocolate coconut macaroons?"

He looked up from his sandwich and almost thought he could see her. Was this the invisible presence that engaged Koko in conversation?

Qwilleran jumped up and went outdoors, taking a brisk walk around the grounds to restore some semblance of peace to his life.

It was Sunday night. A week ago he had been listening to *Otello* when Mrs. Cobb's frantic phone call had interrupted Act One. Since then he had made two more attempts to hear the opera in its entirety. He would try again. Sunday evening was usually quiet in Moose County, and it was doubtful that anyone would be calling. Briefly he considered silencing the two phones, but communication was his life, and the idea of willfully missing an incoming call struck him as a moral lapse.

With a mug of coffee in his hand and two cats in the blue velvet wing chairs, the comfortable scene was set. He pressed the Play button. Again the crash of the opening chords catapulted the Siamese out of the parlor, but they returned and withstood the trumpets, although they laid their ears back.

All went well until Act Three and the aria that Polly had called gorgeous. Just as Othello began the poignant *Dio! mi potevi* . . . the telephone rang. Qwilleran tried to ignore it, but the insistent ringing ruined the music. Even so, he was determined to let it ring itself out. He turned up the volume. The tenor agonized, and the telephone rang. Qwilleran clenched his teeth. Ten rings . . . fifteen rings . . . twenty! Then it occurred to him that only a desperate person would persist so long, only someone who knew he was at home. He turned down the volume and went to the bedroom phone.

"Hello?" he said with apprehension.

"Qwill, this is Kristi," said a nervous voice. "Don't run the column about my goats."

"Why not, Kristi?"

"Something terrible has happened. Eight of them are dead, and the others are dying."

"My God! What happened?"

"I fed them at five o'clock and they were okay. Two hours later I went out there and three were lying dead." There was a catch in her voice. "The rest were struggling to breathe, and one of them fell over right at my feet. I can't—I can't—" Her words turned into sobs.

Sympathy welled up in Qwilleran's throat as his thoughts flew to Koko and Yum Yum. He knew how precious animals can be. "Easy now, Kristi," he said. "Easy! What did you do?"

She sobbed for a while and sniffed moistly before saying, "I called the vet's emergency number, and he came right away, but by that time all the kids were gone and most of the does." She choked up again.

He waited patiently for her to recover.

"The bucks are all right," she said. "They were penned separately."

"Do you have any idea what caused it?"

"The vet says it's poison—probably insecticide in the feed. Their lungs—" She stopped and cried again. "Their lungs filled with fluid, and they suffocated. The vet is sending samples to the lab. It's almost more than I can bear! The whole herd!"

"How could it possibly have happened?"

"The police call it vandalism."

Qwilleran felt a tingling sensation on his upper lip, and he knew the answer to his next question. "Do you have any idea who would commit such an unthinkable crime?"

"I know who did it!" Her grief gave way to anger. "The stupid fool I used to be married to!"

"Did you tell that to the police?"

"Yes. They've been looking for him ever since he walked away from a minimum-security camp near Lockmaster. He thought he could hide out here, or else I'd give him money and a car. I told him he was out of his mind. I didn't want anything to do with him! *Oh, why didn't I turn him in?*" she cried, ending with a heart-rending wail.

"This is shocking, Kristi! Did you have any idea he'd sabotage the farm?"

"He threatened me this morning, and I warned him I had a gun. I didn't expect anything like this. I could kill him! It's not just the loss of two years' work, but . . . all those sweet animals! Buttercup . . . Geranium . . . Black Tulip! They were so dear to me!" she said with a whimper.

"I wish there were something I could do. Is there anything I can do?" he asked.

"There's nothing anyone can do," she sighed. "Just don't run the column. The poisoning will be in the paper tomorrow. One of the reporters called me."

"Phone me, Kristi, if any trouble develops, no matter what it is."

"Thank you, Qwill. Good night."

Qwilleran turned off the stereo. He had heard enough tragedy for one night.

Early Monday morning his telephone began to ring, as the grapevine went into operation. Mildred Hanstable, Polly Duncan, Larry Lanspeak and others called to say, "Did you hear the newscast this morning? . . . Do you know what happened to your neighbor? . . . Isn't that the woman you were going to interview? . . . The board of health has removed all goat products from the market . . . They think it was poison."

It was a rude start to another busy day. Even before he had prepared his first cup of coffee Qwilleran saw Mr. and Mrs. Tibbitt drive up in their ponderous old car, followed closely by Al's Fix-All truck. That was the accepted system in Moose County; workmen always arrived six hours late, or before breakfast. Qwilleran greeted them moodily.

"I'm going to do a little dusting," Rhoda announced.

"I'm going to have a cup of coffee," said Homer.

"Will you join me?" Qwilleran asked, waving a coffee mug.

"No, thanks. I'll mix a cup of my own

blend in the office." Homer patted his hip pocket and maneuvered his angular limbs briskly in the direction of the office.

Great guy! Qwilleran thought. He gulped a roll and coffee while the locksmith worked on the door and then joined Tibbitt in the museum office.

"Someone swiped my feather duster," Rhoda complained.

"I did!" said her husband. "I threw it in the trash. You can use a dustrag like everyone else. Spray it with that stuff that's supposed to pick up dust."

"Once a principal, always a principal," she explained to Qwilleran. "He likes to be boss." She took a duster from the cleaning closet and left the office, flicking it temperamentally at chairs and filing cabinets as she passed.

Qwilleran said to Homer, "Someone once told me there's no such thing as a locksmith in Moose County because there are no locks. So who's the guy working on my door?"

"A locksmith would starve to death in these parts," said Homer, "but this fellow fixes refrigerators, phonographs, typewriters —anything. Why do you want a lock between you and the museum? Has old

223

Ephraim been bothering you? A door won't stop him, you know. Not even a stone wall."

"I don't worry about dead prowlers," Qwilleran said. "I worry about the live ones."

"Halloween's coming, and you can expect pranksters. When I was a young lad we used to spook houses around Halloween, especially if it was someone we hated, like a strict teacher or the town skinflint."

"How do you spook a house? That wasn't in our bag of tricks in Chicago, where I grew up."

"As I recall," said the old man, "you stick a big nail or something under a loose board on the outside of a house, with a long string attached. Then you pull the line taut and run a stick over it like bowing a violin. It reverberates all through the house. Screaming in the attic! Moaning in the walls! I doubt whether it would work with the aluminum siding and plywood they use nowadays. They're eliminating all life's little pleasures. Everything's synthetic, even our food."

"One of life's little pleasures, I gather, was carving initials on school desks," said Qwilleran. "Mrs. Cobb's telephone stand is an old desk with the initials H.T. carved on the top. Would you know anything about that?"

"In the lower righthand corner? That's my desk!" Homer exulted. "It came from the old Black Creek School. The teacher gave me what-for with a cane for carving that little masterpiece. If I'd been smart I would have carved someone else's initials. Adam Dingleberry had that desk before I did he was four years ahead of me—and he carved the initials of the preacher's son. He had a madcap sense of humor. Still does! Got expelled from school for playing practical jokes. No one gave him credit for originality and creativity. Are there any other initials on the desk?"

"Quite a few. I remember B.O. I suppose those letters didn't have any significance in those days."

"That's Mitch's grandfather, Bruce Ogilvie. He came after me. He won all the spelling bees with his eyes closed—couldn't spell with 'em open."

Qwilleran said, "In this north country it seems that lives are interwoven. It gives the community a rich texture. Life in the cities Down Below is a tangle of loose threads."

"You should write a 'Qwill Pen' column about that," Homer suggested.

"I think I shall. Speaking of the 'Qwill

Pen,' Rhoda tells me you know something about old barns."

"Yes, indeed! That's another tradition that's disappearing. They build steel things that look like factory warehouses. You can't convince me that the cattle are happy in those contraptions! But there's still a good barn on this property." He crooked an arm toward the north window. "It'll still be standing long after the steel barns have blown away."

"I haven't had a chance to look at it," Qwilleran admitted.

"Then let's go out there. It's a beauty!" Homer stood up slowly as if unlocking his joints one by one. "Contrary to popular opinion I'm not put together with plastic bones and steel pins. What you see is all original parts. Rhoda," he called out, "tell Al to leave his bill and we'll send him a check."

Walking toward the barn the two men made slow progress, although Homer's flailing arms and legs gave an impression of briskness. Qwilleran looked back toward the farmhouse and saw a small fawn-colored bundle on the kitchen windowsill; he waved a hand.

The Goodwinter barn was a classic style

with a gambrel roof, its boards once painted red and now a red-streaked silvery gray. A lean-to had been added on one side, and the remains of a squat stone silo stood at the opposite corner like a gray ghost.

They walked in silence. "Can't walk . . . and talk . . . at the same time," said Homer, flinging his limbs rhythmically.

The barn was farther from the house than Qwilleran had realized, and larger than he had imagined. The closer they approached it, the loftier it loomed. A grassy ramp led up to enormous double doors.

He said, "Now I know what they mean by big as a barn door."

They were pausing at the foot of the ramp for Homer to catch his breath before attempting the ascent. When he recovered from the exertion he explained, "The doors had to be large so a loaded hay wagon could drive into the barn. The man-size door cut in the big door is called the eye of the needle."

As he spoke, a corner of the latter flapped open, and a pregnant cat stepped through the cat-hatch and waddled away.

"That's Cleo," he said. "She's on my committee in charge of rodent control. Looks like another litter of mousers is on the way. You can never have too many barncats."

"What's the function of the lean-to?" Qwilleran asked.

"Ephraim built it to house his carriages. He had some elegant ones, they say. Later his son kept his Stanley Steamer in there. After Titus Goodwinter was killed, his widow bought a Pierce Arrow—with windshield wipers, mind you! Everyone thought that was the cat's pajamas!"

The weathered wood barn perched high on a fieldstone foundation, and as the land sloped away to the rear, the foundation became a full story high.

"That's what they called a byre in Scotland," Homer said. "The Goodwinters kept cattle and horses down there in the old days." They climbed the grassy ramp slowly and entered the barn through the eye of the needle, the old man pointing out the door hardware—simple hooks and eyes of hand-wrought iron, the work of a local blacksmith.

The interior was dark after the sunshine outdoors. Only a few shafts of light slanted in from unseen windows high in the gables. All was silent except for the muted cooing of pigeons and beating of wings.

"Better open the big doors so we can see,"

said Homer. "This place gets darker every year."

Qwilleran suddenly realized he had never been inside a barn. He had seen them in the distance while speeding down a highway, and an apple barn was included with the Klingenschoen property, but he had not inspected it. Now, gazing upward at the vast space under the roof, crisscrossed with timbers, he felt the same sense of awe he had experienced in Gothic cathedrals.

Homer saw him gazing upward. "That's a double haymow," he explained. "The timbers are sixty feet long, fourteen inches square. Everything's put together with mortise-and-tenon construction—no nails. All white pine. You don't see white pine any more. It was all lumbered out."

He pointed out the marks of the hand axe and hewing adze. "The main floor was called the threshing floor. The boards are four inches thick. It takes a solid floor like this to support a loaded hay wagon—or those danged printing presses."

It was then that Qwilleran noticed the contents of the barn. Wooden packing crates and grotesque machines resembling instruments of torture stood about the straw-strewn floor.

"This is only part of it," the old man went on. "The rest of the crates are down in the stable. Senior Goodwinter was obsessed with handprinting. Every time an old printshop went out of business or modernized, he bought their obsolete equipment. Never got around to taking inventory or even opening the crates. He just kept on collecting."

"That's where I come in!" said a jarring voice behind them. Vince Boswell stood silhouetted in the open doorway. "My job is to find out what's in those crates and catalogue the stuff so they can start a printing museum," he said in his penetrating voice. It was easy to believe he had been an auctioneer. "Yesterday I uncrated a wooden press that's eighteenth century."

"You carry on," Homer told him. "I want to go back to the house before my legs give out. I'm getting a pain in my knees." He retreated down the grassy ramp.

At that moment a doll-size figure came trudging toward the ramp, wearing doll-size blue jeans and a wisp of a red sweater. She carried a green plastic pail in one hand and a yellow plastic spade in the other. She was followed by an anxious mother, running and calling in a small voice, "Baby! Baby! Come back here!"

Vince looked at them and stiffened. "Can't you control that kid?" he demanded. "Get her out of here. It isn't safe."

Verona scooped the child into her arms, the pail and spade flying in opposite directions.

"My pail! My shovel!" Baby screamed.

Qwilleran gathered them up and handed them to her.

"Say thank you," Verona murmured.

"Thank you," said Baby automatically. As they retreated up the lane she looked back toward the barn with longing. There was something disturbingly adult about her, Qwilleran thought, and she was so unhealthily thin.

With a shrug Boswell said, "I'll show you what I've found here, if you're interested." He pointed to a contraption with fancy legs. "That's a Washington toggle press, 1827. I've found old typecases, composing sticks, a primitive cylinder press, woodblocks—all kinds of surprises. I open a crate and never know what I'll find." He picked up a crowbar and wrenched the top off a wooden box. It was packed with straw. "Looks like a hand-operated papercutter."

"I'm vastly impressed," said Qwilleran as he edged toward the door.

"Wait up!" Boswell said in piercing tones. "You haven't seen the half of it yet."

"I must confess," said Qwilleran, "that I'm not greatly interested in mechanical equipment, and some of those presses look diabolical." He nodded toward something that seemed half sewing machine and half guillotine.

"That's a treadle press," said the expert. "And this one's an Albion. And that one's a Columbian. When the counterpoise lever moves, the eagle goes up and down." The Columbian was a cast-iron monster embellished with eagle, serpents, and dolphins.

"Amazing," said Qwilleran in a minor key. "You must tell me more about this fascinating subject some other time." He consulted his watch and headed for the ramp.

"Would you care to have a bowl of soup with the wife and me?"

"Thank you for the invitation, but I'm expecting an important phone call."

Boswell picked up a walkie-talkie from the top of a crate. "Coming home to lunch, Verona," he said. "How about some tomato soup and a hot dog?"

The two of them closed the big doors, latching them with the crude hook and eye, and walked down the grassy ramp. Then

Boswell drove away in his rusty van and Qwilleran strolled back to the house, grateful to escape the stiletto-voiced expert with the textbook patter. Why did he need a walkie-talkie? Why didn't he simply stand on the ramp and yell? How could the delicate Verona endure that deafening delivery? It irked him that she and Baby were expendable, that they could be shipped back to Pittsburgh like unwanted merchandise if Vince was named Mrs. Cobb's successor. That he should even presume to follow in her footsteps was obscene, Qwilleran told himself.

As he opened the door to the west wing, a furry blur whizzed past his ankles and flew off the steps. With a roar Qwilleran made a flying tackle, grabbing the cat's slippery body in both hands. They landed in a pile of leaves.

"Oh no, you don't, young man!" Qwilleran scolded as he carried him back into the house. "Where do you think you're going? To the Jellicle Ball with the barncats? Or are you interested in printing presses?"

As he spoke the words he dropped the cat on the floor, and Koko made a surprised four-point landing. As for Qwilleran, the idea that flashed across his mind at that moment made his moustache curl.

Exactly what, he asked himself, is in those unpacked crates? Printing presses? Or something else . . .

Thirteen

Qwilleran's new-found suspicions regarding the printing presses were relegated to the back burner as he faced the exigencies of the day. There was a long telephone conversation with the CEO of the K Fund and then a follow-up call to Kristi at the Fugtree farm.

"Nothing to report," she said wearily. "The police keep dropping in. They've put up road blocks around the county, expecting Brent to make a getaway in a stolen car, but no car thefts have been reported. Where's your car? I looked for it with the binoculars, and it wasn't in the yard. I was just going to phone you."

"It's locked up in the steel barn, but I appreciate your concern."

"The board of health is here again, and the men who do dead stock removal. It's too painful to watch. I can't bear to see them hauling away my beautiful Black Tulip and my sweet little Geranium."

"It's a terrible thing," Qwilleran said, "but you must put it behind you and think about your next step."

"I know. I must think constructively. That's what I've been trying to do. My friend says he'll help me fix up the house if I want to open a restaurant or bed-and-breakfast. But first I've got to unload all my mother's junk. I don't know whether to have a big garage sale or a big bonfire. And it will take money to get the house into shape. I don't know how much I'll get from the insurance. Oh, God! I don't want the insurance money! I just want to wake up and find Gardenia and Honeysuckle waiting to be milked and looking at me with those soulful eyes. I love goat farming!"

"I know you do, Kristi, but whether you start another herd or a B-and-B, the Klingenschoen Fund would like to help you register the house as a historic place. If you're interested, they're prepared to offer you a grant to cover research and renovation."

"Am I interested! Am I interested! Oh, Qwill, that would be neat—really neat! Wait till I tell Mitch."

"Mitch? Do you mean Mitch Ogilvie, by any chance?"

"Yes. He says he knows you. And Qwill,

could I ask you a big favor? He's applied for the job of resident manager at the museum. Would you put in a few good words for him? He feels about the museum the same way I feel about goats. And he can't be a desk clerk at the hotel forever. He has too much to offer."

"Isn't he the one who tells ghost stories to the kids at Halloween?"

"Yes, and he really makes their teeth chatter!"

"I'd like to talk to him. Why don't you bring him over to the west wing for some cider and doughnuts?"

"When?"

"How about tonight?" Qwilleran suggested. "About eight o'clock."

"I'll bring some goat cheese and crackers," she said in great excitement. "And don't worry—the cheese isn't poisoned."

Next Qwilleran phoned Polly at the library. He said, "I'm driving into Pickax to do errands. Would you care to join me there for dinner?"

"Delighted," she said, "provided it's early. I must go home, you know, to feed my little sweetheart. He has four meals a day on a regular schedule."

Qwilleran recoiled. Many a time he had

said, "I've got to go home and feed the cats," but Polly's simpering was intolerable.

"Why don't you come to my apartment when the library closes?" he suggested. "I'll have the Old Stone Mill send over some food. What shall I order for you?"

"Just a green salad with turkey julienne and some melba toast. I'll take some of the turkey home to my sweetheart. He eats like a little horse."

Qwilleran winced, forgetting how many doggie bags he had toted home to the Siamese, forgetting how the pocket of his old tweed overcoat had once smelled of turkey gravy. True, he often called Yum Yum "my little sweetheart," but he did it in private.

He spent that afternoon writing a "Qwill Pen" column on the museum's new disaster exhibit. About the missing sheet he was mum, but he questioned why there was no mention of the miners lost in the explosion. On display was a photo of a granite monument in the cemetery, erected by public subscription to the memory of the thirty-two, but they were not identified.

He filed his copy at the office of the *Something* and bought cider and doughnuts for his soirée with Kristi and Mitch, arriving at his Pickax apartment in time to order dinner.

238

Although home delivery was not an advertised service of the Old Stone Mill, the chef catered meals for the Siamese when they were in town, and a busboy named Derek Cuttlebrink was used to making daily visits with sushi, shrimp timbales, braised lamb brains and other delicacies.

Polly arrived on foot. Leaving her car in the library parking lot she cut through the rear of the property to the former Klingenschoen carriage house, an ounce of the discretion that she found wise to practice as head librarian in a gossipy town, although it fooled no one. The carriage house, now a four-car garage, was a sumptuous fieldstone building with arched doors and eight brass carriage lanterns posted at the corners. Using her own key, Polly unlocked what had been the servants' door and climbed the narrow stairs to Qwilleran's quarters. There was a warm moment of greeting that would have titillated the Pickax grapevine, and then he inquired about the health of her new boarder.

"He's becoming more adorable every day!" cried Polly. "The things he does are so darling, like sleeping on my pillow with his nose buried in my hair and purring his little heart out. He's gained five ounces, imagine!"

Qwilleran shuddered and picked up a decanter. "May I pour the usual?"

As Polly sipped her sherry she asked about the goat poisoning. "Any more news?"

"Nothing official. We also have a couple of mysteries at the museum. You may not have noticed it during the festivities yesterday, but the Reverend Mr. Crawbanks' sheet has disappeared from the disaster exhibit. Also missing is Iris Cobb's cookbook."

"Really? That's most unusual! The cookbook I can understand, but why the sheet? The young people used to flit about the countryside in white sheets around Halloween, trying to frighten people, until the county outlawed it with what they call the pork-and-beans ordinance."

"And what might that be?"

"It was the result of an incident near Mooseville. A woman sent her teenage son to buy groceries at a crossroads store, and he was walking home on a country road after dark. As he approached the bridge over the ittibittiwassee, a white-sheeted figure rose out of the dark riverbed and started moaning and screaming. The intrepid youth kept on walking until he was a few yards from the ghost. Then he reached into his grocery sack and hurled a can of beans at the spectre—

right between the eye holes. It was a young woman under the sheet, and she went to the hospital with a concussion."

"And I presume the youth went to the majors," Qwilleran said.

Just then the doorbell sounded, and Polly thought it prudent to retire to the bathroom to fix her hair. A tall lanky busboy arrived with Polly's salad and Qwilleran's lambchop—plus two servings of pumpkin chiffon pie with the compliments of the chef.

"Where are the cats?" the busboy asked.

"On vacation," Qwilleran said as he handed him a tip. "Thanks, Derek."

"They've got it made. I never get to go anywhere."

"I thought you were going away to college this fall."

Derek shrugged. "Well, you see, I got this good role in the next play at the theatre, and I met this girl from Lockmaster who's a blast, so I decided to work another year."

"Thanks again, Derek," said Qwilleran, ushering him to the door. "I'll look forward to seeing you in the November play. Don't tell me anything about your role; it's bad luck. The Siamese send you their regards. Give my thanks to the chef. Watch your step with that girl from Lockmaster. Don't trip on the stairs." In slow stages he maneuvered the gregarious Derek Cuttlebrink from the apartment.

Polly emerged from the bathroom, looking not much different. "He's a nice boy, but he hasn't found himself yet," she said.

"He's looking in the wrong place," Qwilleran muttered.

They dined at the travertine table, and Polly inquired how he liked the *Otello* recording.

"A stunning opera! Even the cats have enjoyed it. I've played it several times." Not all the way through, but he withheld that detail.

"How did you like Iago's *Credo?*"

"Unforgettable!"

"And don't you agree with me that *Dio! mi potevi* is gorgeous?"

"My word for it exactly! . . . And what did you think of the disaster exhibit?" he asked, changing the subject deftly.

"The girls accomplished a miracle! That was a difficult subject to dramatize. And the balloting idea was very clever."

"In my opinion they missed the boat. They should have honored the thirty-two victims by name, and I said so in my column."

"No one knows who they were, except for an occasional family recollection," Polly informed him. "There is no official list. We have old copies of the *Picayune* on microfilm, but the issues of May thirteenth to eighteenth are missing, oddly enough."

"Where did you get this film?"

"Junior Goodwinter turned everything over to us when the *Picayune* ceased publication. We also checked the county courthouse files, but death records prior to 1905 were destroyed in a fire that year."

"It would be interesting to know who threw the match," Qwilleran said. "It's doubtful that all the records were destroyed accidentally. Who would want the victims' names forgotten? The Goodwinters? Or would their names give a clue to the identity of the lynch mob? There were probably thirty-two in the gang, one to avenge each victim. A ritualistic touch, don't you think? They were draped in sheets so no one would know the identity of the actual hangman. I imagine they drew straws for the privilege."

"An interesting deduction," Polly said, "assuming that the lynching story is true."

"If Ephraim committed suicide, why would he do it in a public place? He had a big barn. He could have jumped off the haymow. Actually, does anyone really care—at this late date—about the exact fate of the old scoundrel? Why do the Noble Sons of the Noose persist generation after generation?"

"Because Ephraim Goodwinter is the only villain Moose County ever had," said Polly, "and people love to have a bête noire to hate."

She declined the pumpkin pie, and Qwilleran had no difficulty in consuming both pieces. Then he said, "What do you know about Vince and Verona?"

"Not much," Polly said. "They suddenly appeared a month ago and proposed a deal, which the museum board was delighted to accept. Vince offered to catalogue the presses, in return for which they gave him the cottage rent-free. Those presses were a white elephant, so Vince's arrival on the scene was considered a blessing from heaven."

"Don't you consider his offer unusually generous?"

"Not at all. He's writing a book on the history of printing, and this is a unique opportunity for him to see actual equipment that was used a hundred or two hundred years ago."

"I wouldn't mind knowing how he found out about the presses."

"He seems quite knowledgeable about printing."

Qwilleran said, "During my career, Polly, I've interviewed thousands of persons, and I can detect the difference between (a) those who know what they're talking about and (b) those who have memorized information from a book. I don't think Boswell is an 'a.' "

"No doubt the project is a learning experience for him," she persisted stubbornly. "He's always checking out books on the subject. Thanks to Senior Goodwinter, our library has the definitive collection on handprinting in the northeast central states."

Qwilleran huffed into his moustache. "Coffee?" he asked.

"Vince was an auctioneer Down Below," Polly added.

"Or a sideshow barker. His voice would wake the dead. There's one thing about Boswell's operation that puzzles me. Every time I return to the museum from somewhere else, his van is pulling away from the barn. Today I discovered that he uses a walkie-talkie to tell Verona when he's going home to lunch, and I suspect she uses it to tip him off when I turn into Black Creek Lane. One of these days I'm going to trick him—drive away from the museum, park my car somewhere, and sneak back on foot, coming in the back way."

"Oh, Qwill, you're a born gumshoe!" Polly laughed. "All you need is a deerstalker cap and a magnifying glass."

"You may laugh," he retorted, "but I'll tell you something else: Koko spends most of his waking hours watching the barn from the kitchen window."

"He's looking for barncats or fieldmice."

"That's what you may think, but that's not the message I'm getting from the feline transmitter." He smoothed his moustache significantly. "I have a theory, not fully developed as yet, that Boswell is up to no good in that barn. He's looking for something other than printing equipment in those crates. And when he finds it, he drives around to the livestock doors, loads his van, and delivers the goods."

"What kind of goods?" Polly asked with an amused smile.

"I have no evidence," Qwilleran said, "and I'm not prepared to say. If I could spend an hour in that barn with a crowbar,

I might have some answers. Bear in mind that Boswell is the first person to touch those crates since Senior Goodwinter's death a year ago. How did he know about them? Someone in Moose County tipped him off and is probably collaborating in the distribution."

Polly glanced at her watch. Still smiling she said, "Qwill, this is very interesting—confusing, but provocative. You must tell me more about it next time. I'm afraid I must excuse myself now. Bootsie has been alone all day, and the poor thing will want his din-din."

Qwilleran huffed into his moustache. "When do you leave for Lockmaster?"

"Early tomorrow evening. I'll drop off Bootsie on the way. He'll have his special food and his own little commode and his brush. He'll appreciate it if you give him a brush-brush and a kiss-kiss once in a while. He's so affectionate! And he's housebroken, of course. It's adorable to see the little dear scratching in the litterbox and then sitting down with a beatific expression on his smudged-nose face."

Polly returned to her car in the library parking lot, glancing about casually to see who was watching. Qwilleran waited a few discreet minutes and then loaded his bike in

247

the trunk of his own car and headed for North Middle Hummock, where two Siamese were anxiously watching the freezer-chest.

"Guess who's coming to dinner tomorrow," he announced. "Bigfoot!"

Fourteen

 At approximately eight o'clock Monday evening Qwilleran was preparing for his guests, chilling the cider, finding paper napkins, piling a plate with doughnuts enough for ten, and laying a fire in each of the two fireplaces. Without warning Koko came racing into the kitchen from nowhere and hopped onto the windowsill that faced the barn. To Qwilleran's eye the window was nothing but a reflective black rectangle after dark, but Koko saw something that excited him.

Qwilleran cupped his eyes and peered into the blackness. Two lights were bobbing in the barnyard, and his mind flashed back to the bobbing lights on the hats of Homer's ghostly miners. But these lights were different; they darted erratically and swung in wide arcs. As they came closer he could distinguish two faces, and then he recognized Kristi and Mitch. They had walked from the Fugtree farm with flashlights—walked along the Willoway—and were approaching the museum property from the rear.

Qwilleran met them at the entrance, accompanied by the chief security officer.

Kristi said, "It's such a nice night that we decided to walk. The trail alongside the creek is a shortcut but kind of scary at night. Mitch ought to take the kids down there for the Halloween ghost stories this year." She gave Qwilleran an enthusiastic hug and a plastic tub of goat cheese. "I've been high," she said, "ever since you told me about the Klingenschoen offer."

The men shook hands, and Qwilleran said, "You have a fine old Scottish name. My mother was a Mackintosh."

"Yes, the Ogilvie clan goes back to the twelfth century," said Mitch with obvious pride. "My family came here from Scotland in 1861."

"And I happen to know that your grandfather won all the spelling bees with his eyes closed."

"You've been talking to Homer. That old guy has *some memory!*"

Kristi said to Qwilleran, "I'll weave you a scarf in the Mackintosh tartan as soon as I dig out my loom from under my mother's junk . . . Oooooh! What a beautiful cat! Is he friendly?"

"Especially to persons who come bearing goat cheese. Where would you like to sit? In the parlor or around the big table in the kitchen? In either place we can have a fire."

They elected the kitchen. While Qwilleran poured the cider, Mitch put a match to the kindling in the fireplace and Kristi lighted the pink candles that Mrs. Cobb had left on the table. "This is so cozy," she said. "Iris used to invite us over for lemonade and cookies. Mitch, wouldn't you love to live here?"

"Sure would! I'm living over the Pickax drug store right now," he explained to Qwilleran. "I wonder if they've had many applications for Iris's job."

"What are your qualifications, Mitch?"

"Well, I've belonged to the Historical Society ever since high school, and I've read a lot about antiques, and I'm on Homer's committee, supervising the kids who do the yardwork. Plus I have some ideas for special events I could stage if I lived here full time."

"And he gets along with *everybody*," Kristi said. "Even Amanda Goodwinter. Even Adam Dingleberry."

Mitch said, "Old Adam won't be around

251

much longer. He's moved into the Senior Care Facility, but his mind is still sharp."

"And he still gropes girls," Kristi said.

"You should interview him for your column, Mr. Qwilleran, before it's too late."

"Call me Qwill, Mitch. Does Adam have any ghost stories to tell?"

"Everyone around here has had at least one supernatural experience," he said, looking pointedly at Kristi, but she ignored the hint.

"Unfortunately I haven't joined the club as yet," said Qwilleran. "How about the stories you tell the kids on Halloween? Are they classics? Or do you invent them?"

"They're all true, based on events in Moose County and Scottish history. Naturally I add a few hair-raising details."

"Have you ever seen the thirty-two miners?"

Mitch nodded. "About three years ago. I was coming back from a party in Mooseville, and I stopped at the side of the road for a minute, you know. It was near the Goodwinter hill—the old slag pile—and I saw them."

"What did they look like?"

"Just shadows of men, slogging along. I

knew they were miners because they had lights on their hats."

"Did you count them?"

"I didn't think of it until some of them had disappeared over the hill, but here's something funny: It was May thirteenth, the anniversary of the explosion."

"Did you say you were coming home from a party?"

"That had nothing to do with it, I swear."

"Okay, I'll square with you. I've always been skeptical of these stories. I always thought there was some logical explanation. I still do, in the back of my mind, but I'm beginning to be skeptical of my own skepticism. Let me tell you what's been happening here."

He told them about Iris Cobb's terrified call in the middle of the night, about the knocking in the basement and the moaning in the walls, and about her "seeing something" just before her death. He said, "I've been told that Senior Goodwinter—just before he died—saw Ephraim walking through a wall. I'm trying to sort out the evidence, you understand."

Kristi said, "There are lots of rumors about Ephraim. They say he stashed away a lot of gold coins in case he wanted to make a quick getaway, but he died suddenly and now he comes back looking for them."

"The old miser!" said Mitch. "He never gives up!"

"One of my cats," Qwilleran said, "has been acting strangely since we moved here. He talks to himself and stares out the window where Iris saw the thing that frightened her."

"Cats are always doing crazy things," Kristi said.

"Koko," said Qwilleran, "is not your ordinary cat. He always has a damned good reason for doing what he does."

Hearing his name, the cat walked into the kitchen, looking elegant and vain.

"God! He's a beautiful animal," said Mitch.

"He looks so intelligent," Kristi added.

"Koko is not only intelligent but remarkably intuitive. I won't say that he's psychic, but he senses when something is out in left field, and if Ephraim's ghost is prowling around here, Koko is going to find him!"

All three turned to look at the remarkable cat. Unfortunately Koko had taken that moment to attend to the base of his tail.

Qwilleran said quickly, "Would you like to see the basement where Iris first heard the knocking? It's just a junkroom for the museum. Do you know the one I mean?"

"I know about it, but I've never been down there. I'd like to see it," Mitch said.

"I'll take Koko along. He can hear earthworms crawling and butterflies pollenating, and if there's anything irregular down there, he'll sniff it out. I'll put him on a leash so that I have a little control."

He strapped the cat into a blue leather harness and coiled a few yards of nylon cord that served as the leash, and the four of them went to the basement, Koko quite willingly.

In the storeroom a few bare lightbulbs threw garish light over the broken furniture, rusty tools, moldy books, cracked crockery, and cobwebs.

"My mother would love this!" Kristi said.

"This is what Homer calls the magpie nest," said Qwilleran. "Iris was looking for a broken bed warmer when she first heard the knocking in the wall. Here's the potato masher she used to reply." He picked up the small wooden club and rapped the Morse code for SOS on the plastered wall—the only skill he remembered from his year in the Boy Scouts—and followed it with the burlesque tattoo, "shave and a haircut, two bits." Neither message called forth a response, but the plaster cracked a little more.

Meanwhile Koko was snapping at cobwebs instead of investigating.

"Cats never cooperate," Qwilleran explained. "The trick is to ignore him for a while. Let's find something to sit on."

Kristi found a platform rocker that no longer rocked; Mitch perched on a barrel; Qwilleran sat on a kitchen chair with three rungs missing, all the while keeping a furtive eye on Koko, who was beginning to move around stealthily.

"I hear rumbling," Kristi said.

"That's thunder," Mitch told her, "but it's a long way off. It's not supposed to rain tonight."

Koko sniffed a wicker baby buggy without wheels. "Some kid cannibalized it to make a go-cart," Mitch guessed.

When the cat sniffed the potato masher, Qwilleran said, "We're getting warm. He knows Iris handled it. Now watch him!"

Koko was making his way to the cracked plaster wall, hopping over a coal skuttle, slinking under a three-legged chair, climbing up on the monstrous sideboard that stood against the plaster wall. It was a hodgepodge of shelves, mirrors, and carved ornament.

"My mother bought two of those dumb things," Kristi said. "Listen! Thunder again! It's coming closer!"

Koko was standing on his hind legs and stretching to see the wall behind the sideboard.

"He senses something," Qwilleran whispered.

Mitch said, "I think he sees a spider walking up the wall."

"I hate spiders," said Kristi.

With one swift movement Koko jumped up, swatted the insect, brought it down in the cup of his paw, and chomped on it with satisfaction.

"Ugh!" she said.

"Let's go," said Qwilleran, grabbing the cat. "He's not in good form tonight."

"We should think about leaving," Mitch said as they emerged from the basement and saw the sky illuminated with blue lightning.

"I'll drive you home," Qwilleran offered, "so have another glass of cider before you go." The four paraded back to the kitchen.

"This is good stuff," said Mitch. "Did it come from Trevelyan's cider mill? They throw in bruised apples, windfalls, worms and everything. My grandfather insisted on

257

using perfect apples, and it was the flattest cider anybody ever tasted."

The two men talked about leaf raking, the hotel business, and Scottish history, but Kristi was quiet and introspective. Finally she said softly, "Emmaline will walk tonight."

The men glanced at each other and then at her.

She said, "Qwill, would you like to see Emmaline? Mitch has seen her twice."

"Yes, I would," he said.

The downpour had started. They collected their jackets and ran for the steel barn. As they drove up Black Creek Lane torrents of water slapped the windshield. As they turned into the Fugtree drive, flashes of lightning silhouetted the Victorian house against an electric blue sky. No one spoke. They dashed for the side door and arrived in the kitchen wet. Still there was no conversation. Wordlessly Kristi draped their wet jackets over kitchen chairbacks. She turned on no lights, but she beamed a flashlight at the floor to lead them into the foyer. Groping through the incredible clutter they found their way to the massive staircase and sat on the stairs to wait in the dark, smelling the mustiness of the house, feeling the vibration from thunderclaps overhead, hearing the rain slap against the tall narrow windows, seeing the panes glow blue with each lightning flash. They waited.

"She's coming!" Kristi whispered.

No one dared to breathe.

The men stared in rapt silence.

Kristi shuddered and gasped.

Qwilleran found his blood running cold.

The minutes ticked away.

Then Kristi broke into tears. "Wasn't she beautiful?" she sighed.

"Beautiful!" Mitch said in a half-whisper.

"Incredible!" Qwilleran said under his breath.

The three sat quietly for a while, each with private thoughts. The rain relented; the tumult subsided; and Qwilleran brought himself to murmur, "What can I say? . . . Thank you . . . Good night." He squeezed Kristi's hand, touched Mitch's shoulder, and found his way out of the house. "My God!" he said aloud, sitting in the driver's seat, reluctant to turn on the ignition.

At home he dropped into his wing chair and fell into a reverie so deep that he didn't hear the vehicle pulling up to the door. The brass knocker startled him. He jumped up and opened the door, saying, "Mitch! Did you forget something?"

"Just wanted to talk for a minute—without Kristi."

"Come into the kitchen and get that wet jacket off. Do you want a cup of coffee before you drive home?"

"It might be a good idea."

"Put another log on the fire while I make the coffee."

"Sorry to come back so late."

"Forget it! What's on your mind?"

Mitch gave him a searching look. "Tell me honestly, Qwill. Did you see Emmaline?"

"Did you?" Qwilleran asked, returning the intent gaze.

"I've never seen her," the young man confessed.

"To tell the truth," Qwilleran said, "I didn't see her either, but I felt a chill. I sensed an invisible presence. Perhaps I was reacting to Kristi's emotion. Whatever, it was a memorable experience."

They drank coffee for a while without talking. Then Qwilleran said, "Have a doughnut." He pushed the plate across the table.

"Thanks. These are pretty good dough-nuts."

"Kristi's an interesting young woman," Qwilleran said.

"I worry about her—with Brent still at large."

"Is he dangerous?"

"Worse still, he's stupid! He was okay until they went Down Below and he started doing drugs. He fell apart. Used to be a good-looking guy, too. At least, Kristi thought so, I guess."

"If he's that far gone," Qwilleran speculated, "it won't take the police long to track him down. It takes a modicum of intelligence and some animal instinct to be a fugitive."

"You're right!" Mitch pushed the plate back across the table. "Doughnut?"

"Yes. They're not bad."

"Up front, Qwill, do you think I stand a chance of getting the museum job?"

"I'm on your side, Mitch, but it's in the hands of the museum board."

"I've been doing some lobbying, and most of them pledged their support, but Larry and Susan are dragging their feet—that's what it seems like."

"I'll see what I can do on your behalf."

"Sure appreciate it." Mitch stared into his coffee cup and fidgeted.

"Another doughnut, Mitch?" The plate went back across the table.

"Thanks."

Qwilleran read the signals. "Is there something else on your mind?"

"Well, when you were telling us about Iris hearing the noises, I thought of something I should tell you, something I heard recently from one of the old-timers. He got the story from an old blacksmith who used to shoe the Goodwinter horses . . . You know about the big funeral they had for Ephraim?"

"I certainly do! Thirty-seven carriages, fifty-two buggies, or was it the other way around?"

"This blacksmith told the old-timer that Ephraim wasn't in the coffin!"

"Why! Did he know why?"

"The family of the old miser was afraid he'd be dug up—by his enemies, you know—so they went through the motions of burying him in the cemetery, but actually he was secretly buried, here on the farm."

"Where? Do you know?"

"Under the house!"

"Now I've heard everything, Mitch. Do you believe that story?"

"I'm only telling you what I heard, Qwill, on account of what you said about Iris, and the way your cat is acting."

"Hmmm," Qwilleran said, stroking his moustache. "How about another cup of coffee?"

"Thanks, but I've got to be going. I'm on the day shift this week."

Qwilleran and Koko walked their guest to the door and watched the blue pickup drive away. The rain had stopped, but the trees were still dripping, and the night was dark. Koko was sniffing and peering into the blackness, and Qwilleran made a lunge for the cat before he could cross the threshold and disappear into the night.

Fifteen

At midnight Qwilleran retired to the General Grant bed with a paperback novel that Koko had twice knocked off the shelf. He had read *One Flew Over the Cuckoo's Nest* some years before and had seen the movie but he was willing to read it again. He tried, but his eyes only processed the words automatically while his mind reviewed the evening with Kristi, Mitch, and Emmaline. He particularly relished the rumor about Ephraim's burial under the house. Mitch apparently believed the story, but the old-timer who revealed it may have imagined the whole thing, or the blacksmith who related it may have taken a swig after a hard day at the anvil. Nevertheless, Qwilleran liked the story.

The Siamese were curled up on the foot of his bed. In Pickax they had their own room, complete with all conveniences, but at the museum they wanted to sleep on the foot of Qwilleran's bed, a quirk that made him wonder about subliminal influences in the place. All was quiet except for an occasional twitching paw or delicate snore. Shortly after he had turned off the bedside lamp and rolled over, he felt the animals snap out of their deep sleep. Koko was grunting. He turned on the lamp in time to see them listening with ears pricked, necks extended, and heads swiveling like periscopes as they strained to see into the adjoining hall. Then, with one accord, they jumped from the bed with fluid grace and scampered toward the kitchen. They had heard something.

Qwilleran had heard it, too, but he assumed the refrigerator motor had kicked on, or the electric pump was refilling the tank, as it sometimes did in the middle of the night for reasons of its own. Nevertheless, he slipped into his mooseskin moccasins and groped his way to the kitchen, where he heard the gentle sound of a cat lapping a drink of water. That was Yum Yum. Koko was on the windowsill, chattering as he did at squirrels—unusual behavior in the middle of the night.

Qwilleran looked out the window and saw nothing, but he thought it prudent to check the museum. Without turning on lights— simply low-beaming a flashlight on and off

—he inspected the exhibit rooms and the office. Whimsically he thought, it would be a joke on a skeptic like me if Ephraim Goodwinter were to materialize through a wall—and what a column it would make for the "Qwill Pen"! Hopefully he sat down in the office. Once he thought he saw, from the corner of his eye, a wisp of movement, and he turned quickly, but there was nothing there. If he had been less skeptical he might have been more patient, but he declined to spend more than five minutes on ghost watching.

Returning to his apartment he locked the connecting door and went back to bed, where he turned on the radio and heard WPKX signing off for the night. Yum Yum again nestled against his feet, although her partner had not returned. Qwilleran picked up his book and tried to resume reading, but Koko's absence made him uncomfortable. Once more he padded to the kitchen and called him without hearing a reply. The entire apartment was silent, and it was not the living, breathing silence that means a furry body is hiding and listening; it was the dead silence that falls on a place when a missing cat is simply *not there*.

Grumbling under his breath, Qwilleran returned to the museum and found Koko sitting on the registrar's table with other un-catalogued items: a stoneware jug, a hand-cranked apple peeler, an embroidered pillow celebrating the Columbian Exposition of 1893, a wooden blueberry picker, an old print of sailing ships—and Kristi's bible. The merest quiver in the roots of Qwilleran's moustache told him to carry both the cat and the bible back to the apartment.

This time, with two cats pressing against his feet, he had no trouble falling asleep. He slept soundly until the darkest hour of night, when he found himself sitting up in bed and staring at the face of the stern-eyed, sour-faced miser. He tried to speak, but no words came. He tried to shout. Ephraim came closer and closer, and then the General Grant headboard began to topple. He raised both hands in a futile attempt to stop it from crushing him . . .

The dream ended, and Qwilleran found himself sitting up in bed with both arms raised and his head throbbing. The cats were blissfully asleep; the headboard was firmly in place; but his skin was clammy, his throat was sore, and his eyes burned.

After taking aspirin and a large glass of water he finished the night on the sofa and succumbed to deep sleep until the telephone rang and the familiar voice of Arch Riker barked, "Did you hear the news on the radio?"

"No, dammit! I was sound asleep!" Qwilleran complained in a hoarse croak. "With a friend like you, who needs an alarm clock? What time is it?"

"Nine-fifteen. Do you want to go back to sleep or do you want to hear some hot breaking news?" asked the publisher of the *Something*, knowing well what the answer would be.

Qwilleran was instantly awake. "What happened?" he asked in full voice.

"It was on the nine o'clock news. They found the body of a man near where you're living. Were you involved in any fights last night?"

"Who? Who's the man?"

"For an innocent bystander you sound unusually anxious, my friend. They're not releasing his name until they've notified next of kin."

"Where was the body?"

"On Fugtree Road near the Black Creek bridge. That's all I know. Roger's over at the police station getting something for the *Something*."

Qwilleran had no sooner hung up than

Polly Duncan called him with the same news.

He said, "Both the cats and I were alerted last night. Something was happening in the neighborhood, but I couldn't figure it out. After that, I had a nightmare. I saw Ephraim's ghost. I was wishing I had a can of beans. When I woke up I was having a peculiar physical reaction." He described the symptoms.

"It sounds to me," Polly said, "like an allergy attack, probably caused by all those fallen leaves and the heavy rain. Drink a lot of water."

Qwilleran opted for coffee, then called the *Moose County Something*. Roger had just returned from the civic center.

"What did you find out, Roger?" he asked.

"Talk about poetic justice! The murdered man is Brent Waffle," the young reporter said. "He's the guy Kristi Fugtree divorced, and he was the prime suspect in the poisoning of her goats."

"How was he killed?" Qwilleran held his breath, remembering that Kristi had a gun and she was emotional enough to use it.

"Hit on the head with a blunt instrument, but it didn't happen at the bridge. He was

269

dumped there. They can tell by the bleeding or something that he was killed elsewhere."

"Do they know the time of death?"

"The medical examiner figures between five and six P.M. yesterday."

"Who found the body?"

"A road crew going to work on the bridge."

"How about suspects?"

"They're talking to people around your neighborhood. They'll get to you soon, so you'd better rehearse your alibi . . . I've got to go and file my story now. Keep this under your hat till the paper hits the street."

Qwilleran leafed through Mrs. Cobb's phone book, but before he could make another call there was a commotion on the windowsill. Koko was agitated, pacing back and forth on the sill like a caged tiger, uttering a sharp "ik ik ik."

"What's all the fuss about?" Qwilleran asked. He went to the window in time to see something disappearing through the cat-hatch in the barn door, and it was not a cat. On the grassy ramp outside the hatch lay a small bright green object.

Qwilleran rang the Boswell cottage. "This is Qwilleran. I think Baby's in the barn. Better send your husband down to get her."

"Oh dear! . . . I didn't know . . ." said a confused voice. "Vince isn't here . . . I'll get dressed . . ."

"Are you feeling all right, Mrs. Boswell?"

"I was lying down . . . I didn't know . . . I'll get dressed . . ."

"Stay where you are. I'll find her and send her home."

"Oh, thank you . . . I'm sorry . . . I didn't know . . ."

Qwilleran skipped the civilities, pulled on some clothes and ran to the barn. Opening the eye of the needle and squinting into the darkness, he called "Baby! Baby!"—his voice reverberating in the vaulted space. Then he opened the big barn doors, and the flood of light revealed the small girl trudging down an aisle between the crates, clutching a kitten, its four legs protruding awkwardly like a scarecrow.

"I found a kitty," she said.

"Be careful! He might scratch. Put him down gently—very gently—that's the way!"

Baby did as she was told. That was to her credit, Qwilleran thought. She listened to reason and she was obedient.

"I like kitties," she said.

"I know you do, but your mother wants you to go home. She isn't feeling well. Pick

271

up your pail, and we'll walk back to your house."

With a backward look at the kitten as it staggered away on wobbly legs, Baby walked out of the barn and picked up the green pail and yellow spade. Qwilleran closed the barn door, and they started down the ramp.

"That's a nice pail," he said. "Where did you get it?"

"My mommy bought it for me."

"What color is it?"

"It's *green!*" she said impatiently as if she considered her questioner mentally deficient.

"What do you do with your pail?"

"Dig in the sand."

"There's no sand around here."

"We went to the *beach,*" she said with a two-year-old's frown.

They were walking slowly across the barnyard, and Qwilleran realized that the legs of small children are uncommonly short; it would take half an hour to traverse Black Creek Lane. He doubted that he could maintain a dialogue with Baby for half an hour without insulting her intelligence and sounding like a fool himself.

She broke the silence by saying, "I want to go to the bathroom."

"Can you wait till you get home?"

"I don't know."

Dire possibilities flashed through Qwilleran's mind. This was a situation he had never been called upon to face.

Baby had a solution, however. "Do you have a bathroom?" she asked.

Devious child! he thought; she's determined to get in to see the cats. Thinking fast, he said, "It's out of order."

"What does that mean?"

"It's broken."

They walked on, Qwilleran clutching her hand and dragging her along.

"I want to go to the bathroom," she repeated.

Qwilleran took a deep breath. "Okay, I'll get you home in a hurry. Hang on to your pail." he scooped her up as he had seen Verona do, reflecting that she weighed not much more than Yum Yum. With rapid strides, being careful not to jiggle her, he hurried up the lane.

Verona was waiting on the porch, wearing a shabby robe, her hair uncombed, and her face pale. One eye was swollen shut, and there was a purple bruise on her cheek.

"Thank you, Mr. Qwilleran. I'm sorry to trouble you."

Baby tugged at her mother's bathrobe, and a wordless understanding passed between them.

"Excuse me," Verona said.

Qwilleran waited. The black eye aroused his curiosity. When she returned, he said, "Where's Vince?"

"Gone to Lockmaster . . . to the *library?* To do some *research?* He left yesterday *noon?*" The fascinating lilt had returned to her speech.

"What happened to your eye?" Qwilleran asked.

"Oh, stupid me! I walked into a cupboard *door?*"

Qwilleran huffed into his moustache. He had heard that one before. "I found your little girl playing with kittens in the barn. They may be wild. She could get scratched or bitten."

"Poor Baby doesn't have anyone to play with," said Verona pathetically.

"Why doesn't your husband make a sandbox for her? She likes to dig."

"I'll ask him, but he works hard and gets so *tired?* His bad leg, you know, gives him *pain?*"

"When do you expect him?"

"I think he'll be home for *supper?*"

Jogging back to the museum Qwilleran thought, Why would Boswell go to the Lockmaster library when the Pickax library has the definitive collection of material on handprinting? What else might attract him to Lockmaster? The medical center? The race track? Or some covert business in connection with the crates in the barn? His fleeting suspicion about the content of the crates returned, and he thought, I'd like to spend an hour with a crowbar in that barn!

Upon arriving home he found Koko on the telephone table, an indication that it had been ringing. Kristi might have tried to phone. He called the Fugtree farm.

"I've heard the news!" he said to her. "I don't know what to say!"

She spoke with surprising belligerence. "I know damn well what to say. Why didn't someone kill him before he poisoned my goats?"

"Do the police have a suspect?"

"Of course," she said bitterly. "I'm the prime suspect, and Mitch is a close second."

"How do I get on the list?" Qwilleran asked. "I was on the Willoway Sunday morning, and I heard him threatening you. I threw a rock into the stream, but I felt like throwing it at his head."

"Well, I imagine the police will be talking to you as a matter of course."

"I'll keep in touch. Let me know if there's anything I can do."

Soon afterward, Larry Lanspeak phoned. "What the devil is happening in North Middle Hummock, Qwill? First Iris's death, then two thefts in the museum, then a herd of goats poisoned, and now a mysterious dead body."

"Not guilty!"

"We've had an application for Iris's job from a woman in Lockmaster who's highly qualified, but she's too old, considering she's already had one heart attack. God knows we don't want another manager dropping dead on the kitchen floor."

"I still think Mitch is your man, Larry," said Qwilleran. "I spent some time with him last evening, and I'm impressed. He has good ideas, and he'd bring some youthful spirit to the job. Old people like him and young people like him."

"I value your opinion," said Larry, "but —taking the long view—I still favor Boswell, and Susan goes along with my thinking. As manager he can continue cataloguing the presses, help us set up a Museum of Handprinting and assume the title of curator. In its scope I daresay it will be unique in the United States, if not the world! Of course, the final decision is up to the board of governors. We're having a meeting this week."

Qwilleran said, "Excuse me, Larry. There's a sheriff's car pulling up at the door. I'll talk to you later."

The deputy standing on the doorstep was the one who had responded to Qwilleran's call ten days before. "Mr. Qwilleran, may I ask you a question or two?" he asked politely.

"Certainly. Will you step inside? I don't want the cats to run outdoors." Both of them were standing beside him, sniffing the fresh air.

The deputy asked, "Did you see or hear anything suspicious, sir, in the vicinity of Fugtree Road?"

"I can't say that I did. This old house is built like a fort, you know, and the windows were closed. I had friends in during the evening, and we were talking and not paying much attention to the outside world . . . although . . . there was one thing I might mention," Qwilleran added as an afterthought. "Sometime after midnight I was reading in bed when the cats alerted me to a faint rumbling sound. I checked the apartment and also the museum and found everything in order."

"Did you look outdoors?"

"Briefly, but everything was quiet so I went back to my reading."

"What time was that?"

"WPKX was signing off."

At that moment there was a rumbling sound in the hallway, and both men turned to look for its source. It was coming from the floor at the far end of the hall. One of the Oriental rugs was humped in the middle, and the hump was heaving.

"That's my cat," Qwilleran explained. "He burrows under rugs and talks to himself."

The deputy produced a photograph of a man, full-face and profile. "Have you seen this person in the vicinity in the last two or three days?"

"Can't say that I've ever seen this face." It was the face of a once-handsome but now debauched thirty-year-old. "Is he the man you're looking for?" Qwilleran asked with feigned innocence.

"This is the victim. We're interested in his movements in the last few days."

"I'll let you know if anything comes to mind."

"Appreciate it."

Qwilleran closed the door after the deputy, straightened the crumpled rug, and went to look for Koko. This time he was on the dining table, guarding the bible and twitching his whiskers.

"Aha! Leather!" Qwilleran said aloud. The binding was elaborately embossed cowhide with gold-tooling, and the fore-edges of the pages were gilded. Probably a hundred years old, he guessed. Opening the bible to check the date of publication, he went no farther than the flyleaf. The page was covered with hand-written family records, and some of the names and dates demanded Qwilleran's immediate attention.

Sixteen

 While the cowhide binding of the historic bible may have attracted Koko, it was the flyleaf that occupied Qwilleran's attention for the next few hours. He forgot to have lunch, and the Siamese respected his concentration and refrained from interrupting, although Koko stood by for moral support. This grand book had once rated a place of importance and reverence on someone's parlor table. More recently it had been relegated to the Fugtree jumble of relics, acquiring some of the mansion's moldy aroma. It was this fustiness that had caused Koko's whiskers to twitch, Qwilleran assumed.

Inside the cover was a salescheck from the Bid-a-Bit Auction House dated August of 1959, stating that Mrs. Fugtree had paid five dollars for the "Bosworth Bible." Making a quick check of the Moose County telephone book, Qwilleran found no Bosworths listed, the family had either died out or moved away. Also inside the cover was an envelope of yellowed newspaper clippings, obviously from the old *Pickax Picayune*. In typical nineteenth-century style the news items, obituaries, and social notes all resembled classified ads, and the typefaces were microscopic, suggesting that readers had better eyesight in those days.

He scanned the clippings and laid them aside, then turned his attention to the flyleaf. Having heard members of the Genealogical Society talk at great length about their adventures in tracing their lineage, he knew it was customary to keep family records in the bible. He knew nothing of his own ancestry except that his mother's maiden name was Mackintosh, yet he found the Bosworth family tree fascinating.

Unfortunately the generations were not charted in the scientific way. Births, deaths, marriages, and calamities were recorded as they occurred, with the year noted. A house burned down in 1908; a leg was amputated in 1911; someone drowned in 1945. It was a chatty journal as much as a family tree. In the early years entries were written with a wide-nibbed pen dipped in ink that had faded somewhat—later, with a fountain pen that occasionally leaked—and finally, it appeared, with a good-quality ballpoint.

The handwriting suggested that the same person had kept the records for more than fifty years, and the dainty script led Qwilleran to believe it was a woman. The last entry was dated 1958, a year before the bible was sold at auction, no doubt in the liquidation of her estate. No member of the family had claimed the nostalgic document. He soon guessed her identity and decided that he liked her. She included squibs of news: A bride had a large dowry or tiny feet; a newborn had red hair or big ears; a death notice was followed by a terse comment, "drank." There was no room on the flyleaf for wasted words, but the newspaper clippings enlarged on the vital statistics.

Qwilleran tackled the investigation with the same gusto he applied to a good meal, and Koko knew something exciting was taking place. He sat on the table and watched intently as the clippings were sorted in neat piles: weddings, births, christenings, business announcements, obituaries, accidents, etc., occasionally putting forth a bashful paw to touch, then withdrawing it when Qwilleran said, "No!"

What first flagged his attention was a date. The first name on the page was Luther Bosworth, born 1874. The similarity to Vince's surname was noted and dismissed; the important factor was the date of death—1904. If Luther died on May 13 in that year, he was obviously one of the explosion victims, only thirty years old. But would a miner own such a pretentious bible? The cottages provided for miners were little more than shacks, and the mine owners operated company stores that kept the workers constantly in debt.

A further check showed that Luther married in 1898. His bride, Lucy, was only seventeen. Six years later she was widowed and left with four small children. What did single parents do in those days? Send their children to an orphanage? Take in washing?

"I think Lucy is the one who kept these records," Qwilleran said to Koko. "Damnit! Why didn't she state exact dates? And how did she get this expensive bible?"

"Yow!" said Koko, ambiguously.

"Okay, let's see if we can figure out what happened to Lucy's four kids." The flyleaf provided the following information:

One son died in 1918. "France" was the notation, making him a World War I casualty.

A daughter died in 1919. "Influenza." A cross-reference in the *Picayune* revealed that seventy-three residents of Moose County died in that post-war epidemic, including two doctors who "worked until they dropped."

Two children, Benjamin and Margaret, survived to carry on the family lineage, but only Benjamin could carry on the family name. Qwilleran traced his line first, and what he found had him pounding the table with the excitement of discovery.

Benjamin Bosworth had three children. One of them, named Henry, died in 1945. "Navy—drowned at sea" was his grandmother's notation. Henry's widow moved to Pittsburgh in 1956, taking her son. The boy had suffered an accident in 1955, and the *Picayune* file elucidated in its usual terse style: "A farmhand employed by the Trevelyan Orchard fired a shotgun to deter youths from robbing the apple trees Wednesday night, resulting in three scared boys and one broken leg. Vincent Bosworth fell from a tree and sustained a compound fracture."

In obvious glee Qwilleran pounded the table and said, "Well, Koko, what do you deduce from that?"

The cat shuffled his feet self-consciously and made no comment.

"I'll tell you what I deduce! Vincent Bosworth, still suffering from a badly repaired fracture—not polio!—returns from Pittsburgh after many years with his name changed. Why did he come back? And why did he change his name? And why does he blame his limp on polio? Vince is the great-grandson of Luther and Lucy!"

Qwilleran was so elated that he had to get out of the house and walk. He took two turns around the grounds, taking care not to shuffle his feet through the fallen leaves. The damp earth excuded a heady aroma; the garden club's rust and gold mums were still blooming stubbornly; a barncat was sunning on the grassy ramp; there was no sign of Boswell and his van. Altogether it was a pleasant day.

Returning to his genealogical investigation he said to Koko, "This is more fun than panning for gold. Now let's see what happened to Luther's daughter Margaret."

According to the flyleaf, Margaret married one Roscoe DeFord. Lucy's proud comment was "Lawyer!" The *Picayune* mentioned a reception for two hundred guests at the Pickax Hotel and a honeymoon in Paris— not bad for a miner's daughter, Qwilleran thought, if that's what Luther was. The

DeFord name was still evident in Pickax, although not in the practice of law.

Working faster, driven by suspense, he identified the progeny of Roscoe and Margaret DeFord: four children, ten grandchildren. One of the latter was named Susan, born 1949.

"Well, I'll be damned!" said Qwilleran. He remembered the gold lettering on the Exbridge & Cobb window. In one corner were the names of the proprietors: Iris Cobb and Susan DeFord Exbridge.

"So Susan Exbridge and Vince Boswell are second cousins!" he said to the faithful Koko. "Who would guess it? She's so suave, and he's such a boor! But blood is thicker than water, as they say, and that's why she's backing him for the museum job. Obviously she doesn't care to have it known that they're related."

This discovery called for a celebration. He prepared coffee and thawed a couple of chocolate brownies from the bountiful freezer, and he gave the Siamese a handful of something crunchy that was said to be nutritious and good for their teeth. He was eager to resume his search now. There was one more clue to pursue: the fate of Luther's widow.

"When we last heard from her," he said,

"she was a twenty-three-year-old widow with four young children and an impressive bible. Was she deeply religious? Was she pretty? Too bad we don't have a picture of her."

His enthusiasm was contagious, and both cats were now in attendance, seated on the table in statuesque poses. Yum Yum's notorious paw occasionally disturbed the order of the clippings.

"Ple-e-ease! If you're going to participate, do something constructive . . . Listen to this! In the same year that Luther died, Lucy went into business—and she wasn't taking in washing!"

A business announcement in the *Picayune* stated: "Lucy Bosworth, widow of Luther Bosworth, announces that she has purchased the Pickax General Store from John Edwards, who is retiring because of ill health. Mrs. Bosworth will continue to handle the best quality edibles, apparel, hardware, sundries, notions and homemade root beer at reasonable prices. Open daily 7 A.M to 10 P.M. Closed Sundays until noon."

"The party store of 1904!" Qwilleran exclaimed. "With checkers around the potbellied stove instead of video games . . . Wait a minute! What do we have here?"

287

A written comment in the margin of the clipping, in Lucy's recognizable hand, said, "Cash."

"Interesting," said Qwilleran. "If Luther was a miner, where did Lucy get the money to pay cash for a going business? Miners didn't carry insurance in those days—*that* I know! Did Ephraim make restitution to the victims' families? Not likely, unless forced to do so. Did Lucy sue? Victims weren't big on litigation in the good old days. Did she blackmail the old tightwad? And if so, on what grounds?"

"Yow!" said Koko with an emphasis that reinforced Qwilleran's conjecture.

He continued deciphering the entries on the flyleaf. In 1904 Lucy bought the store. In 1905 she remarried. Her new husband was Karl Lunspik, and her parenthetical remark in the bible was "Handsome!"

"Ah!" he said. "Handsome man marries widow with four small children! For love? Or because she owns a successful business and an expensive bible?" The next facts caused his moustache to bristle:

In 1906 Karl and Lucy Lunspik had a son, William.

In 1908 their name was legally changed to Lanspeak.

In 1911 the Pickax General Store was renamed Lanspeak's Dry Goods.

In 1926 their son, William, joined the business, and it became Lanspeak's Department Store.

William had five children and eleven grandchildren, one of the latter being Lawrence Karl Lanspeak, born 1946.

"Fantastic!" yelled Qwilleran, to the alarm of the Siamese, who scattered. "They're all second cousins—Larry and Susan with their country club connections and status cars . . . and Vince Boswell with his rusty van and irritating manners. Larry is the great-grandson of the unsinkable Lucy Bosworth!"

He picked up the phone and called the store. As soon as Larry heard Qwilleran's voice, he said, "Have you seen today's paper? They've identified the body. The guy that poisoned the goats!"

"I know," said Qwilleran. "The police have been around asking questions."

"I hope you didn't give your right name," Larry quipped.

"Speaking of names, I've made a discovery at the museum. When do you plan on coming out here?"

"Tomorrow, but why don't you come into

town tonight and have dinner with Carol and me? Meet us at Stephanie's."

"Sounds good," Qwilleran said, "but I'm tied up tonight. Thanks just the same. See you tomorrow." He refrained from mentioning that Polly was bringing Bootsie to spend the night.

Turning away from the phone he heard a faint knocking in the front of the apartment that startled him. The usual summons from that direction was the clanging of the brass door knocker. The Siamese froze with their ears forward, and when he left the kitchen to investigate, they hung back. Walking down the hall, he heard the knocking again. He glanced through the glass in the front door but saw no one standing there and no car parked in the yard. It was true, he told himself, that old houses make strange noises.

As he turned his back, the knocking was repeated. Even in broad daylight it was eerie, and to Mrs. Cobb's ears in the middle of the night it must have been terrifying. He strode back to the front door and yanked it open. There on the top step was Baby, carrying her green pail and raising her yellow spade, ready to strike again.

"Hi!" she said.

Qwilleran groaned with relief and annoyance. "What are you doing here? Does your mother know where you are?"

She offered him the green pail. "This is for you."

There was a note in the pail, as well as a chunk of something wrapped in waxed paper. The note said, "Just thought you'd like some meatloaf for a sandwich. Made it yesterday. It's better the second day."

"Tell your mother thank-you," he said, handing back the pail.

Baby was peeking around his legs. "Can I see the kitties?"

"They're having their nap. Why don't you go home and have your nap?"

"I had my nap," she said, turning away and gazing speculatively toward the barn.

"Go home now," he said sternly. "Go right home, do you hear?"

Without another word Baby walked down the steps and marched up the lane on her short legs, carrying her green pail. He watched her until she was almost home. She never looked back.

Qwilleran prepared a meatloaf sandwich for himself and gave some to the cats. All three devoured it as if they had been on a week-long fast. Then he hauled his bike out of the steel barn and went for a ride.

There was an unusual amount of traffic on Fugtree Road—gawkers, driving out to see where the body was found, hoping to see blood. A county road crew was working on the bridge, and a blatant orange sign warned that the road was closed for construction, but Qwilleran wheeled past the barrier and talked to the foreman, a burly man in a farm cap, with a cheekful of snuff. The foreman recognized the famous moustache.

"Right down yonder," he said, pointing to the rocky slope where Qwilleran had first scrambled down to the Willoway. "Dry blood all over his face. Looked like one o' them Halloween get-ups."

"Do the police have any idea who did it?" It was a truism in Moose County that anyone in a farm cap possessed inside information or was willing to invent some.

"I hear they gotta coupla suspects, but they didn't charge anybody yet. He was killed somewheres else and dumped. There was a lotta muddy tire tracks on the pavement when we come on the job."

"Who was the murdered man?"

"The guy that poisoned the goats—escaped con, local kid—went Down Below and got inta trouble. I'm tellin' ya," said the foreman with an emphatic spit, "if it was my goats, I'da went after 'im myself with a shot-gun!"

Seventeen

Qwilleran returned from his bike ride just as Polly was parking her car in the farmyard. "I'm a little early," she apologized, "because I want to reach Lockmaster before dark." She handed him a cardboard cat carrier. "Here's my precious darling. Take him indoors before he catches cold. I'll collect his impedimenta."

The carrier had a top handle and round airholes and a printed message on the side: "Hi! My name is Bootsie. What's your name?" From one of the holes a wet button-size nose protruded, then quickly withdrew, only to be replaced by a brown paw that might have belonged to a cocker spaniel.

Polly entered the apartment carrying a can of clinical-looking catfood with much fine print on the label, a cushioned basket, a brush, and a shallow litterbox containing shreds of torn paper. "This is his own commode," she said. "He's trained to paper. I use paper toweling—not newsprint because

the ink might come off on his little derrière
. . . And here's his special food, a formula
computerized to suit his needs. Give him
three level tablespoons, no more, no less, for
each meal, and don't let him have anything
else. Spread it thinly over a saucer, and I
suggest you place the saucer in a secluded
corner so he won't feel threatened."

"How about drinking water? Can he have
the stuff out of the tap?"

"Tap water will be satisfactory," she said
with a serious nod, "and here's his sleeping
basket. Put it in a warm place, elevated a
foot or two off the floor . . . And thank you
so much, Qwill! Now I must dash. Let me
say goodbye to the little dear." Tenderly she
lifted Bootsie from the carrier and touched
her nose to his wet one. "Kiss-kiss, sweetums. Be a good kitten." To Qwilleran she
added, "Tomorrow is his birthday, by the
way; he'll be eleven weeks old."

She gave Qwilleran a fond but hasty farewell, handed him the innocent kitten, and
hurried out to her car. He stood holding the
handful of purring fur, wondering what had
become of the Siamese. They had avoided
the opening ceremonies, as well they might,
and until he knew their whereabouts he was
reluctant to let the kitten out of his grasp.

Koko and Yum Yum, it was eventually discovered, were on top of the seven-foot Pennsylvania German *Schrank,* sitting side by side in compact bundles, looking petrified.

"Oh, there you are!" Qwilleran said. "Come down and meet Bigfoot."

He placed the kitten carefully on the floor. The tiny thing looked vulnerable with his skinny white neck, skinny brown tail, floppy feet and smudged nose, but once he found himself free of restraints he took a few staggering steps and then shot out of the room like a missile. By the time Qwilleran found him he was on the kitchen counter, eating the leftover meatloaf, waxed paper and all. Seeing the big man, he raced to the front of the apartment with exaggerated leaps like a grasshopper, bouncing from chair to table to desk to bed to dresser. Koko and Yum Yum were still on top of the *Schrank,* gazing down in apparent disbelief.

For the next few hours Bigfoot created chaos with his wild flight—slamming into furniture, breaking a piece of antique glass, leaping and falling and landing on his back, climbing Qwilleran's pantleg and pouncing on his lap. After a nervewracking dinner hour he telephoned Lori Bamba in Mooseville and cried "Help!"

He wasted no time inquiring about the baby's health or Nick's job-hunting. He said, "I don't know how I fell into this trap, Lori. Polly Duncan has a new kitten and I agreed to cat-sit, but he turned out to be a wound-up, hyperactive, jet-propelled maniac! He's driving us all crazy with his whizzing around and pouncing, and all the time he's purring like a Model T with two cylinders missing."

"How old is he?" asked Lori.

"Eleven weeks tomorrow. I'm supposed to sing 'Happy Birthday' to him."

"Remember, Qwill, he's very young, and he's being exposed to a strange house with two big cats. He's apprehensive. Fright causes flight."

"Apprehensive!" Qwilleran shouted. "Koko and Yum Yum are the ones who are apprehensive. They're on top of the seven-foot wardrobe and won't come down, even to eat. Bigfoot ate his own medically approved food, and then he ate their turkey loaf with olives and mushrooms, and then he swooped in and knocked a piece of salmon right off my fork! . . . And let me tell you something else. Instead of claws he has needles. When I sit down he pounces on my lap and sinks those eighteen needles. Propriety prevents me from describing the effect. Ask your husband to tell you."

Lori was listening sympathetically. "Where is the kitten now?"

"I finally locked him up in his carrier, but I can't leave him in that cramped box for twenty-four hours. Isn't there some kind of feline Mickey Finn?"

"With all that food in his stomach and with the security of the carrier, he should go to sleep soon, Qwill. Leave him there until he calms down. Then at bedtime shut him up in the kitchen with his water dish and litterbox and something soft to sleep on."

"I'll try it. Thanks, Lori."

She was right. Bigfoot was quiet for an evening of serenity, and the Siamese ventured down from their safe perch. The domestic peace was short-lived, however.

Shortly before midnight Qwilleran took the carrier to the kitchen, closed the door and released Bigfoot. For a while the kitten staggered about the floor like a drunken plowman, squeaking and purring at the same time. Then he became quiet and mysteriously absent from view. It should have been obvious that he was lurking in ambush.

Qwilleran was preparing the kitten's bed-time meal—three tablespoons of unappetizing gray hash smeared thinly on a saucer—when he was suddenly attacked from the rear. Big-foot had pounced on his back and was clinging to his sweater.

"Down!" he yelled, shrugging his shoulders in an attempt to dislodge his attacker, but his sweater was a chunky knit pullover, and Bootsie was firmly hooked into the yarn and squealing at the top of his minuscule lungs.

"Down! . . . Ow-w-w-w!" Every time he yelled, the needles sank deeper into his flesh and the squeals accelerated.

"Shut up, you idiot!"

Qwilleran reached behind his back, first over his shoulders and then around his midriff. The former approach netted him a handful of ears; the latter, only a wisp of a tail. He pulled gently on the tail. "Ow-w-w-w! Damnit!"

Hearing the commotion, the Siamese ventured down from the top of the *Schrank* and yowled outside the kitchen door.

"And you shut up, too!" he bellowed at them.

Stay calm, he told himself and tried sitting quietly on the edge of a chair. It worked, to a degree. Bootsie stopped squealing and gouging but made no attempt to disengage his claws. He was content to spend the night, suspended like a papoose.

After five minutes of inactivity Qwilleran reached the end of his patience. As Lori said, fright causes flight. He jumped to his feet, roaring the useful curse he had learned in North Africa, flapping his arms and galloping about the kitchen like a witch doctor. The curse ended in a prolonged howl of pain as Bigfoot gripped Qwilleran's back for the wild ride.

It was after midnight. In desperation he telephoned the Boswells' number. When he heard Verona's gentle hello, he shouted, "Let me talk to Vince! I'm in bad trouble! This is Qwilleran."

"Oh, dear! Vince hasn't come home," said the soft voice with an overtone of alarm. "Is there anythin' I can do?"

"I've got a cat on my back—with his claws hooked into my sweater! I need someone to pry him loose . . . Ow-w-w-w!"

"Oh, gracious! I'll come right away."

He walked slowly to the front door, trying not to upset Bigfoot, and turned on the yard-lights. In a matter of minutes that seemed like hours Verona appeared, running and clutching a flashlight. A heavy jacket was thrown over her shabby bathrobe.

Opening the door in slow motion, he warned her, "Don't make any sudden movement. See if you can grasp him about the middle and raise him gently to unhook the claws. Try releasing one paw at a time."

Verona did as she was told, but when one paw was freed, another clutched with renewed determination.

"I'm afraid it's not workin'. May I make a suggestion?" she asked in her deferential way. "We could take your sweater off over your *head?* If I roll it up in the back, we should get the kitten and all."

"Okay. Take it easy. Don't alarm him."

"Oh, he's a nice kitty. He's such a nice kitty," Verona cooed as she rolled the sweater over the little animal and then over Qwilleran's head. "Oh, gracious!" she said. "Your shirt is all *bloody?*"

He ripped it off.

"And your back is a mess of bloody *scratches?* Do you have an antiseptic?"

"There's something in the bathroom, I think."

Leaving Bigfoot rolled cozily in the sweater, they trooped to the bathroom and found a liquid which Verona applied liberally to the scratches while Qwilleran winced and grunted.

"Does it smart? We don't want to get an infection, do we? There now, put on somethin' so you don't take a *chill?*" Her voice was music to his ears.

"I don't know how to thank you, Mrs. Boswell," he said as he put on a fresh shirt. "I was reluctant to bother you at this late hour, but my only other recourse was the volunteer fire department in North Kennebeck."

"No bother. No bother at all. Do you have any more scratches that need antiseptic?"

"Uh . . . I don't think so," Qwilleran said. "Where's Vince?"

"Stayin' in Lockmaster a bit longer. He didn't finish at the *library?*"

He looked down at the pathetic little woman with her hair uncombed, her black eye turning yellow, her ridiculous garb—khaki jacket, faded bathrobe, old sneakers. "Would you like a cup of coffee?"

"I should go home," she said. "I left Baby sleepin' and she might wake up . . . but . . . do you have any milk?"

"Milk? I'm afraid not. I'm not a milk drinker. Mrs. Cobb left a carton but it turned sour and I threw it out."

"I've run out of milk for *Baby?* I thought Vince was comin' home and could do some *shoppin'?*"

"There's a package of that powdered stuff here. Could you use that?"

"Oh, I'd appreciate it so *much?*"

"If Vince isn't home tomorrow morning, I'll pick up some groceries for you. Make a list of what you need."

Verona redded with embarrassment. "He didn't leave me any money."

"That's unforgivable! Let's see what we can find here." Taking a shopping bag from the broom closet he filled it with cheese-bread, blueberry muffins, banana-nut bread, vegetable soup, tuna casserole, chili, and—reluctantly—his favorite dish, macaroni and cheese. "I'll drive you home," he said, picking up a jacket and feeling for his keys.

It was a short ride, hardly more than two city blocks. After a brief silence Verona said, "I saw your big *kitties?* They're beautiful! I'd love for Baby to see them someday."

"All right," he said. "Bring her over on Thursday afternoon. And thanks again, Mrs. Boswell, for coming to my rescue."

"Call me Verona," she said as she climbed out of the car. He waited until she was in the house and then drove away, asking himself how a nice woman like Verona could get mixed up with a cad like Boswell.

Back at the apartment Bigfoot was still rolled up in the sweater, and when Qwilleran unrolled him the kitten remained in deep slumber with an angelic look on his smudge-nosed face. He was purring in his sleep.

Eighteen

Bigfoot and the Siamese were socializing politely when Qwilleran rode away on his bicycle Wednesday morning, headed for West Middle Hummock. As he passed the Fugtree farm he wondered when the police would return to question him about his Monday evening visitors.

Brent Waffle was killed before eight o'clock, according to the medical report. Kristi and Mitch arrived via the Willoway promptly at eight. They might have encountered Waffle on the trail, argued violently, bashed him with a flashlight—or two flashlights—and left his body on the bank of the stream. Perhaps they remembered the Buddy Yarrow case on the Ittibittiwassee River, when the coroner ruled that Buddy slipped and hit his head on a rock. Then, after midnight, Mitch would drive down one of the access roads to the Willoway and remove the body to the public highway, a site farther removed from the Fugtree property. The rumbling that

Qwilleran had heard at a late hour could have been Mitch's truck on the gravel road.

If this scenario were true, he reflected, the amateur murderers had been remarkably cool during the evening. And if it were true, why would the body—left on the Willoway during the torrential rain—be covered with dried blood when found by the road crew? More likely, Waffle had been killed indoors. Perhaps the guy had returned to the scene of his crime and was hiding in one of the vacant goat barns, perhaps eyeing Kristi as his next victim. Perhaps the bucks—Attila, Napoleon and Rasputin—had created a disturbance and alerted her. Then she and Mitch went to investigate, and it was two against one.

Qwilleran hoped his speculations were wrong. They were good kids, with promising lives ahead of them. It was the mesmerizing effect of pedaling his bike that produced such fantasies, he told himself.

At a country store in West Middle Hummock he bought apples, oranges, and milk and dropped them off at the Boswell cottage. Verona, still in a bathrobe, was tearfully grateful.

"Where's Vince?" he asked.

She shrugged and shook her head sadly.

"Call me if any problem arises."

Baby, clutching her mother's bathrobe, said, "I'm going to see the kitties tomorrow."

When Qwilleran arrived at the museum the yard was filled with cars: the Tibbitts' old four-door, Larry's long station wagon, and Susan's gas-guzzler (part of her divorce settlement) among others. It appeared that the board of governors was in session, no doubt deciding on a new manager.

Qwilleran changed quickly from his thermal jumpsuit, counted the noses of three sleeping bundles of fur, and joined the group in the museum. The meeting had not yet been called to order. Some of the officers and committee heads were milling about the exhibit area; others were having coffee in the office.

"Join us, Qwill!" Larry called out. "Have a doughnut!"

"First, a word with you, Larry." Qwilleran beckoned him out of the office and conducted him to the apartment. "I want you to see something I've discovered."

"What is it?"

"Something that belonged to your great-grandmother."

307

"Which one? I had four. So did you, as a matter of fact."

"Mine didn't write family secrets on the flyleaves of their bibles," Qwilleran retorted. "Have a chair."

They sat at the big table, and Qwilleran picked up the large, leather-bound, gold-tooled book. "This rare artifact was sold at a Bid-a-Bit auction to Mrs. Fugtree, whose daughter presented it to the museum. It was identified as the Bosworth Bible, because the first name recorded on the flyleaf was Luther Bosworth, who died in 1904."

"Let me see that!" Larry held out his hand.

"Not so fast! From studying the inscriptions I deduce that Luther's widow, Lucy, kept the family records in the bible. She apparently died around 1958, because there are no entries beyond that date, and Mrs. Fugtree made her purchase in 1959."

"You've been a busy boy," said Larry, "but what's the point?"

"The point is that, according to Lucy, you and Susan and Vince Boswell are second cousins, but of course you know that; everyone in Moose County is a genealogy nut."

"I believe there is some sort of relationship," Larry said evasively. "Ow-w-w-w! *What's that?*" He was shaking his leg.

"Sorry. That's Bigfoot. I'll lock him up. He's Polly's cat." Qwilleran put Bootsie in the broom closet.

"Okay, Sherlock, what else did you discover?" Larry asked. "You look smug."

"I learned some facts about your store. Your great-grandmother bought the Pickax General Store in 1904, shortly after Luther died. She paid cash for it. Soon after, she married Karl what's-his-name and changed the store name to Lanspeak's Dry Goods. It would make a newsy column for the 'Qwill Pen.' I'm sure you could fill in the details."

Good actor though he was, Larry could not keep his face from flushing nor his forehead from perspiring. "Let me see that thing!"

Qwilleran clutched the bible possessively. "One more thing, Larry, and then I won't delay you any longer. You and Susan have been pushing Vince Boswell—or Bosworth, as the case may be—for Iris's job, but are you sure he projects the image you want for the museum? Even though he's your relative he lacks a suitable personality and lacks class, to put it bluntly, and there may be other marks against him if my hunches check out." He smoothed his moustache in a significant gesture. "If the board is meeting today to discuss the matter, it might be wise to postpone your decision."

"What are you trying to say, Qwill? What's the big mystery?"

"Vince has gone to Lockmaster, leaving Verona without transportation, without money, and even without milk for the child. He left Monday, and there's no telling when he'll return. Does he play the horses? The race season just opened in Lockmaster."

"I don't know about that."

"Obviously the man has little sense of responsibility. Is that the kind of manager you want? By the way, why did he change his name from Bosworth?"

"To tell the truth, I never asked him," said Larry.

"Was Luther Bosworth a miner? Was he a victim of the May thirteenth explosion?"

"No, he was sort of a handyman—a caretaker on the Goodwinter farm. All I know is what my great-uncle Benjamin said. Ephraim thought very highly of Luther."

"But you're not descended from Luther; your great-grandfather was Karl."

"Correct."

"Karl was a handsome man."

"How do you know?"

"Read your family bible, and you'll find out." Qwilleran presented it to Larry with a flourish, unaware of some clattering and thumping in the broom closet.

"Now let me ask you a question," Larry said. "According to the paper, the murder victim was Kristi Fugtree's ex-husband. Everyone says he's the one who poisoned her goats. She's now seeing a lot of Mitch Ogilvie. Do you think Mitch had anything to do with it?"

"Not very likely. He and Kristi were here Monday night, drinking cider and discussing the restoration of the Fugtree mansion as a historic place."

"I hope to God he's not involved," said Larry. "Now I've got to go back to the office and start the meeting."

"One more question, if you don't mind, Larry. What do you know about sandboxes for kids?"

"People around here make them with two-by-fours and get free sand on Sandpit Road. Why do you ask?"

"We have a budding archaeologist at the Boswell cottage with no place to dig."

Out came the reliable notebook. "The yard crew can rig something up. There

311

might be some two-by-fours in the steel barn. I'll take care of it."

As he left there was a minor explosion in the broom closet, accompanied by the sound of shattering glass. Qwilleran yanked open the door. Bootsie was sitting on the shelf with the light bulbs, purring.

Polly Duncan returned earlier than expected to pick up the kitten. "When the meeting ended, I didn't stay to socialize," she explained. "I was lonesome for my little sweetheart. Was he a good boy?"

"No problem. I have a few scars, and the value of the Cobb glass collection is down a few hundred dollars, and the Siamese will never be the same, but . . . no problem."

Polly paid no attention. "Where is he? I can hardly wait to see him. *Where is he?*" Both she and Qwilleran searched the apartment, checking all the warm places and soft places. They found Koko and Yum Yum on the blue velvet wing chair but not a hair of the kitten. Qwilleran could tell by Polly's terrified expression that she thought the Siamese had eaten Bigfoot.

"Here he is!" he called from the bathroom, just in time to save Polly from nervous collapse.

Bootsie was in the turkey roaster that

served as a commode for the Siamese, sound asleep in the gravel.

Polly seized him. "Bootsie darling! What are you doing there? Were you lonesome? Did you miss me? Kiss-kiss . . . Did he use his litterbox, Qwill?"

"He seemed to prefer the turkey roaster."

"I hope he wasn't too frightened to eat."

"No, he ate *very well*, let me assure you. Did you run into Vince Boswell down there? He's supposed to be doing research at the library."

"I didn't see anyone from Pickax. If they were there, they were all at the track. The races are on this week. Now we must pack our luggage and go home."

Qwilleran produced Bootsie's basket, litterbox, brush, and carrier with alacrity.

"Say goodbye to Uncle Qwill, Bootsie," said Polly, lifting the kitten's thin foreleg and waving the floppy brown paw. "Look at that lovely paw—just like a beautiful brown flower. Do you think I should clip his claws?"

"Don't do anything rash," said Qwilleran.

When they had left, he heaved a sigh of relief, and the Siamese walked around, stretching. The three of them enjoyed a peaceful dinner of chicken cordon bleu from the freezer, and at dusk they settled down in the parlor for some music—the cats on the blue wing chair and Qwilleran on the brown lounge chair opposite, a mug of coffee in his hand. Both telephone bells had been turned off. No matter what the crisis or emergency he was determined to hear Polly's opera cassette without interruption.

As the first three acts unreeled he realized he was actually enjoying this music. Whatever sardonic remarks about opera he had made in the past, he was willing to rescind. The Siamese were listening, too, possibly hearing notes and nuances that escaped his ear. He was following the English libretto, and the suspense was mounting in the fourth act. During the poignant "Willow Song" Desdemona cried, "Hark! I hear a wailing! Hush! Who is knocking at that door?" And Emilia replied, "It is the wind."

At that precise moment a rumbling growl came from the depths of Koko's chest. He jumped to the floor and ran into the hall. A moment later there was a frantic pounding at the front door, the brass knocker clanging and fists beating the door panels.

Qwilleran rushed to open it.

"Help me find Baby!" screamed Verona,

wild-eyed with anxiety and gasping for breath. "She got out! Maybe the barn!"

He grabbed a jacket and the battery-operated lantern, and they ran across the barnyard. A mercury-vapor lamp on a high pole flooded the entire yard, but Verona had run all the way down the lane without a flashlight. She had forgotten it in her panic.

"How long has she been gone?" Qwilleran shouted.

"I don't know." She was short of breath.

"Where's Vince?"

"Not home yet."

They raced up the grassy ramp to the eye of the needle.

"Step inside, but don't go any farther," Qwilleran ordered. "It's dark in there. Too many obstacles. Call her name."

"Baby! Baby!" Verona called in a terrified voice.

"Louder!"

She started forward.

"Stay back! And I mean it! Call her name!"

"Ba-aby! Ba-aby!"

Qwilleran flashed his light up and down the straw-covered aisles between the crates and presses. There was no movement except for a barncat darting to cover. In one corner of the barn an industrial palette was leaning against the wall. Qwilleran had seen this wooden platform on his previous visit, flat on the floor, and he had wondered if Boswell used a forklift. Now it was leaning against the wall.

"Stay where you are!" he warned Verona as he went to investigate. "Don't stop calling."

The up-ended palette had been covering a square opening in the threshing floor, and a ladder led down into the stable. Qwilleran flashed his light down the hole and saw a green pail. He climbed down the ladder and quickly up again.

Putting his arm around Verona he said, "Come back to the house. We have to call the ambulance."

"She's hurt! Where is she? I've got to see her!"

"You can't. Wait till the ambulance comes."

Verona fainted.

Qwilleran carried her back to the apartment and placed her on the bed, where she lay—awake but motionless and staring at the ceiling. He covered her with a blanket and elevated her feet, then called the emergency number and Dr. Halifax.

"Doc, I've got a mother and child here. The baby's unconscious," he said. "I think the mother's in shock. I've called the ambulance. What should I do in the meantime?"

"Keep them both warm. Have the ambulance bring them both to the Pickax hospital. I'll be there. What's the name?"

"Boswell. Verona Boswell."

"Don't know the name. That's not a Moose County name."

The paramedics put Baby on a stretcher and told the sheriff's deputy who was standing by, "Looks like she fell down a ladder and landed on the stable floor. Stone floor. Possible broken neck, looks like."

Such a puny neck, Qwilleran thought. Hardly bigger than Koko's.

After Verona had been carried out on a stretcher, Qwilleran went to the barn again with his lantern and flashed it down into the stable. The green pail was still there. He closed the eye of the needle and returned to the museum. As soon as he opened the apartment door, something whizzed past his feet and disappeared around the corner of the house faster than the eye could discern. He dashed off in pursuit, bellowing, "Koko! Come back here!"

The cat was headed for the barn at a speed four times faster than Qwilleran's fifty-yard dash. Clearing the ramp in two leaps Koko disappeared through the cat-hatch as if he had been a barncat in one of his other lives. Qwilleran swung the great doors open to take advantage of the lightpole and called his name.

A twinge on his upper lip told him that Koko would leap down the ladder. Qwilleran followed. The stable was a low-ceilinged, stone-floored room with more crates and more presses and more straw. He flashed the light around the stalls and listened intently until he heard a familiar rumbling growl ascending the scale and ending in a shriek. He traced it to the far end of the stable, near the back doors where the horses and cows would have been led into their stalls. Koko was there, hovering over something wedged between two crates—a litter of squirming newborn kittens and a mother cat, bedded down on a piece of soiled cloth.

Qwilleran seized Koko about the middle, and the cat seemed quite willing to be seized. As they headed for the ladder he almost tripped over the crowbar that Boswell used to open crates. He flashed his lantern around the floor. In one corner a pile of straw was hollowed as if someone had slept there. He saw beer cans and empty cigarette packs. That fool Boswell! Qwilleran thought. Goofing off and *smoking* in a bed of dry straw!

The cat under his arm was wriggling to get free, and he let him go. With his nose to the floor Koko followed a scent that led him into the pile of straw, led him to a bundle of something rolled to make a pillow, led him to a patch of dried blood on the pillow and the straw. The bundle was the same dark green Qwilleran had seen on the Willoway, stenciled LOCKMASTER COUNTY JAIL.

Clutching Koko and the lantern Qwilleran hurried back to the apartment and made three phone calls: first to the night desk of the *Moose County Something*, then to the sheriff's department, and finally to the president of the Historical Society.

Nineteen

The early-morning newscast on WPKX included this announcement: "A suspect in the bludgeoning murder of Brent Waffle is being sought by police in several northern counties following the discovery of incriminating evidence and the suspect's disappearance from the area. According to the sheriff's department, the name of the suspect will not be released until he is apprehended and charged."

There followed brief reports on a three-car accident at the blinker in downtown Kennebeck and a controversy at the Pickax city council meeting regarding a Halloween curfew. The newscast ended with the following: "A two-and-a-half-year-old child fell and was seriously injured on the property of the Goodwinter Farmhouse Museum last evening. A trap door in the barn floor was left uncovered, and the child fell to the stone-paved floor of the stable below."

After that eye-opening news hit the airways, Qwilleran received phone calls from all the usual operators on the local grapevine, one of the first being Mr. O'Dell, the white-haired janitor who serviced Qwilleran's apartment in Pickax. He said, "It's the windows I'm thinkin' of washin' if you'll be comin' back to the city soon."

"I have no immediate plans," Qwilleran said. "I promised to stay here until they find a new manager."

"A pity it is, what's happenin' out there," said Mr. O'Dell. "First Mrs. Cobb, a good woman, God rest her soul! And herself barely cold in her grave when the little one, innocent as a lamb, fell. Sure an' it's a black cloud that hangs over the Goodwinter farm, an' I'm givin' you some advice if you've a mind to take it. No good will come of it if you take it into your head to stay there. The divil is up to tricks for eighty or ninety year since, I'm thinkin'."

"I appreciate your advice, Mr. O'Dell," said Qwilleran. "I'll give it some serious thought."

"An' shall I be washin' the windows?"

"Yes, go ahead and wash the windows." Qwilleran was in no hurry to move back to Pickax, devil or no devil, but he knew it would relieve Mr. O'Dell's mind if the windows were clean.

Arch Riker had other ideas. "Why don't you move back to town and stop playing detective?" the publisher said. "Readers are complaining. They expect to see the 'Qwill Pen' on certain days."

"It's been nothing but emergencies, obstacles, and distractions for the last two weeks," Qwilleran said. "I was all set to write a goat column when the herd was poisoned and the front page got the story. I was planning to do a piece on the antique printing presses, but the so-called expert has left town and will wind up in prison."

"Excuses, excuses! Find an old-timer and rip off some memoirs for Monday," Riker suggested. "Do it the easy way until you get back on the track."

Taking the publisher's suggestion and Mitch Ogilvie's tip, Qwilleran called the Senior Care Facility in Pickax and asked to interview Adam Dingleberry. The nurse in charge recommended a late-morning visit, since the old gentleman was always drowsy after lunch, and she specified a time limit of thirty minutes for the nonagenarian, by doctor's orders.

Arriving at the Facility, Qwilleran found

the lobby bright with canaries—those yellow-smocked volunteers wearing "We Care" lapel buttons. They were fluttering about, greeting visitors, wheeling patients, tucking in lap blankets, adjusting shawls, smiling sweetly, and showing that they cared, whether the patients were paying guests like Adam Dingleberry or indigent wards of the county. There was no hint that the cheerfully modern building was descended from the County Poor Farm.

One of the canaries ushered Qwilleran into the reading room, a quiet place equipped with large-print books and cleverly adjustable reading lamps. He had been there on previous occasions to conduct interviews and had never seen anyone reading. Patients who were not confined to their beds were in the lounge, watching television.

"He's a little hard of hearing," said the canary who wheeled the elderly mortician into the room, a wizened little man who had once been the tallest boy in school and a holy terror, according to Homer Tibbitt.

The volunteer took a seat apart from them, near the door, and Qwilleran said in a loud, clear voice, "We've never met, Mr. Dingleberry, but I've seen you at meetings

323

of the old-timers, and Homer Tibbitt tells me he went to school with you."

"Homer, eh? He were younger than me in school. Still is. He's only ninety-four. I'm ninety-eight. How old are you?" His voice had the same high pitch as Homer's, and it cracked on every tenth word.

"I'm embarrassed to say," Qwilleran replied, "that I'm only fifty."

"Fifty, eh? You have to walk around on your own legs. When you're my age, you get trundled around everywhere."

"That gives me something to look forward to."

In spite of his shrunken form and leathery wrinkles, Adam Dingleberry had sharp bird-like eyes that darted as fast as his mind. "The city fathers are tryin' to outlaw Halloween," he said, taking the lead in the conversation. "In the old days we used to wax windows and knock over outhouses till hell-won't-have-it. One year we bricked up the schoolhouse door."

Qwilleran said, "May I turn on my machine and tape some of this?" He placed the recorder on the table between them, and the following conversation was preserved for posterity:

The museum has a desk from the Black Creek School, carved with initials. Would any of them be yours?

Nope. I always carved somebody else's initials. Never finished the grades. They kicked me out for smearin' the teacher's chair with cow dung. My paw give me a whuppin' but it were worth it.

Is it a fact that the Dingleberry family has been in the funeral business for more than a hundred years?

Yup. My grampaw come from the Old Country to build shafthouses for the mines. Built coffins, too. When some poor soul died, Grampaw stayed up all night whittlin' a coffin—tailor-made to fit. Coffins warn't like we have now. They was wide at the top, narrow at the foot. Makes sense, don't it? It took a heap o' skill to mitre the joints. Grampaw were mighty proud of his work, and my paw learned coffin-buildin' from him, only Paw started buildin' furniture.

What kind of furniture, Mr. Dingleberry?

Wal, now, he used to build a desk with long legs and a cupboard on top. Sold tons of 'em! The Dingleberry desk, it were called. They was all a bit different: doors, no doors, one drawer, two drawers, false bottom, built-in lockbox, pigeonholes, whatever folks wanted.

Did your father sign his work?

Nope. Folks knowed who built their desk. No sense in puttin' a name on it. Like today, they slap names all over. My grandsons have names on the outside of their shirts! Next thing, they'll be puttin' the Dingleberry name inside the casket!

How did your father become a mortician?

Wal, now, his desk—it were such a good seller, he hired fellas to build 'em and tables and beds and coffins—whatall folks wanted. So Paw opened a furniture store. Gave free funerals to folks that bought coffins. He had a fancy black hearse and black horses with black feathers. Funerals were a sight in them days! When me and my brothers come along—they're all dead now—we opened a reg'lar funeral parlor, all proper and digni- fied but not high-fallutin', see? Got rid o' the horses when automobiles come in. Folks hated to see 'em go. Then my sons took over, and my grandsons. They went away to school. I never finished.

Do you remember the Ephraim Goodwinter funeral?

(Long pause.) Wal, now, I were a young lad, but my folks talked about it.

Was his death a suicide or a lynching?

(Long pause.) All I know, he were strung up.

Do you know who cut down the body?

Yup. My paw and Ephraim's son, Titus. They had a preacher there, too. Forget his name.

Mr. Crawbanks?

That's him!

How do you know all this?

(Long pause.) I warn't supposed to be there. My paw told me to stay to home, but I hid in the wagon. The preacher, he said some prayers, and Paw and Titus took off their hats. I crossed myself. I knew I'd get a whuppin' when we got home.

Did you see the corpse? Were the hands tied or not?

Couldn't see. It were near daybreak—not much light.

Did anyone have a camera?

Yup. Titus, he took a picture. Don't know what for.

How was the corpse dressed?

That were a long time ago, and I were too bug-eyed to pay attention. They throwed a blanket over him.

A suicide would have to stand on a box or

something and then kick it away. Do you re-
member seeing anything like that?

(Long pause.) Musta sat on a horse and
give it a kick. Horse went home all by itself.
Empty saddle. That's when they come
lookin' for the old man. That's what Titus
said.

Did you believe that?

I were a young boy then. Didn't stop to
figger it out.

Did your father ever talk about it?

(Long pause.) Nope. Not then. (Long
pause.) What d'you want to know all this
for?

Our readers enjoy the memoirs of old-timers.
I've interviewed Euphonia Gage, Emma Hug-
gins Wimsey, Homer Tibbitt . . .

Homer, eh? I could tell you some things
he don't know. But don't put it in the paper.

I'll turn off my tape recorder.

Qwilleran flipped the button on the machine
and placed it on the floor.

"I want a drink of water," the old man
demanded in his shrill voice. As the canary
hurried from the room, he said to Qwilleran.
"Don't want her to hear this." With a leer
he added, "What d'you think of her?"

"She's an attractive woman."

"Too young for me."

When the canary returned with the glass of water, Qwilleran took her aside and said, "May I have a few minutes alone with Mr. Dingleberry? He has some personal matters to discuss."

"Certainly," she said. "I'll wait outside."

Nervously Adam said, "Where'd she go?"

"Right outside the door. What did you want to tell me, Mr. Dingleberry?"

"You won't print it in the paper?"

"I won't print it in the paper."

"Never tell a living soul?"

"I promise," said Qwilleran, raising his right hand.

"My paw told me afore he died. Made me promise not to tell. If folks found out, he said, we'd both be strung up. But he's gone now, and I'll be goin' soon. No percentage in takin' it to the grave."

"Shouldn't you be passing this secret along to your sons?"

"Nope. Don't trust them whippersnappers. Too goldurned cocky. You've got an honest face."

Qwilleran groomed his moustache with a show of modesty. Strangers had always been eager to confide in him. Looking intensely interested and sincere, he said, "What did your father reveal to you?"

"Wal, now, it were about Ephraim's funeral," old Adam said in his reedy voice. "Longest funeral procession in the history of Pickax! Six black horses 'stead of four. Two come all the way from Lockmaster. They was followed by a thirty-seven carriages and fifty-two buggies, but . . . *it were all a joke!*" He finished with a cackling laugh that turned into a coughing spell, and Qwilleran handed him the glass of water.

"What was the joke?" he asked when the spasm had subsided.

Adam cackled with glee. "Ephraim warn't in the coffin!"

Qwilleran thought, So Mitch's story is true. He's buried under the house! To Adam he said, "You say Ephraim's body wasn't in the coffin. Where was it?"

"Wal, now, the truth were . . ." Adam took a sip of water, which went down the wrong throat, and the coughing resumed so violently that Qwilleran feared the old man would choke. He called for help, and a nurse and two canaries rushed to his aid.

When it was over and Adam was calm enough to leer at the nurse, Qwilleran thanked the staffers and bowed them out of the room. Then he repeated his question. "Where was Ephraim's body?"

Cackling a laugh that was almost a yodel, the mortician said, *"Ephraim warn't dead!"*

Qwilleran stared at the old man in the wheelchair. There was a possibility that he might be senile, yet the rest of his conversation had been plausible—that is, plausible by Moose County's contrary standards. "How do you explain that bit of deception?" he asked.

"Wal, now, Ephraim knowed folks hated his guts and they was hell-bent on revenge, so he fooled 'em. He sailed off to Yerp. Went to Switzerland. Used another name. Let folks think he were dead." Adam started to cackle.

Qwilleran handed him the glass of water in anticipation of another attack of convulsive mirth. "Take a sip, Mr. Dingleberry. Be careful how you swallow . . . What about the rest of the Goodwinter family?"

"Wal, now, Ephraim's wife moved back east—that were the story they told—but she followed him to Yerp. In them days folks could disappear without no fuss. Damn gover'ment warn't buttin' in all the time. Way it turned out, though, the joke were on Ephraim. When he writ that suicide note,

331

he never knowed his enemies would take credit for lynchin' him!"

"What about his sons?"

"Titus and Samson, the two of 'em lived in the farmhouse and run the business—run it into the ground mostly." His voice soared into a falsetto and ended with a shriek of hilarity.

"If your father participated in this hoax, I hope he was amply rewarded."

"Two thousand dollars," said Adam. "That were big money in them days— mighty big! And five hun'erd every quarter, so long as Paw kep' his lip buttoned. Paw were a religious man, and he wouldn'ta done it but he were in debt to Ephraim's bank. He were afraid of losin' his store."

"How long did the quarterly payments continue?"

"Till Ephraim kicked the bucket in 1935. Paw always told me it were an investment he made, payin' off. He were on his deathbed when he told the truth and warned me not to tell. He said folks would be madder'n hell and might burn down the furniture store for makin' fools of 'em." Adam's chin sank on his chest. The half hour was almost up.

"That's a thought-provoking story with interesting ramifications," Qwilleran said.

"Thank you for taking me into your confidence."

The old man showed another spurt of energy. "There were somethin' else on Paw's conscience. He buried the Goodwinters' hired man, and they paid for the funeral—paid plenty, considerin' it were a plain coffin."

Qwilleran was instantly alerted. "What was the hired man's name?"

"I forget now."

"Luther Bosworth? Thirty years old? Left a wife and four kids?"

"That's him!"

"What happened to Luther?"

"One o' the Goodwinter horses went berserk. Trampled him to death—so bad they had a closed coffin."

"When did this happen?"

"Right after Ephraim left. Titus said he shot the horse."

There was a tap on the door, and the canary opened it an inch or two. "Visiting time almost up, sir."

"Don't let her in," Adam said.

Qwilleran called out, "One more minute, please." The door closed, and he said to Adam, "Do you know why the Goodwinters paid extra for the funeral."

Adam wiped his mouth. "It were hush money. Paw wouldn'ta took it if he warn't beholden to the bank. Paw were a religious man."

"I'm sure he was! But what were the Goodwinters trying to hush up?"

Adam wiped his mouth again. "Wal, Titus said the man were trampled to death, but when Paw picked up the body, there were only a bullethole in the head."

There was another tap on the door. The old man's chin sank on his chest again, but he revived enough to make a swipe at the skirt of the canary when she came in to wheel him to his room.

Driving back to North Middle Hummock Qwilleran was thinking, Mitch Ogilvie was right on one point: Old Adam knew a thing or two. The story of the double hoax was plotted with enough dovetailing details to make it convincing—in Moose County, at any rate, where the incredible is believable . . . And yet, was it really true? Adam Dingleberry had a reputation as a practical joker. Telling a cock-and-bull story about Ephraim could be his final joke on the whole county. Telling it to the media would be a virtual guarantee that it would be leaked. What headlines it would make! GOODWINTER

Hanging a Hoax! Mine owner Died Abroad in 1935! The wire services would pick it up, and Qwilleran's byline would once more be flashed nationwide. But how would Moose County react? The Noble Sons of the Noose—whoever they were—might trash the Dingleberry funeral home with all its lavish decor, not yet paid for. They might even go after Junior Goodwinter, managing editor of the *Something*, a nice kid in spite of being the great-grandson of the original villain. Qwilleran had a responsibility here, and a decision to make. The double hoax might be a triple hoax.

Twenty

 Arriving at the farmhouse, Qwilleran made straight for the stereo, followed by two Siamese with waving tails. "Adjust your ears," he instructed them. "You're about to hear an astounding tale."

If the cats were expecting Verdi, they were disappointed. Adam's high-pitched voice crackled from the speakers: "Yup. My grampaw come from the Old Country to build shaft-houses for the mines . . ."

Their ears swiveled nervously until they heard a deep voice saying, "What kind of furniture, Mr. Dingleberry?" At the familiar sound Koko rose on hind legs and pawed the player while Yum Yum purred enthusiastically.

"Thank you," Qwilleran said to them. "I admit I was in good voice."

The old man was saying, "They was all a bit different: doors, no doors, one drawer, two drawers, false bottom, built-in lockbox, pigeonholes, whatever folks wanted."

"Yow!" said Koko, and Qwilleran felt a familiar quiver in the roots of his moustache. He turned off the sound.

Mrs. Cobb's ugly desk was a Dingleberry; no matter what its value on the local market, Qwilleran still thought it ugly. It had tall legs, a cupboard with doors, no pigeonholes, one drawer, not two. Did it have a false bottom? He removed the drawer and inspected it, shook it, pressed the bottom in several places, felt around the perimeter with his fingertips, hit the sides with the flat of his hand, shook it again. The bottom was thicker than normal, and something was shifting inside it.

"I may need some help here," Qwilleran said, and the cat sniffed and pawed while the man ran his hand over the surfaces and pressed experimentally at vital points. Unaccountably the bottom of the drawer popped up at one end, and Qwilleran pried it out.

There were no jewels concealed in the false bottom; no doubt Mrs. Goodwinter had taken them to Switzerland. There were documents, however, that gave him a psychological chill, as if he were invading a tomb, and he built a fire in the fireplace before spreading the musty papers on the hearth rug. There were bills, receipts and promissory notes. He recognized the writing on one such document:

> *Rec'd of Titus Goodwinter the sum of three thousand dollars ($3,000) in compensation for the accidental death of my husband. Signed this day of Oct. 31, 1904.*
>
> *Lucy Bosworth*

Had Titus dictated it? Had Lucy written it under duress? Or had she been an accomplice in the plot? The receipt led Qwilleran on a wild gallop of speculation regarding the young woman's relationship with her husband and, for that matter, with Titus, who was a notorious womanizer. It was clear that the payoff financed the purchase of the Pickax General Store, $3,000 being an enormous sum in the days when a family of six could live nicely on five dollars a week. The blood money, so to speak, may have paid for the impressive bible as well, a status symbol of its day.

There were other documents of historic interest if one had the time to study them, including promissory notes at abnormally high interest rates, signed by names well-known in Moose County, among them the thriftless Captain Fugtree.Ephraim's banks may have operated legitimately, but in his private money-lending he was guilty of usury.

The handwriting on a receipt dated October 28 caught Qwilleran's attention. It was the same small bold script found in Ephraim's suicide note, but it was signed by the financially captive storekeeper and undertaker, Adam Dingleberry's "Paw." Driven by debt to set aside his religious scruples, he had signed the following:

Rec'd of Ephraim Goodwinter, the sum of two thousand dollars ($2,000) in consideration of which the undersigned agrees to bury an empty coffin with full ceremony in the Goodwinter plot in the Pickax Cemetery, payee to conceal the arrangements noted above from all living souls and future descendants, on condition of which payer agrees to make quarterly payments of five hundred dollars ($500) until such time as payer departs this life. Signed and accepted this day of Oct. 28, 1904.

Joshua Dingleberry

A similar agreement with Titus Goodwinter,

covering the interment of Luther Bosworth, also bore Joshua's signature.

The Siamese, attracted by the heat from the burning logs or the stale aroma of the documents, were in close attendance, and Koko was particularly interested in a folded sheet of paper that had been handled by dirty hands. It was a rough diagram with measurements and other specifications noted in faded penciling that Qwilleran could not decipher even with his reading glasses. Using a magnifying glass from the telephone desk he was able to identify the central element as a half-circle with dimensions given in feet. Two rectangles connected by a pair of parallel lines were marked SW and NW, but no dimensions were specified. Folded in with the diagram was a misspelled bill from the Mayfus Stone Quarry on Sandpit Road: "4 lodes stone to pave carage house." The date was May 16, 1904, and it was marked "pd."

"Three days after the explosion!" Qwilleran observed. "What do you two sleuths make of that? The carriage house is not paved; it's plank like the threshing floor. And what's this?"

Folded in with the diagram was a small slip of paper in Ephraim Goodwinter's unmistakable hand:

Rec'd of Ephraim Goodwinter the sum of one thousand dollars ($1,000) in consideration of which the undersigned agrees to do stonework as specified, privately and without help and without revealing same to any living soul, work to be completed by August 15 of the current year. Signed and accepted this day of May 16, 1904.

> *Luther Bosworth*
> *X (his mark)*

"Luther couldn't even write his name!" Qwilleran exclaimed. "How do you like that?"

Hearing no reply he looked for the cats. Yum Yum was asleep on the hearth rug with her tail curled comfortingly over her nose. A hump in one of the other Orientals indicated that Koko was in hiding again. In consternation Qwilleran went to the telephone and called a number in Mooseville.

"Hello, Lori. This is Qwill," he said. "How's everything? . . . Glad to hear it. How's the baby? . . . Are you sure he isn't eating the cats' food? . . . Speaking of cats, I'm sorry to trouble you again, but I'd like to ask you a question about Koko's latest aberration. He's accustomed to wall-to-wall carpet in our Pickax apartment, you know, but here we have bare wood floors scattered with small rugs, and he's always hiding under them—something he's never done before . . . Well, there are different kinds: Orientals in the parlor and entrance hall, hooked rugs in the bedroom, braided rugs in the kitchen and dining area—all old and handmade. Koko prefers the Orientals, which are the thinnest and the most valuable. He's always been a snob . . . No, he tunnels under them in a neat, workmanlike way, making a hump in the rug. *Wait a minute!* Excuse me, Lori. I just got an idea! I'll call you back."

Qwilleran hung up, tamping his moustache with fervor. He grabbed a flashlight, rushed out to the barn, barged through the eye of the needle, frightening a barncat, plunged down the ladder into the stable, flashed his light into the southwest corner. There he found another wooden palette like the one on the threshing floor above. This one also leaned against the wall, but it was surrounded by rubble. When he pulled it aside he was gaping at a hole in the foot-thick stone wall. The opening was about four feet wide and three feet high, an arched tunnel of crumbling masonry with a floor of hard-packed clay. The arch was roughly mortared quarry stone. As far as the beam of the flashlight penetrated there was arched stone.

Qwilleran dropped to his knees and started to crawl. This was Ephraim's escape tunnel, he realized, evidently planned when public outcry alarmed him. The bill for the stone was dated three days after the explosion—the same day that Luther signed his X and agreed to build the tunnel secretly while the family traveled abroad.

Had Ephraim actually used this escape hatch on the night of October 29? It was quite possible. Qwilleran imagined furious hordes shouting obscenities in front of the farmhouse and throwing rocks at the windows, while Ephraim craftily crawled through the tunnel. No doubt, the trusted Bosworth had a horse ready—two horses, one for Ephraim's son—the saddlebags packed with valuables. Under cover of darkness the pair would ride along the Willoway, heading for Mooseville, where Ephraim would board a passenger boat to Canada across the lake. His wife, meanwhile, was taking refuge at the parsonage with Mr. and Mrs. Crawbanks. A deal had already been made with Enoch Dingleberry, and Ephraim's sons would carry out the remainder of the charade: killing Luther, who knew too much, then blaming the horse; staging the hanging with a hastily rigged effigy; announcing the suicide and producing the suicide note; mourning at their father's funeral. Little did they know that the rumor mill would go into operation, with their enemies taking credit for Ephraim's demise. What started the rumor, of course, was Mr. Crawbanks' discovery of the white sheet, recently left there by some Halloween prankster.

Composing this melodrama occupied Qwilleran's mind while he crawled slowly and painfully through the tunnel. It was rough on the hands, and he had a bad knee dating back to his years in the armed service. He sat down and pondered. What he needed was a pair of heavy gloves and some padding for his knees.

Carefully he backed out of the cramped space, brushed himself off and climbed the ladder. He could hear the playful shouts of the teenage yard crew as they raked leaves, bagging them and loading the bags in Mitch's blue pickup. They were working on the north side of the house, and Qwilleran sauntered through their midst en route to the west wing.

Mitch hailed him. "Hi, Qwill! Nice day for a walk."

Once inside the apartment he contemplated his strategy. Gloves were no problem; he had brought a pair of lined leather gloves from Pickax, and he was willing to sacrifice them for the tunnel investigation. How to pad his knees presented a challenge, however. He canvassed the apartment looking for likely material. All he could find was a stack of pink terry towels with Iris Cobb's monogram. They would have to do. Now he needed some kind of heavy cord to bind the towels around his knees.

Koko was following him around, sensing an adventure, and his eager presence gave Qwilleran an idea. It might be advantageous to take the cat to the tunnel, letting him walk ahead, prudently restrained by a leash. Miners used to lower canaries down the mineshaft to test for toxic gasses. If Koko sniffed any noxious fumes, he wouldn't succumb; he would raise holy hell as only an outraged Siamese can do. Koko had a blue leather harness, and the leash was a twelve-foot length of nylon cord, some of which could be used to bind the pink towels. Congratulating himself on his ingenuity, Qwilleran

345

cut the leash down to a manageable six feet and reserved the remainder for binding.

The yard crew was rapidly working its way around to the west side, and he hesitated to walk to the barn wearing leather gloves, leading Koko on a leash, and carrying an armful of pink towels. After pacing the floor for a while he went outdoors and asked Mitch for a plastic leaf bag.

"Going to do some raking, Qwill?"

"No, just bundling up some stuff to store in the barn."

Now he was all set. Into the plastic bag he threw the pink towels, a second flashlight, gloves, the harness and two short lengths of cord. He stuffed Koko inside his shirt and added a loose jacket for camouflage. "This won't take long," he explained to the cat, "and I would appreciate your cooperation. Keep your mouth shut and don't exercise your claws."

Qwilleran waited until the volunteers gathered around Mitch's truck for a guzzle break. Then he slung the sack over his shoulder and headed for the barn. He could feel some wriggling inside his shirt, and he heard a few muffled yiks, but the barnyard was traversed without arousing suspicion. Avoiding exposure on the grassy ramp he scuttled around the east side of the barn and entered the stable through the livestock door in the rear. So far, so good!

First he trussed Koko, purring, into his harness and tied him to a printing press. Then he applied himself to wrapping legs with bath towels and cord, an idea that proved less achievable than it sounded. In fact, after the first attempt he found it impossible to bend his knees, and it was necessary to untie the cords and start again. Koko, becoming impatient, uttered some piercing yowls.

"Quiet!" Qwilleran growled. "I'm working as fast as I can."

At last they were ready. Koko in his blue harness and Qwilleran in his pink kneepads entered the tunnel, the cat leading the way and the man crawling after him. It was slow work. The clay floor of the tunnel was scattered with stones and chunks of mortar. Tossing them aside with one gloved hand and wielding the flashlight with the other, Qwilleran was obliged to hold Koko's leash in his teeth, trusting the cat not to make a sudden leap forward.

It was a slow crawl and a long crawl. After all, the original diagram showed the tunnel extending from the stable, under the carriage house and across the barnyard to the basement of the west wing. Qwilleran had read about such a tunnel in Europe, connecting a convent with the outside world: the convent was haunted, and human bones were eventually found in the tunnel. There were no bones in the Goodwinter tunnel, only beer cans and gum wrappers and some unidentified items that Koko saw fit to sniff. Qwilleran found the air in the tunnel stuffy, smelling of mold and mice, but Koko was experiencing a catly high.

They crawled on. The farther they progressed, the more rubble they encountered, and the faster the cat wanted to travel, yikking and tugging at his leash.

"Arrgh!" Qwilleran growled through his teeth.

"Yow!" replied Koko impatiently.

They were nearing the southwest terminal, but there was no light at the end of the tunnel—just a wall of chipped stone. Scattered about were broken rocks, chunks of mortar, and a few discarded tools—chisels, hammers, and a drill. Also there was a great deal of dust. They crawled to the end, Qwilleran choking and trying to cough without unclenching his teeth.

Koko was the first to find it—a small,

square, boxlike object in a dark corner of the tunnel.

A *bomb!* Qwilleran thought. *Dynamite!*

Twisting the end of the leash around one gloved hand, he used the other to flood the contraption with light. Then he moved toward it on his knees and found a button to press. For a moment there was dead silence in the tunnel, then . . . a hair-raising screech . . . an angry growl ending in a vicious snarl . . . the moans of the dying . . . the bong of a death knell . . . ghostly wailing and rattling . . . *screams!*

Koko shot off like a rocket, and Qwilleran on the other end of the leash went sprawling on the clay.

Twenty-one

When Qwilleran emerged from the barn with his sackful of pink towels and yowling cat, Mitch Ogilvie cupped his hands and yelled across the barnyard, "Your phone's ringing!"

For two hours Qwilleran had been on hands and knees with hunched back, and he responded stiffly. Nevertheless, he made his way to the apartment quickly enough to catch the caller before she hung up.

"Oh, there you are, Qwill!" said Carol Lanspeak. "I let it ring fifteen times because I thought you were outdoors on a nice day like this. Were you outdoors?"

"Yes," he said, breathing hard.

"I've been to the hospital to see Verona. Baby is going to make it—and Verona's pregnant."

"I didn't know. How is she?"

"Not too good. She wants to go 'down home' and have Baby convalesce there. Larry's taking care of her expenses and giving

350

her something to live on. Vince left her without a cent! That brute!"

"Have they found him?"

"I don't think so. The police have been talking to Verona, and Larry has asked his attorney to advise her."

"I feel sorry for Verona."

"So do I. We never really got to know her. She was so quiet and retiring. She volunteered for our cleaning committee and was very reliable. The reason I'm calling, Qwill —she has something she wants to tell you. She says it's important. Do you think you could go to the hospital tonight? I'm taking her to the airport tomorrow."

"I'll go. Thanks for letting me know."

"By the way, the board has voted to give Mitch the job," said Carol.

Polly Duncan was the next to call. "They've found him!" she said without any formalities. "Somewhere in Ohio. My assistant's mother-in-law heard it on the air and phoned the library."

"He's guilty of more than just killing a hophead, I surmise."

"What do you mean?"

"I'd like to drop in to see you tonight— and discuss a few things," Qwilleran said.

"Come for dinner, and I'll whip up a curry."

"Uh . . . thanks, Polly, but I have an appointment in Pickax. See you after eight o'clock."

"Don't have dessert," she said. "We'll have pumpkin pie and coffee."

On the way to Pickax Qwilleran experienced a pang of remorse that he had not allowed Baby to visit the cats; it was pure selfishness on his part, he admitted. And now it wouldn't ever happen. It was perhaps a need for penance that led him to have dinner at the Dimsdale Diner. After some watery soup and oversalted cabbage rolls and unrecognizable coffee, he drove to the hospital.

He found Verona in a private room, sitting in a chair and picking at a meal tray. "I'm sorry to interrupt your dinner," he said.

"I don't feel like eatin' anythin'," she said, pushing the tray away. "Have they caught him?" Her soft voice had lost its lilt and was now a dreary monotone.

"They found him somewhere in Ohio."

"I'm glad."

"Cheer up. Baby is going to be all right, and your eye is looking better. The bruise is fading."

She touched her face. "I didn't bump into a door. We were arguin' and he hit me."

"When did it happen?"

"When he was leavin'—Monday night."

"You told me he left Monday noon."

"That's what he told me to say." She turned away and looked out the window.

"Carol Lanspeak said you have something you want to tell me, Mrs. Boswell."

"That's not my name. I'm Verona Whitmoor."

"I like that better. It has a pleasant musical sound, like your speaking voice," he said.

She looked flustered and lowered her head. "I'm so ashamed. I was cleanin' the museum, gettin' it ready for Sunday, and I went in Iris's kitchen when you weren't there and took the cookbook."

"I knew you were the one," said Qwilleran, "after you sent me the meatloaf. It was her recipe."

"Vince liked her meatloaf so much, and I was tryin' to please him."

"I'm surprised you could read her handwriting."

"It was hard, but I figured it out. I meant to take it back, but then everythin' happened." She looked pitifully vulnerable and undernourished.

"Ms. Whitmoor, shouldn't you have something to eat? That apple pudding looks good."

"I'm not hungry."

"How did you happen to meet Vince?" Qwilleran asked.

"I was workin' in a restaurant in Pittsburgh, and he used to come in. I felt sorry for him because he was always in pain—with his bad leg, you know. He was wounded in Vietnam."

Qwilleran huffed scornfully into his moustache.

Verona went on. "We got friendly, and he invited me to come up here on a vacation. He said I could bring Baby. He didn't tell me about the money—not then."

"What money?"

"His mother came from here, and she told him about some money hidden under the barn, but he had to dig for it. His grandfather knew all about it. But the diggin' was hard, and he was always afraid someone would find out what he was doin'. That's why he killed the man in the barn." Verona put her face in her hands, and her thin shoulders shook with her sobbing. Such an outburst of emotion over the murder of a tramp caused Qwilleran to ask:

"Did you know the man who was killed?"

She shook her head, and the tears continued to pour forth. He placed the tissue box on her lap and waited patiently. What could he say? Perhaps her emotions were a confused combination of grief and relief that she and Baby were free of Vince. It was a long, painful scene. When he finally persuaded her to talk, her faltering voice mumbled a few words at a time.

He described the emotional ordeal when he arrived at Polly's cottage at eight o'clock. Bursting into the house he said, "I knew that guy was a fraud! He was no expert on printing presses, and he lied about his bad leg— told Larry it was polio, told Verona he got it in Vietnam. Actually it was the result of a boyhood escapade. And get this! He and Larry and Susan are second cousins!"

"Sit down and have some pie," Polly said, "and start from the beginning."

"I've just been to the hospital to see Verona," he said.

"Did she know anything about the murder of Waffle?"

"Not until the police told her, but she

knew what Boswell was doing in the barn. He was digging for Ephraim's gold coins!"

"How naive! Where did he hear that hoary fable?"

"His great-grandfather was Ephraim's hired man, and the story had been handed down in the family. He believed it. Changed his name so the town wouldn't connect him with the original Bosworth. Cataloguing the presses was only a cover. It happily presented itself when he contacted Larry about a vacation up here with his 'wife and child.' But he was constantly afraid someone would blow his cover. So when Brent Waffle hid out in the stable, I suppose Boswell considered him a threat and killed him with a crowbar."

"What happened to your contraband crate theory, Qwill?" Polly said teasingly.

"Forget it. I was off-base."

In his state of animation Qwilleran failed to notice that the pumpkin pie had been frozen and insufficiently thawed, or that Bigfoot was sitting on his knee. He said, "On the night the body was dumped, the cats heard a noise, and so did I—a rumbling sound. It was Boswell's van, driving around the far side of the barn to pick up the body in the stable. After that, he took off, having instructed Verona to lie for him. He also gave her a poke in the eye."

Polly offered him more pie, and he declined. "One slice is more than enough, but I'll have another cup of coffee." After a few gulps he said, "Boswell was using a drill in his search for the loot, and the vibration was loosening lightbulbs. I believe it also cracked the plastered wall in the basement. That's where Iris first heard sounds of knocking. He was using a hammer and chisel to gouge out the mortar . . . Are you ready for the worst?"

"Is there more?"

"Plenty, but it took me awhile to get it out of Verona. She was on a crying jag, and I thought she was upset about Baby and her condition. Actually she was agonizing over Iris's death. I happened to have a small inconspicuous recorder with me. Would you like to hear my conversation with Verona firsthand?"

Polly demurred. "It doesn't seem quite decent. It was a private conversation."

"Would it be more decent if I repeated it verbatim?"

"Well . . . if you put it that way . . ."

Verona's faltering speech was punctuated with sniffles and whimpers, but Qwilleran's voice was the first on the tape, and he grimaced when he heard himself repeating Boswell's corny line. "My God! Did I say that?" he said.

Don't be afraid to talk to me about your grief, Ms. Whitmoor. That's what neighbors are for.

I feel terrible about it. When Iris died, I wanted to die, too.

She was a wonderful woman. Everyone loved her.

She was so kind to Baby and me. No one else . . . (long pause).

Did you know she had a heart condition?

She never talked about herself, but I knew she was worried about somethin'.

Did she tell you about the mysterious noises in the house?

Yes, she did. And when I told Vince he got nervous. He said she was too nosy. He was poundin' and drillin', and she could hear it and thought it was ghosts or somethin'. (Soft crying.)

What did he do about it?

He tried to figure out ways to get her out of the house, so he could work, but she loved the museum and loved her kitchen. She was always cookin' and bakin'. (Long pause.)

Go on, Ms. Whitmoor.

One day he came home with a Halloween cassette—spooky sounds, you know. He said he had an idea. He said she was a silly woman, and he could frighten her enough so she would quit the job, and then we could live in the manager's apartment and he could dig all he wanted to.

Did his idea work?

She got very upset, but she didn't leave. Vince talked about it all the time. He was like a crazy man, and when he got into a tantrum like that, his leg would hurt worse.

Do you remember the night Iris Cobb died?

(Prolonged wailing.) I'll never forget it! Not till I die!

What happened?

(Whimpering.) He gave me a sheet with two holes in it. (Sobs.) He told me to get under the sheet . . . and stand outside her window . . . and he would play the spooky sound effects. I didn't want to, but he said . . . (long pause).

What did he say?

He said some threatenin' things, and I was afraid for Baby, so I did what he wanted. (Anguished wailing.) I didn't know what he was goin' to do! . . . Oh, Jesus forgive me! . . . I didn't know he was goin' to smother Iris with that pillow! (Hysterical sobs.)

Qwilleran switched off the tape. He said to Polly, "Her crying went on until I thought she was going into convulsions. In fact, the nurse came in and gave her something to drink and said I'd better leave. So I did, but I waited in the visitors' lounge and after a while I went back. I thanked her and told her she was a good woman and she should go down south and start a new life. I held both her hands, and she almost smiled. Then I asked her a question: Why was Iris's apartment in darkness? That question had been nagging me ever since I found her body on the kitchen floor."

"Did Verona have an answer?"

"She said she was the one who went in and turned off lights and the microwave. Homer Tibbitt had impressed upon the cleaning volunteers that they should always turn everything off—because of the danger of fire."

Polly said, "I feel limp! This is an unnerving story—and bizarre!"

"You want to hear something really bizarre?" Qwilleran said. "When I first took Koko into the museum, he went directly to a certain bed pillow in the textile collection. I didn't know it at the time, but that pillow had been removed from the exhibit without authorization and then returned . . . And that's not all. When he ran out to the barn last night he found a litter of kittens on a soiled white sheet with burn holes. Obviously Boswell had stuffed it between the crates after it had been used to frighten Iris. It had been raining, and the sheet had dragged on the wet ground; the edges were muddy . . . And one more incredible instance, Polly! Twice—not once, but twice —Koko knocked a novel off the bookshelf in which a character is smothered with a pillow!"

When Qwilleran returned to the farmhouse, the Siamese met him with yowling complaints and bristling fur. It was chilly in the apartment. "Is the thermostat too low?" he asked them, "or has Ephraim's shade been drifting around?" He started a crackling blaze in the parlor fireplace, got into his old Mackintosh bathrobe, and dropped into a lounge chair for contemplation.

He had refrained from telling Polly about Adam Dingleberry's story and about the documents he had found to confirm it. The papers were returned to the false bottom of the old Dingleberry desk, and the secret would be safe for a few more decades. Moose County could go on believing that Ephraim died on October 30, 1904—one way or the other—and the Noble Sons of the Noose could continue their fraternal shenanigans. Qwilleran suspected that the Noble Sons, thirty-two of them with lights on their caps, staged a ghostly march across the Goodwinter slag heap every year on May 13.

In the blue wing chair, the Siamese were indulging in a mutual grooming session. Had they chosen that chair because it was Mrs. Cobb's favorite or because they knew the upholstery enhanced the blue of their eyes? Qwilleran watched them—beautiful creatures, vain, and mysterious.

He said to Koko, "When you sat in the kitchen window, staring at the barnyard, did you know something irregular was happening out there?"

Koko, intent on flicking a facile tongue around Yum Yum's left ear, paid no attention. Why, Qwilleran asked himself, are cats either smotheringly attentive or infuriatingly indifferent? He went on—doggedly:

"When you tunneled under rugs were you

trying to tell me something? Or were you just amusing yourself?"

Koko extended his services to Yum Yum's snowy throat, and she raised her chin in ecstasy. Qwilleran could remember when Koko expected the female to do the laundering. Times had changed.

"And how about all that muttering and mumbling?" he demanded. "Were you talking to yourself or conversing with an invisible presence?"

Both cats settled down with paws tucked under in contentment, totally oblivious.

As Qwilleran sat brooding in his chair and dimly perceiving the blue wing chair opposite, he could almost feel Iris Cobb's presence. At that precise moment two brown noses lifted, four brown ears swiveled, two sets of whiskers twitched. Something was about to happen. Qwilleran braced himself for a pink apparition, bearing cookies. Ten seconds later, the telephone rang.

Qwilleran took the call in the bedroom. "Hello? . . . Of course I remember you! How's everything Down Below? . . . I don't know. What's the proposition? . . . A penthouse, did you say? Sounds good, but I'll have to discuss it with my bosses. Where can I reach you? . . ."

He returned to the parlor and addressed the blue wing chair. "How would you guys like to spend the winter in the Crime Belt instead of the Snow Belt?"

The chair was vacant. They had sensed another change of address. Qwilleran's eyes automatically rose to the top of the Pennsylvania German *Schrank*. Not there. But he noticed a hump in the hearth rug and another hump in the rug before the sofa. Both humps were eloquently motionless.